The Moon by Night

MADELEINE L'ENGLE

The Moon by Night

SQUARE
FISH

Farrar, Straus and Giroux

SQUARE
FISH
An Imprint of Macmillan

Library of Congress Catalog Card Number: 63-9072

ISBN: 978-0-312-37932-2

Originally published in the United States by Farrar, Straus and Giroux
Square Fish logo designed by Filomena Tuosto
First Square Fish Edition: 2008
10 9 8 7 6 5 4 3
www.squarefishbooks.com

To Hugh, Jo, Maria, and Bion

The Moon by Night

Introduction

"Who are you in this book?" we would constantly ask our grandmother, Madeleine L'Engle, about every book that she wrote. Her books have protagonists that many people can identify with, generation after generation, whether it is the brave and clever, gawky and frustrated Meg Murry, or the vulnerable and awkward, but at the same time, sensitive and intuitive Vicky Austin. Madeleine also strongly identified with her characters, and said many times that she was both Meg and Vicky. There was so much that was recognizable as her and her life in her stories, and we wanted to be able to map her fiction to her biography, thereby fixing and understanding her place, and by extension, ours, in the family and the wider world.

Most children want to be told stories about themselves. We were no different, and so, reading the Austin books was always a special thrill, because the narrative is peppered with incidents and details that also featured in family lore, like the adorable malapropisms of Rob Austin and Vicky's bicycle accident. The Austin family house in the quiet New England village of Thornhill (as described in *Meet the Austins*) is ever-present as a touchstone of their domestic peace, and is modeled on Crosswicks, a pre-Revolutionary War farmhouse in northwestern Connecticut where our grandparents and their children lived in the 1950s. The cross-country road trip in *The Moon by Night* copies the Franklin family itinerary of 1959, during which Madeleine started writing *A Wrinkle in Time*. In *The Young Unicorns*, the Austin kids unravel a mystery at the Cathedral of St. John the Divine, where our grandmother was the librarian and writer-in-residence for more than forty years.

There is enough similarity of detail in the books to have caused us some confusion: If our grandmother is Vicky, how can she have the bicycle accident that left our own mother with a Y-shaped scar on her chin? If some of the details confounded our sense of reality, we never questioned the underlying truth of the characters and our grandmother's relationship to them. If Madeleine were Vicky, then we felt understood. Because we were Vicky, too.

People would joke that *Meet the Austins* could have been called *Meet the Franklins* (Madeleine's married name), and yet, we knew that Vicky and the Austins couldn't be a simple translation of our grandmother's life, because of the family tension and pain surrounding these books about this family. Madeleine's own children were often shocked at how their own lives were appropriated and rewritten for publication, and felt judged against this very happy and practically perfect family. The line between fact and fiction can sometimes be blurry for writers, and the temptation to inscribe a certain version of and authority on events is strong.

All of Madeleine's writing, fiction and nonfiction, was an example of how all narrative is fiction, and all fiction can be true. She wrote and lectured extensively on the difference between truth and fact, arguing that it is through story that we human beings approach the truth, not through facts, which can only get us so far. As her granddaughters, this was both liberating and confusing, but we happily suspended our disbelief, and some of our best-loved stories are ones that are culled from her real life, from her days in the theater, from her early years with our grandfather, and the mysterious decade of the fifties.

The five books that are now presented as The Austin Family Chronicles were written over a period of thirty years. A prolific writer of more than sixty books in a variety of genres, Madeleine created a web of characters that grew, changed, and surprised her. As we re-read these books over our lifetime, what strike us are the very different responses we have to this family. At eleven, we thrilled to the references to things that our mother or aunt or uncle would confirm were true. At seventeen, we were cynical about the blur between fact and fiction, and thought we could read our grandmother as if she were a book. In our mature adulthood, we recognize how rich and complicated our grandmother was, and that fact can be the springboard for fiction, and fiction can inform who we are and tell us about ourselves.

Charlotte Jones Voiklis and Lena Roy
March, 2008

One

"Vicky!"

It was John's voice and he was calling for me. I suppose somewhere on the inside of my mind I realized it, but with the outside of my mind all I heard was the constant crying of sea gulls and the incoming boom of breakers. I hadn't even seen that the early morning sun had moved across the sky, and the tide had pushed the waves closer up to my feet. I'd forgotten that there was any such thing as time, and almost why I'd come sliding down the steep path to the cove and climbed up on the sun-baked rock.

I wanted to be alone and I wanted to think. Indoors there was excitement and confusion and I guess a lot of happiness. I was the only one who seemed to be unhappy because nothing would ever be the same again. Up to a few days ago my life (and fifteen years is quite a considerable hunk of time—well, I'm not quite fifteen, but I'm on the way) had been all of a piece, exciting, sometimes, and even miserable, but always following the same and simple pattern of home and school and family. And now it was all being thrown away, tossed to the four winds. I wanted to leave all the chatter and babble and be alone to sort things out. Just a few minutes alone down at the beach—was that so very much to ask?

"Vicky! VICK-EEEE!"

Now even the outside of my mind couldn't confuse John's angry shouting with a sea gull's squawk. I looked up. He was scrambling down the path, but much more slowly than usual, because he was dressed in grey flannel slacks and a freshly ironed white shirt and was carrying his jacket over his arm. I waved at him.

He sounded furious. "Vicky! Victoria Austin! Get up here! Don't you know what time it is?"

Of course I didn't know what time it was. I'd left my watch with my clothes when I put on my bathing suit. I wouldn't dare use that as an excuse with John, though. He knows perfectly well that I can tell by the sun, that I can tell by the tide. What he wouldn't know was that I had been lost in time, and that my few minutes had stretched out to what was obviously over an hour and I hadn't even realized it.

I jumped off the rock onto the soft sand instead of climbing down. We've always jumped off the rock, so maybe what I was doing at that moment was hanging on to my childhood instead of trying to leap out of it the way I usually do. I hurried across the sand and started up the almost vertical path that leads to the top of the bluff. There's a winding road you can take, full of hairpin bends, but we've always taken the path cut down through the scrubby bushes. The bushes were very useful in helping me to

8

pull myself up the path quickly, and in keeping me from looking at my rightfully enraged older brother. He had climbed back up to the top of the bluff and was standing there waiting for me. When he spoke his voice was coldly angry. "Have you no sense at all? We've been looking for you for the last half hour. With everything there is to do why do you have to pick this particular day to go mooning off by yourself?"

I didn't answer. He was right and I was wrong and there wasn't any point in shouting in the face of that calm fury. I stared down at my bare feet as I hurried along the dusty road.

A hundred yards down the road was my grandfather's house, if you can call it a house. It's an old stable painted a lovely barn red. The horse stalls are still there but now they're all filled with shelves of books, so it's more like a library that somebody lives in than a house. There's one bedroom with Grandfather's huge four-poster bed, and up above the stalls is a loft with six army cots.

I ran ahead of John, into the stable, hoping I could rush through and up the ladder to the loft without seeing anybody. But of course the first person I saw was my father. I practically knocked him down in my hurry.

He grabbed me by both elbows. "Vicky, your mother has needed every bit of help she could get this morning and you simply went off without a word to anyone. Now get up to the loft and get changed and please do not keep us waiting."

John tries to copy Daddy when he's angry. He couldn't have a better model. I mumbled, "I'm sorry, Daddy," and scurried up the ladder. It seemed odd not to have to climb over the recumbent body of our Great Dane, Mr. Rochester, who usually spent most of the time when we were at Grandfather's lying at the foot of the ladder and being miserable because he couldn't climb it. But that was part of it all, part of the reason I'd wanted to go down to the beach to look at the ocean and rest my eyes where the ocean and the sky became one. This time Mr. Rochester wasn't with us.

Up in the loft Suzy and Maggy were standing in front of the mirror, preening. Suzy's my younger sister, and Maggy's just a year older and has lived with us for the past couple of years, but won't after today. Another reason.

Suzy and Maggy are just about the same size and Suzy is a buttercup-colored blonde, and Maggy's hair is blue-black. Up until this winter people used to look at me pityingly when I was with the two of them. But Uncle Douglas always said I was an ugly duckling type, and suddenly with my fourteenth birthday all my angles and sticky-out bones and unmanageable hair seemed to come to some sort of agreement and I no longer felt wistful if I happened to look into a mirror when Suzy and Maggy were around. As a matter of fact, I enjoyed mirrors very much.

"Well, jeepers, Vicky!" Suzy accused as my head appeared in the loft. "Where have *you* been?"

I thought for a moment about not climbing the rest of the way up, but there wasn't any place else to go. I decided maybe a change of subject would be nice, so I said, "You look gorgeous. Both of you."

It worked. They started looking in the mirror again. Too old to be flower girls, too young to be bridesmaids, they stood dressed, Suzy in pale blue, Maggy in the softest rose, Aunt Elena's hand-maidens, as Uncle Douglas called them. My dress was a very light, clear yellow, and I loved it, though it wasn't nearly as dressed-up a dress as Suzy's or Maggy's, and I wasn't going to be a handmaiden. I was just going to sit in the pew with Mother, and Rob, my little brother. John was best man, Daddy was going to give Aunt Elena away, and Grandfather, of course, was going to perform the ceremony. It was a very family wedding.

Uncle Douglas is Daddy's younger brother, and Aunt Elena has been mother's best friend since they were at boarding school in Switzerland together. Hal, Aunt Elena's first husband, a test pilot, was killed several years ago, and we'd all been hoping for a long time that Uncle Douglas and Aunt Elena would get married. So why wasn't I glowing like Suzy and Maggy?

If everything else could have been the same, if we could have gone back to Thornhill after the wedding, if everything could have gone on as usual, I would have lit up the beach with joy. But nothing was ever going to be the same again. Before we left for Grandfather's I'd said good-bye to the house, to the dogs and the cats and an entirely brand new completely different life lay ahead. I was scared stiff.

"Hurry up and get *dressed*," Maggy said in a bossy way. "It's almost time to go. *I* helped make the punch."

I went into the shower, stripped off my bathing suit, and sluiced off the salt water, being very careful to keep my hair dry, because I'd washed and set it the night before. I'd even remembered to be careful of it while I was in the ocean. I hadn't gone swimming. I just sat in the shallow water and let the cool waves ripple over me. The water flowed comfortingly about my body, the sun beat warmly down upon my head, and the sea stretched out and out until it seemed that sea and sky would never meet. It was hard to tell where the horizon lay, because sea and sky seemed to blend together in one great curve. In Grandfather's cove the beach repeated the curve, the sea gulls circled overhead, the small waves that broke against my body were lacily scalloped, and there weren't any straight hard lines anywhere to be the shortest distance between two points.

Maggy pounded on the bathroom door. I knew it was Maggy because of the way she pounded; a pound on a door can be just as personal as a footstep or a tone of voice. This pound was a little more violent than usual, because of course Maggy was frantic with excitement. I'd been sitting down at the beach brooding while Maggy had been helping Mother make punch, and of course everything was going to be more different from now on for Maggy than for the rest of us.

Since her parents' death Maggy had lived with us even though Aunt Elena was her guardian, because Aunt Elena is a pianist and had to be away so much on concert tours. Now Maggy was going to live with Aunt Elena and Uncle Douglas, in California, and this was wonderful for her. But if I were Maggy I'd have been more scared, I think, than excited.

I got out of the shower and got dressed and had to shove Maggy and Suzy away from the mirror long enough so that I could fix my hair properly and put on a small amount of lipstick. My nose had turned rather red while I'd been sitting on the beach. I hadn't thought of that when I'd gone off looking for solitude. Well, it wasn't *my* wedding. No one would be looking at *my* nose.

"Girls!" Mother called from downstairs. "Commander Rodney's here."

We hurried down the ladder. Commander Rodney is a particular friend of ours, though most particularly of Rob's. Two years

12

ago when Rob was only four he stowed away on one of the Island ferries. We thought he was lost and went to the Coast Guard headquarters where Commander Rodney helped us find him.

Rob, dressed in navy blue shorts and a blazer and looking very snazzy, was holding on to Commander Rodney's hand and talking a blue streak. John and Grandfather appeared to be studying a large book and looking very calm. Daddy pried them out of the book and sent us off with Commander Rodney, who was to take us to the church.

During the drive I seemed to be the only one who didn't want to talk. This is supposed to have been my moody year, my difficult year, and if anybody noticed my silence, which is unlikely, they probably put it down to that.

I didn't want to talk. I wanted to think. Among all the other changes, Uncle Douglas would never be the same again, popping up for week-ends and being completely ours even when he brought girls up for us to look over in case he ever got serious about marrying one of them. I'd wanted terribly to have Uncle Douglas marry Aunt Elena, but now he would be hers, and Maggy would be his daughter, he would have his own child. I've always felt very special with Uncle Douglas because he's stuck up for me and understood me even when nobody else has. He was the one who'd made me believe I wouldn't always be an ugly duckling, and that one day everything would come clear for me and I'd develop a talent for something particular and know what I wanted to do in the adult world the way John and Suzy always have known. But it couldn't be the same with Uncle Douglas and me any more. This, like everything else, was going to change.

I was sitting next to Grandfather in the car and suddenly for no reason at all he put his hand on my knee and patted it and I felt—how can I explain it—loved and cherished sounds soppy but I think it's exactly what I mean, only in a non-soppy way. And suddenly, whammo, I began to feel happy.

At the church everything was confusion and excitement and then Rob and I were sitting quietly in our pew and Commander Rodney was sitting behind us with his wife and kids and the church began to fill up.

Because we were sitting down front we couldn't see who was coming in, but I knew just who it would be: Grandfather's friends from the Island, not the summer people, because those hadn't started coming up yet, but the year-round people, like Commander Rodney and his family, and the retired ones, like Grandfather: Dr. Wood; he's a physicist; and Isaac Ulrich, the violinist; and lots of interesting people like that. Then there would be the Rosses from the drug store, and old Mr. Codd from the grocery store, and Mr. Dolittle, the butcher. They would come in, all dressed up and not looking in the least like their every day, ordinary selves; but then neither did we, and neither did the church. It was full of candles and flowers, and a sense of expectancy filled the nave and seemed to mix in with the sunlight coming softly through the windows. They were partly open, a soft breeze came through, and the sound of the sea was always there in the background as it was everywhere on the Island.

Old Grandma Adams started playing, "Jesu Joy of Man's Desiring" on the organ. It's one of my very favorite pieces of music in the world. I relaxed into listening and then there was Mother walking down the aisle looking just beautiful and so young it kind of scared me; it's much more comfortable to have her just Mother and not any age at all. As soon as Mother had sat down the Wedding March began and in came Suzy and Maggy, followed by Aunt Elena on Daddy's arm. Aunt Elena's dress was very much like Suzy's and Maggy's, except that it was moonlight color, not silver, not seagreen, but shimmering with both.

Suzy and Maggy won't sit next to me in the movies because I cry. I cried so at *West Side Story* that I was a pulp, and they didn't want anyone to know they were even with me. I had an awful time not crying at Aunt Elena's and Uncle Douglas's wedding, because it was so beautiful. When Grandfather read the wedding service it was as though it were being done for the very first time, as though those words had never been spoken before. Uncle Douglas's and Aunt Elena's voices were low, but very clear. I think the part that brought me closest to crying was when Grandfather took Aunt Elena from Daddy, put her hand in Uncle Douglas's, and Uncle Douglas said after him, "I take thee, Elena, to my wedded wife, to have and to hold from this day forward, for better for worse, for richer for poorer, in sickness and in health, to love and to cherish, till death us do part, according to God's holy ordinance; and thereto I plight thee my troth." And then when Aunt Elena, taking Uncle Douglas's hand, said, "I take thee, Douglas, to my wedded husband, to have and to hold from this day forward, for better for worse, for richer for poorer, in sickness and in health, to love and to cherish, till death us do part, according to God's holy ordinance; and thereto I give thee my troth."

Aunt Elena must have said those same words once before to Hal, and death had parted them. My own hands were very cold,

15

and I wondered if her hand, holding Uncle Douglas's, was cold, too, and what she was thinking. But she looked at him with love and trust and her voice never trembled and I realized all of a sudden that she probably felt all the wonderful things I felt about Uncle Douglas, and a few more besides.

Then the wedding was over. Uncle Douglas kissed Aunt Elena and it seemed everybody was kissing everybody else. Commander Rodney's oldest son, Leo, who's a slob, kissed me, and I had to get into the car to go back to the stable before I could wipe it off.

Back at the stable everybody spilled in and out of the house, on the porch, on the grass, and now at least I did help, serving punch, passing sandwiches, with Leo at my heels saying, "Let me take this, Vicky," "I'll do that," until I wanted to shove him over the cliff. Why couldn't he be more like his father?

Suzy and Maggy were dancing around, getting in everybody's way, but so happy and pretty nobody minded. Aunt Elena glowed and Uncle Douglas beamed and Daddy started pouring champagne and everybody was eating and laughing and talking and then I felt a hand at my elbow and it was Uncle Douglas. He said softly in my ear, "We're going to slip away now, Vic. Tell Maggy we'll see her tomorrow. And we'll see you in California in a month. No, love, don't kiss me, I don't want anybody to know we're going. I'll give you a big kiss by the Pacific ocean instead of the Atlantic. Okay?" And he was off around a corner of the stable.

Two

That night the four of us and Maggy went down to the beach for a cook-out. We'd helped get the stable all cleaned up after the reception, and Mother and Daddy and Grandfather said they were too full of lobster salad, and stuff to feel like eating, so we left them sitting out on the screened porch talking.

We had a picnic basket full of hamburgers and hot dogs and sodas and some charcoal to add to the driftwood. It would be our last night with Maggy as part of the family. The next day some friends of Grandfather's were going to drive her down to New York where she was to meet Uncle Douglas and Aunt Elena and fly out with them to California.

Now right in the midst of sounding all sentimental I must admit that life with Maggy wasn't always easy. In fact there were times when we could cheerfully have wrung her neck. But you get used to somebody in two years, and even her faults were familiar and comforting and part of the quiet, secure life in Thornhill. I sat on my rock and turned away from the sea, and looked at Maggy with the rosy glow of sunset behind her, and wished she weren't going to fly out to California the next day, but that we were all going to drive back to Thornhill. I didn't feel like talking, and it seemed that nobody else did, either, not even Maggy. Usually she never stops talking; it doesn't matter whether she has anything to say or not, it's just yak, yak, yak, right in the middle of homework or somebody else's conversation at the dinner table.

But Maggy stood there, barefooted in the soft sand, shifting her weight from one foot to the other in a rhythmic sort of way, just as quiet as the rest of us. Rob went off to the hard sand at the water's edge to dodge the little waves and collect shells. John built the fire, and after a while Suzy said, "Well!" very brightly, but that was as far as she got.

I don't mean to give the impression that, except for Maggy, we're usually a quiet family. We're anything but, and Rob must have felt that there was something funny about our silence, because he turned away from the water, dropped his shells, came over to my rock and leaned against me.

John looked up from where he was crouched beside the fire, feeding it little bites of driftwood, and said, "We'd better decide who wants hot dogs and who wants hamburgers because we haven't got too much time."

Everybody began talking about food, and things were better. That's something I've noticed about food: whenever there's a crisis if you can get people to eating normally things get better.

John had hot dogs cooked black; Suzy had hot dogs medium; I had hamburger rare ("I've seen cows hurt worse than that and get better," John remarked for the several-hundredth time);

18

Maggy had a hamburger cooked until it might have been a piece of old shoe; and Rob had a hot dog roll with three toasted marshmallows for filling. With the food, tongues loosened and we began to jabber about the wedding, Maggy began to brag about living in California, and Rob fell asleep. As the last light drained from the sky the fire seemed to grow brighter, and then we saw the beam from Grandfather's big flashlight as he stood up at the head of the bluff waving it down at us. We called up that we'd be right along; John put the fire out; we cleaned up our stuff and staggered up the path. Suddenly we were all very tired, and John and I half had to carry Rob, who couldn't seem to wake up.

When we got back to the stable Mother went up to the loft with the little ones. John and I went out to sit on the screened porch for a few minutes with Daddy and Grandfather. There was no light on the porch itself, but lights shone through from the kitchen windows, and moths of all sizes batted against the screens, trying to get in. The great beam from the light house swung around, once every minute, bathing us all in its brilliance. John was sitting on the old couch next to Grandfather, and suddenly, in the sweep of light, I had the funniest feeling that he didn't seem to be my own brother, familiar as an old shoe, someone I fought with frequently, but who could be depended on always to be there when I needed him. To help me with my math homework, for instance: John's a whizz at math and it's always been a struggle for me. Or at high school dances: if I needed him John was always there to see that I had plenty of partners and didn't get stuck, or have to spend long minutes in the girls' room taking off and putting on lipstick to kill time before going out to the dance floor again.

Grandfather must have been thinking about John, too, because he turned to him and said, "What with all the festivities for Elena and Doug I haven't had a chance to congratulate you. We're all very proud of you, son."

John gets terribly embarrassed when anybody praises him, and, since he's an outstanding kind of person, that happens far oftener than he'd like. As the lighthouse beam swept across his face I could see that he was blushing. "I'm scared stiff," he said. "Do you think I'll do all right?"

John's the first boy from our regional high school to be accepted at Massachusetts Institute of Technology. As a matter of fact his acceptance came through early and that was one reason the principal of our school made all kinds of exceptions and gave him his diploma ahead of time with a special little ceremony at Assembly, so he could be best man for Uncle Douglas and not miss any of our trip. We were all getting out of school several weeks early, but John was the one it made the most difference to, because he would have been Valedictorian of his class, and graduation week is something you really don't want to miss. As for me, I was glad not to be getting this final report card, because it had been much my worst year. I've always done well at school, but this year I'd study hard for a test, and get a D, a mark I'd never turned up with before; and then I wouldn't study for another test at all and get an A, and none of it made very much sense.

Mother came out onto the porch just then. Rob, she told us, was asleep before he got into bed. Suzy, who has always had the ability to get right to sleep whenever she feels like it, had hardly waited to say good-night. Maggy, ever since her thirteenth birthday, has felt that she should go to bed at least as late as John does, and she was furious at still having to go up with Suzy, and was lying there in the dark glowering.

"But she has a big day ahead of her tomorrow," Mother said. "She'd better get some rest."

John stretched luxuriously. "As for *us*, we can lounge around on the beach all day."

Daddy, who was sprawled on an old wicker chaise lounge, grunted, "Aside from the time you'll spend helping me get the station wagon ready."

Mother shoved Daddy over and sat by him, then turned to me. "What got into you this morning, Vicky? Why did you run off when I needed you?"

I looked at the screen door, where a moth was clinging, his wings momentarily flattened against the criss-cross pattern of the wires. "I'm sorry. I just wanted to go down to the beach for a while to think. I didn't mean to stay so long."

I expected Mother or Daddy to let me have it then, but all Mother said was, "I guess we all feel the need to go off and sort things out, Vicky. This is a pretty big step for all of us. For Daddy and me, too, you know. Next time you want to disappear for a while check with me first, will you?"

I was grateful not to be getting a bawling out. Here *I* was going around moping and if I sat down to think about it I'd probably have to admit that it was harder on Mother than anybody, and she wasn't making any kind of fuss at all. From the way she behaved on the outside you'd have thought that moving from our own house, that stood on its hill about a mile outside a small New England village, to an apartment right in the middle of New York City was no more important than a trip to the Island.

Well, it was a lot more important than that. None of us could remember living anywhere except Thornhill, or having Daddy be anything but a busy, always overworked country doctor. We knew he'd spent what few spare moments he had in research, and that he'd kept in close touch with his old professors and colleagues at medical school, but when he came back from a meeting in New York and told us that he'd accepted a post teaching and doing research at his old school we all flipped. Well, we flipped if it can mean just plain shock and doesn't mean we were wild with joy. We weren't. At first we weren't anything but stunned. We didn't even realize all at once that it meant leaving Thornhill, that it meant moving to New York. But Thornhill's over a hundred miles from New York. Daddy couldn't very well commute.

Funnily enough it was Rob who was the first to catch on to what it really meant. He got terribly upset, the way he sometimes does, and burst into tears and said that he wouldn't move to New York, that Daddy couldn't leave Thornhill, and then he got very white and suddenly looked very grown up and not at all the baby we always thought him, and said, "You're not going to sell the house! Daddy, you can't sell the house!"

"No," Daddy said. "We hope we won't ever have to sell the house, Rob. We're renting it for the next year to the doctor who's taking over my office. He and his wife are people you'll all like, they've got a darling baby, and they'll take care of the animals for us."

"The animals!" Rob got positively green with dismay. "Aren't they coming with us?" He put his arms around Rochester's neck. Rochester's rear end wriggled with affection; then, as Rob's grip tightened with intensity Rochester gave him a big slobbery kiss of friendship and apology and pulled away so abruptly that Rob sat down hard on the floor.

Daddy laughed and said, "We can't very well take the animals on a camping trip, Rob."

We all went into a state of shock again. "CAMPING TRIP!"

Now Mother and Daddy were both laughing, and Daddy said, "We thought it might soften the blow if we bought a tent and sleeping bags and took a trip out to California to see Uncle Douglas and Aunt Elena and Maggy. It'll be a break between our two lives. Once I really get going in New York I'm not going to be doing much vacationing for a while."

This was easy to believe. Daddy *never* was able to do much vacationing. And the idea of going all over the United States was fabulous because we'd never done much traveling. To the Island to visit Grandfather. A trip to Washington, D.C., last spring vacation. That was pretty much it. John and I liked the idea of travel, and Suzy was thrilled with the thought of all the new insects and animals she'd see. Suzy has wanted to be a doctor ever since she could talk, but sometimes I think she'd much better be a veterinarian.

Rob went off and came back clutching Elephant's Child, his filthy and favorite stuffed animal. Elephant's Child has a music box that plays Brahms' Lullaby and Rob has had him since he was a baby and even starting school couldn't change his feelings about Elephant's Child. John says Rob will probably take Elephant's Child off to college with him and play Brahms' Lullaby in the dormitory at night. And Rob, being Rob, probably will, and be so matter of fact about it that nobody will even laugh.

"Yes, Rob," Daddy said, "you may take Elephant's Child."

Aside from being pleased about new bugs and things on the camping trip Suzy didn't say very much, but you could tell that she was thinking and sorting things out in her own mind the way she does, and the next night when I'd gone to bed early to study for a Social Studies test the next day, one of those stupid, multiple choice things, she came in wearing her polka dot pajamas and plunked herself down on the foot of my bed.

"Maggy's asleep," she said morosely.

I kept on reading. "Oh. That's good."

"Vicky," Suzy said passionately, "what does he want to do it for?"

"Who?" I asked stupidly. "What?"

She punched at my book. "Daddy. Why does he want to go to New York?"

"You know," I said. "He ex*plained* it all. He's gone as far as he can with his research here, and if he really wants to go back to New York and be with a big hospital again——"

"The hospital here's one of the best in the country!" Suzy defended.

"Yes, but it's a *litt*le hospital, Suzy, and it doesn't have a medical school or a nursing school—oh, you want to be a doctor, you ought to understand, you of all people——"

"We've been *per*fectly happy here," Suzzy said. "Daddy, too."

"I know, but I just ex*plained*, and his practice is getting so big and he's so busy and you *know* he's been saying for years he doesn't have enough time for study and research."

"We'll have to leave all our friends—and go to new schools——"

It was all perfectly true, and I argued to convince myself as much as Suzy. "Well, maybe it's like John. John's learned everything he can at Regional and next year he's going on to M.I.T. Maybe that's how it is with Daddy. He's gone as far as he can here and he has to take the next step."

"At least John's not dragging the rest of us *with* him," Suzy said. "I think it might have occurred to Daddy that we might be involved in this, too."

We were all certainly involved in it; it was probably the most involved spring we ever had, with Daddy and John poring over the Montgomery Ward catalogue and brooding over various tents and sleeping bags and air mattresses, and Mother being demanding about cooking equipment, and Aunt Elena coming up to Thornhill with designs for her wedding dress and Suzy's and Maggy's handmaiden dresses, and Uncle Douglas deciding to paint another portrait of Mother before moving out to California, and Daddy finishing up a million things at home and at the office and the hospital.

So it was no wonder, now that Uncle Douglas and Aunt Elena were safely married, we sat out on Grandfather's screened porch and felt that we couldn't possibly move an inch, even to go to bed. And maybe that was why Mother didn't blast me for disappearing in the morning before the wedding.

I thought it would be nice if I did something to make up for it, so I said, "If anybody feels like lemonade or coffee or tea or anything before bed I'll make it."

Mother leaned against Daddy and yawned. "Thanks, Vicky, but let's all just go to bed. Come on, Wally."

Daddy yawned, too. "Come on yourself."

"Father can't go to bed until we get off the porch," Mother

said. "Come on, Wallace. I'm so tired I'm like a piece of cooked spaghetti. Give me a shove."

Daddy gave her a shove and she slid off the chaise longue and onto the floor, and then we were all laughing, and John pulled her up. We kissed Grandfather good-night, Mother and Daddy went to sleep in Grandfather's big double bed, John and I went on up to the loft, and for some reason just being silly out there on the porch had made me feel better. Even if everything around us was different from now on, where we lived and school and everything, as long as Mother and Daddy were the same, as long as the family didn't change, then there was still something to hang on to.

Three

The next day we saw Maggy off and then lazed around on the beach. In the afternoon Daddy and John got the car ready and practiced setting up the tent on the small patch of lawn in front of the stable, while Mother, Suzy, Rob, and I stood around criticizing. John got mad, and Rob thought he really meant it and went and flung his arms around him to comfort him, which slowed things down. But the tent was really quite easy to manage. It hangs from tubular aluminum poles that fit together, so that there isn't any pole in the middle of the tent at all. The back of the tent lifts up and hitches over the end of the station wagon with the tail gate down. Mother, Daddy, Rob, and John were to sleep in the tent, and Suzy and I in the back of the station wagon, and we'd all be under one roof.

The next morning we got up at five o'clock and put the last things in the car. It was a soft morning, with the light a kind of fuzzy, golden-pink, the sort of hazy early morning that always brightens up and clears into a beautiful day. We hugged and kissed Grandfather good-bye and got into the car. Suzy and I wore Bermuda's and knee socks and sweaters, and John and Rob and Daddy wore jeans. Daddy doesn't like women in pants and Mother never wears them, but she looked comfortable and all ready for the trip in a plaid skirt and white blouse and red cardigan.

In the very back of the station wagon Daddy had made a kind of bed out of the sleeping bags and air-mattresses, and so forth, with a couple of extra blankets spread over the top. Rob immediately curled up there with Elephant's Child in his arms. Suzy crawled in by him, so she could lie on her stomach and look out the back window. John and I sat in the middle seat with the stove, the pots and pans, the big water thermos jug, and the ice box. There *was* room for us, but not an inch extra. Mother and Daddy sat in front with the food box and Mother's big straw bag of odds and ends, and a wooden box of books. Mother said she knew she wasn't apt to read them if she brought them, but she was even less apt to read them if she left them behind, so she was going to bring them.

Daddy stood by the car checking everything off on his list: tools, hatchet, saw, fire extinguisher, laundry rope, big-batteried lantern, everything he'd decided that we couldn't possibly do without. Then he, too, said good-bye to Grandfather, got in and started the car, and suddenly my stomach felt very empty, as though we hadn't had any breakfast at all.

For once we were glad when the ferry trip to the mainland was over, because now that we were really all packed up and in the car we wanted to get going. When we reached the mainland we headed for a parkway and started playing the alphabet game.

You know, you divide up by who's sitting on which side of the car, and you have to find the letters of the alphabet, in order, one by one, on signs. John and Daddy and Suzy were way ahead until they came to Q, and then Mother and Rob and I caught up with them and won. Then we played Animal Rummy, and Rob saw a white horse and won that. And of course we sang. We always do a lot of singing.

Daddy and Mother and John were going to take turns with the driving, although there were quite a lot of states John wouldn't be able to drive in after dark because he wasn't eighteen. However, we didn't plan to do much driving after dark, so it didn't matter.

Daddy had picked a route that avoided all the big towns and just went through their outskirts. Rob thought this over seriously, then asked, "Daddy, if those were the out skirts we just went through, where are the out pants?"

We had a snack of fruit and cookies in the middle of the morning, and ate our lunch in the car, too, just sandwiches, so it was easy. Whenever we stopped at a gas station we would all get out and use the wash rooms and Mother would give us some lemonade from the big jug. In the afternoon we stopped and had milkshakes, and all through the trip we found that this was much the best and easiest way to do it——have snack and lunch while we were driving, and then stop in the afternoon when we were restless to get something to drink. We had to play it by ear all along, because we'd never been on a camping trip before, and we really didn't know anything about it.

John and Suzy and I'd been to Scout Camp, but Daddy, of course, had been much too busy to think about anything like

29

camping trips, or even picnics. Why eat a meal outdoors, I'd heard him say, where you have ants and mosquitoes and smoky fires, when you can be so much more comfortable at home? As for views, what could rival the view from our own windows?

Aunt Elena and Uncle Douglas had thought Daddy was nuts not to take the tent and go up Hawk Mountain for a week-end for a dry run. "Really, Wallace," Aunt Elena said, looking up from designing her wedding dress, "you can't just go off on a camping trip cold when you've never had anything to do with tents before."

Uncle Douglas grinned and said, "Wally thinks he can just snap out '*hatchet*' or '*tent peg*' the way he does '*suture*' or '*scalpel*' at the hospital, and somebody'll be hovering over him to slap them in his hand. You'd really better take a week-end up Hawk, Wally."

Daddy threw back his head and laughed. "In the first place, you're confusing me with young Dr. Malone. In the second place if we spent even one night up on Hawk I'd come back and put all the camping equipment in the attic and never touch any of it again."

So that first day when we set off none of us had ever slept in a tent, since the scout camps we'd been to had shacks. All our equipment was new and shiny and we couldn't wait to use it. Uncle Douglas had sent Mother some wonderful cooking equipment from Abercrombie and Fitch in New York. First of all there was a folding two burner stove with canned gas. Then the pots and pans. They all fitted in a canvas bag. There was a big aluminum pot and in the bottom of this went a frying pan. On top of the frying pan went six tin plates. Then there was a medium sized pot, then a smaller pot, then a big coffee pot top, and in this a stack of tin cups. Then came the coffee pot top, and for a grand lid over everything a big frying pan. The handles of the frying pans came off and slipped down in the canvas bag. The way it was put together reminded me of a wooden doll Aunt Elena had given me once years ago for Christmas. You opened the wooden doll, and inside was another wooden doll, and inside another and another and another, all neatly fitted together like our cooking equipment. Mother was as pleased and delighted with the nest of pots and pans as I'd been with the doll.

The first night of the trip Daddy planned to stop near Washington. Since we'd been to Washington the year before, and seen as many sights as you can pack into a few days, we were going to skip the city. Daddy had the car radio on, and every once in a while there would be a weather report; showers by nightfall were forecast. Daddy would look at Mother and Mother would look at Daddy, but the sun kept on shining until we got on the Pennsylvania Turnpike, and even then it didn't look very bad.

But after we left the Pennsylvania Turnpike and were heading for Gettysburg it started to sprinkle and then it began to pour. It rained so hard that the windshield wipers had a hard time keeping up. The sky was black and gloomy all around. There didn't seem to be a break in the clouds anywhere. It was after four o'clock, and Daddy'd said we'd plan to stop by five or five thirty each afternoon at the very latest.

He turned to Mother. "Do you think we should go to a motel?"

We all sat very still and waited. Mother looked at the rain streaming down the windshield and the wipers bustling back and forth. She picked up the AAA booklet of campsites, and then she looked at the map of Pennsylvania that had campsites on it. "Our very first night?" she asked Daddy. "It seems like an awful admission of defeat."

"Mighty wet for putting up tents and building fires," Daddy said.

"We could use Douglas's stove," Mother suggested.

"But not to sleep in," Daddy said.

Mother looked back at us kids. "How do you feel about it?"

John said, "I'd rather not go to a motel," and I nodded.

"Oh, please!" Suzy clasped her hands in her intensity. "*Please!*"

Rob looked very solemn and as though he were about to burst into tears, but he didn't say anything.

Mother looked at the campsite book and at the map again. "This is the only campsite anywhere around. Caledonia State Park. If we don't stay there we'll have to drive another hour or so, and that would make it pretty late."

"Let's try it. Please!" Suzy begged.

I concentrated hard. I guess we all did. But to me it seemed that if this first night of the camping trip, which was the first step of our new life, turned out all right, then the rest of it would be all right, too. But if the first night of the camping trip was a mess, then everything, the trip, New York, all of it, would be a mess, too. I know that's silly and superstitious and I certainly didn't mention it out loud, but it's the way I felt.

"Okay," Daddy said. "We'll go on to Caledonia State Park and if the weather's still impossible we'll give up—and gracefully, kids—and go to a motel."

"But it'll unbalance our budget," John said, and I could have hugged him for it. "There're a heck of a lot of us for a motel."

"The budget is geared for an emergency or two," Daddy told

32

him. "But I agree with you. We're on a camping trip and we want to sleep in our tent. But we don't want to start on the wrong foot the very first night."

Mother folded the map. "We'll just wait and see. That's one thing we have to remember about this trip. For once in our lives we're not on a schedule of any kind. We don't have to plan anything ahead. We'll just take it all as it comes." She looked around at me, and I must have been looking tense, because she said, "and whether it's a sleeping bag or a motel bed we'll have fun, Vicky."

—Not a motel. Please, not a motel.

It seemed to me that the rain was beginning to slacken. — Go away, rain. Stop. Please make it stop. Please.

I'm sure it wasn't due to my concentration, but when Daddy pointed out the entrance to Caledonia State Park the rain began to let up, and when we reached the Park office it had slowed down to a trickle, so Daddy paid a dollar, got a permit, and drove off towards the transient campsites. And just as we drove into the grove of pines where the campsites were the sun burst through the clouds, great shafts of light shot down through the trees, and the floor of pine needles turned golden.

It was an omen!

Daddy stopped by a picnic table near a brook, where somebody had made a fireplace out of several flat stones, and we all jumped out and stretched our legs, which felt cramped and a little wobbly from the long day's driving. Then we all set about our jobs. John and Daddy were to put up the tent and take care of the fire. I was to help Mother unpack the food and start dinner. Suzy and Rob were to blow up the air-mattresses, which they did by taking turns with a little black rubber foot pump, and then I was to help them slide the air-mattresses into the sleeping bags and get things organized in the tent. It was really lucky, as well as being an omen, that the rain had stopped, because the ground at the campsite was hard and shale-ey, not a bit like the soft patch of lawn in front of Grandfather's stable, and John and Daddy had an awful time hammering in the aluminum pitons that hold up the tent. They never did get them in all the way; they were afraid that if they kept on hammering the aluminum would bend or break. "But they'll hold up the tent until morning—I *think*," Daddy said.

This was one of the few American campsites where we were allowed to go off into the forest and collect our own wood. Mother told me to go along with the others because she didn't really need me to help with dinner, so we crossed the little wooden bridge over the brook and Daddy and John took the hatchet while Suzy and Rob and I collected kindling. Rob was so excited and happy that he couldn't just walk, he had to jump and skip. When Rob's happy he seems to shine, almost as though you could actually see light pulsing from him. The rays of his light seem to spread out and touch you so that you can't help glowing with pleasure yourself.

Rob and Suzy went running on ahead while I stood there in the woods suddenly feeling happier than I had in a long time. The leaves of the trees and bushes were all quivering with silver drops of rain, the sunlight sifted down softly, the birds were singing, and I felt all full of life and hope. Maybe nothing would ever be as comforting and secure as it used to be when I was a child in Thornhill, but it was going to be exciting.

When we got back with the firewood Mother needed water

to cook with, as well as water to heat for dishwashing. (As chief dishwasher I was the one most apt to miss the electric one at home. For camping we had only a good-sized white plastic pan.) Rob and I found the water, which was a spigot coming out of a cement base. We splashed water into our pots and I was so happy that I didn't even get cross when Rob slopped water all over me. After we'd brought Mother all the water she needed we scouted around and found the lavatories, which were sort of glorified privies, and were already quite dark inside. We'd need our flashlights when it came time to get ready for bed.

We had a wonderful dinner. I don't think food has ever tasted better than it did that night in the dusk of the pine grove, eaten off our tin plates, with Rob bouncing up and down on the wooden bench, so excited he couldn't keep still. We had a thick, juicy steak. Salad with *three* big tomatoes. Potato salad. And we roasted marshmallows for dessert. While we ate we could hear the faint bubbling of the water for the dishes heating over the fire, and afterwards Mother and I washed the dishes while Suzy and Rob got ready for bed. Then John and I took our turn. When we walked through the campgrounds to the lavatories there were lights in almost all the trailer windows, and they looked warm and cozy. I hadn't realized that people in trailers would have lights, while people in tents wouldn't. This camp had mostly trailers, and there weren't many children.

After I'd brushed my teeth I tried to look at myself in the mirror by flashlight, to see if I'd changed any in the exciting past couple of days. I wasn't exactly looking for grey hairs, but I thought that I might look a little older, more sophisticated, if not a raving beauty. But the flashlight made me look sort of weird, and the mirror in the camp bathroom was one of those wavy ones that distort you, anyhow, so I stuck the end of the flashlight in my mouth, puffed out my cheeks, looked at my ghoulish reflection, and decided to scare Suzy and Rob when we got to bed.

Just as I got back to the tent it started to rain again. "Perfect timing if ever I saw it," Mother said.

Suzy and I climbed into our sleeping bags on the tail gate of the station wagon, with our heads towards the tent. Rob and John got into their bags, and Mother and Daddy into theirs, which was two sleeping bags zippered together to make one big one. It took less room in the tent, which was important, and also gave Mother and Daddy more room to stretch than would an ordinary sleeping bag.

Mother adjusted the lantern, pulled a book out of her wooden box, and said, "What with John's and Vicky's homework it's been a long time since we've been able to do any family reading at bedtime, and this will probably be our last chance in a while. Would you like something?"

John grinned. "You and Rob would be shattered if we didn't. Sure, Mother. What've you got?"

"I thought *A Connecticut Yankee* might be fun for a start," Mother said, and we all settled down to the first chapter.

It made me feel younger. I wasn't sure whether I wanted to feel younger or older. All I knew was that at almost fifteen it's very difficult to be satisfied with the age you are, because you aren't really any age. I mean, you get fascinated with boys, but it isn't really time yet. It's too early to think about marrying and babies and stuff like that, though lots of the kids at Regional who weren't going on to college *were* thinking about it, and there were even a couple of marriages in John's grade. But *I* wasn't ready, that's for sure, and I guess I'm not very good with boys, yet. Suzy can giggle and look cute and when she gets into high school she'll have dozens of boys asking her for each dance. This past year I'd always ended up with an invitation, but people weren't exactly falling over themselves trying to date me. Suzy says it's because I'm too serious about things, and she's probably right. I laugh a lot, because we always seem to in our family, but I don't think my sense of humor is my strong point.

After Mother had finished reading she said, and I thought there was a double kind of questioning in her voice, "How about prayers?"

When we were little we always used to love bedtime, when Mother would read to us, and then we'd all say prayers together. But when John got into high school and had more and more home-work piled up on him, he dropped out. This year I went over to the regional high school, too, and started staying up later to study, so I didn't go up with the others, either. Suzy and Maggy didn't have to turn their lights out till an hour after Rob, but they kept on with the reading and everything. And it wasn't just that. Our grandfather is a minister and I love him more than anyone in the world except Mother and Daddy and Uncle Douglas, but all of a sudden this winter I'd begun to resent having to go to Sunday school, and church every week, and I'd quit saying prayers any-how most nights, partly because I wasn't sure anyone was listening—after all, why *should* anyone—and partly because by the time I'd done my homework and got into bed I was too sleepy, anyhow. I'm not sure how John felt. He's not like me. He never griped about church and all and I don't think not understanding

God ever bothered him, but I think maybe he thought he was too big for prayers at Mother's knee and all that stuff, too.

This time he didn't say it would upset Mother and Rob if we didn't, he just said, "Sure," and looked over at me, as though to make certain I wasn't going to say anything.

So we said prayers and then Rob said his God-bless. We always used to say a God-bless, but Rob was the only one who did that night, and nobody urged anybody else to, thank heavens. I've always loved Rob's God-blesses. He talks very sternly to God during them, telling Him just where to get off, and he spends a great deal of time blessing a great many animals and people. I guess Mother'd had to cut him down on it some, because instead of naming all the cats we've ever had, the way he used to, he asked God to bless Mr. Rochester and Colette, our dogs, and then, "and bless Hamlet and Prunewhip and all the cats and dogs who have been, will be, and are." Then he did the same with people, just blessed the family, and then asked God to bless all the people on all the planets who have been, will be, and are. Then he said, "And God, help the situation in the world. Please don't let there be any wars. Please just make everybody die of old age." And then, "And God, thank you because we've had a wonderful day, and please make tomorrow be just as wonderful, and keep us safe. God, I'm very consented. Bless me and make me a good boy. Amen."

I think if everybody could be like Rob about prayers I wouldn't be so embarrassed by them.

We all said good-night and rolled over comfortably in our sleeping bags. Mother and Daddy kept the lantern on for a little while and read, but it wasn't long before they turned it off and it was dark in the tent. It seemed very peculiar all to be going to bed at the same time and in the same place. I lay in my sleeping bag and listened to the rain pattering on the canvas roof of the tent, and to the gentle splashing of the brook outside. It was hard to tell which was rain and which was brook, and, to add to it, the wind and the rain in the pines sounded like the ocean, so that we might almost have been back at Grandfather's. I've often noticed the way the sound of wind in pines is like the rolling of the waves on the beach. If you close your eyes and listen you can pretend you're at the seashore. But I didn't feel like pretending anything now. It was exciting being in our tent, sleeping out in the wilderness on the rather bouncy air mattress (Daddy said it would take a little experimenting to find out just how much air we needed) and looking around the dark tent. The canvas flaps had to be zipped up over the net windows because of the rain, but the front of the tent had a canvas porch, and from where I was lying on the tail gate I could look through the open netting of the door to the woods. The night sounds all seemed to be different from the night sounds at home, not just the brook and the rain on canvas and through pines, but the frogs and insects seemed to be singing in a different key and rhythm.

I heard a hiss in Daddy's direction and whispered, "What's that?"

"Shh!" he whispered back. "I'm letting a little air out of my mattress."

"May I?"

"Yes, but don't let too much out, because you can't put any back in."

"Go to sleep, Vicky," Mother whispered.

"I'm too excited."

"We're all excited, but Daddy wants to get an early start to-morrow, so try to relax."

I turned my mattress valve and let a little air hiss out. Then I stretched out in the sleeping bag sheet. Mother had made sort of inner bags out of old sheets for us. These had tapes on the bottom and could be tied to tapes at the foot of the sleeping bags, so the sheets wouldn't wrinkle up too much when you tried to turn over. And we all had small foam-rubber-filled cloth pillows, each in a different pattern so we could tell them apart, that could be tossed in washing machines along the way, and of course didn't take up as much room as regular pillows. There are lots of little things like that to a camping trip that I never thought of when we first started making plans.

Suzy mumbled something in her sleep. From one of the tents or trailers somebody called out, "Harry!" The rain shshed gently through the trees and the sound was a lullaby. I closed my eyes and went to sleep.

The next morning we were up early. On school mornings Mother has to pry us out of our beds, but the moment we heard Mother and Daddy stirring we were all very wide awake and excited immediately. John built the fire and Mother made scrambled eggs and hashed brown potatoes, and brewed coffee in the open pot that came with Uncle Douglas's cooking set. At home Mother uses an electric percolator; we have friends who make drip coffee and chemex coffee and instant coffee and espresso coffee and I've never given a hoot about coffee, I've always had milk or cocoa for breakfast. But this coffee! In an open pot you just bring the water to a boil, throw in the coffee (I suppose you

40

have to measure it), and an egg shell if you happen to have one handy, then take the pot off the fire and let it sit on the side of the fireplace till the grounds settle. Well! Nothing has ever smelled quite as wonderful as that open pot coffee at Caledonia State Park, and it even tasted good, with lots of milk and sugar.

We learned that morning that it took us longer to break camp than to set it up. Daddy said we'd undoubtedly learn short cuts and be able to cut down on the time, but we'd have to get going earlier in the morning.

As soon as we got in the car Mother got out her little notebook in which she was keeping lists of everything. Not for any real reason. Just for fun. We did want to know how much we spent each day, and we wanted to jot down every place that was interesting that we went through. The first day we spent $9.95 on tolls, gas, Cokes, and the camping permit. The second day it was $11.84 on tolls, gas, tickets to Monticello (Rob thought it was a musical instrument), gas, sodas, and firewood. At Peaks of Otter State Park in Virginia you had to buy the firewood, but it only cost fifty cents, and the campgrounds were much nicer than Caledonia, with special places marked out for the tents and for parking cars, really nice picnic tables, and well built stone fireplaces with good grills at each campsite. That night we had spaghetti and got to bed earlier than the first night, and were ready for bed, too. There were only a few other campers there, and none very close to us, so Mother got out her guitar and we sang, first loud songs and silly songs, then the kind of sad folk songs, and then she slipped in some hymns. Not that I'm really against hymns, but you know what I mean.

One thing I *do* like about hymns, most of them we can sing

in parts. John and Daddy sing bass, which makes the bass louder than anything else, but you can't stop them. Suzy and Rob sing the melody, and they both have sweet, clear voices. Rob's is really terrific for such a little kid. He never flats or gets off tune or anything. Mother sings tenor, sometimes where it belongs and sometimes an octave high, so it's sort of like a descant, and I struggle along with the alto. I'm the weak link in the part-singing deal. I'm pretty good on the alto of "All Through the Night," and "Now the Day Is Over" is a cinch. It's the Bach ones I'm apt to goof on, but they're really my favorites.

Mother put the guitar down and said, "Let's end up with 'I will lift up mine eyes unto the hills.' After the glorious hills we've seen today it seems the perfect way to say good-night."

As far as the Bible goes (and I suppose you might say it goes pretty far, even if not with me at this point) I like the psalms best, and that's one of my particular best ones, so that was okay.

We cut five minutes off breaking-camp time the next morning and headed for Tennessee.

Don't let anybody kid you. Tennessee's quite a state. When I look back on that night at Cosby Camp Site in the Great Smokies National Park I still get gooseflesh.

Four

But the day started peacefully enough. We drove through more beautiful mountains and *more* beautiful mountains, till I stopped looking. In the afternoon it began to cloud up, and the weather reports started mentioning possible showers. But this was becoming routine for afternoons and didn't bother us any more. We stopped at a market and bought food for dinner: pork chops, turnip greens, lettuce. We still had potatoes and tomatoes and milk, and we'd replenished our ice the day before with a twenty-five pound chunk which would last forty-eight hours.

As we got near the Great Smokies National Park we passed an inn called the Black Bear Inn. It had a sign with a big picture of a bear on it, and Rob cried out, "A bear! A bear!"

"Where?" Suzy yelled, reaching for *her* notebook, because she was keeping lists, too, only her lists were of animals and insects and (she hoped and I didn't) snakes.

Daddy pointed to the sign and said, "Take a good look, kids.

That's probably as close to a bear as you'll get till we reach the Rockies."

As we drove into the park the wind began to whip at the trees, and dark clouds scudded across the sky. It wasn't actually raining, but the air felt wet. There were puddles at the sides of the road, so we knew it must have showered here earlier.

"We'd better set up camp and get dinner quickly," Mother said.

We had our choice of campsites. At Caledonia it was almost crowded; and at Peaks of Otter, in Virginia, there'd been other families. Here we were the *only* people in the largest campgrounds we'd been to so far. I suppose the reason there wasn't anybody else there was that we'd started out almost a month ahead of usual camping time. School was still open most places and people wouldn't be going on vacations yet.

It was a beautiful campgrounds, with big stone tables and benches, and really good fireplaces for each campsite. But it was lonely, and for some reason I felt edgy and almost scared. I didn't quite know why, and I certainly didn't say anything about it. But I wished the ranger's house were nearer the campgrounds instead of way down the mountain.

The ground was soft and wet; it must have rained *hard* here. But this at least made the tent pegs lots easier to drive into the ground, so John and Daddy got the tent up quickly. The late afternoon was chill, so we built an extra big fire. We put on our sweaters and stayed close by the tent instead of running off to explore the way we usually did. The sky was full of low, black clouds, making it dark for this time of day. The wind was rising, whipping the trees so that the younger ones bent against its lash and the small branches tossed wildly.

As soon as dinner was ready we sat down at the big stone table. Because we were the only people there we sang grace, one we do to the Tallis Canon, a very joyful noise. Despite my current feelings about loud singings of grace it made me feel better. Also there's something very matter-of-fact about pork chops. Heroines of mystery novels are never mentioned eating a dinner of pork chops just before something terrible is about to happen.

Being a little nervy hadn't blunted my appetite, and I was gnawing on my chop bone when we heard a car coming up the hill to the campgrounds very fast. It whizzed by us—it must have been going seventy-five miles an hour on that narrow, winding road—zoomed all the way around the campgrounds, and went by us again. As it passed something was flung out of the window and shattered against the side of our station wagon with a sound like an explosion. We all stood up. I thought it was a bomb.

Daddy started towards our car. He moved with such quickness and decision that he was half way there before the rest of us had untangled ourselves from the picnic table and started to follow him. I still had my pork chop bone in my hand and was trembling like an aspen.

"It was just a Coke bottle," Daddy said, his voice very quiet and matter-of-fact. But it wasn't his regular, at home voice. It was his Dr. Austin voice, the kind of voice he uses when patients get hysterical, or some kind of emergency comes up that has to be handled quickly and without fuss.

We could still hear the car zooming on around the road that circled the campgrounds. I knew it was coming by us again, and no matter how calm Daddy was, I was very frightened. There was a dent in the fender where the Coke bottle had hit it, dark stains of Coke splashes, and broken glass all over.

Daddy said, sharply, "Everybody get back to the picnic table. Quickly. Sit there and eat as though nothing had happened."

I knew the car would come by again, and they might throw something else. This time it might hit one of us instead of the station wagon. We scurried up the side of the hill to the picnic table. Mother put her arm around Rob and pretended to eat salad. John said, "Those dumb hoods," and drank some milk.

"How do you know it was hoods?" I asked.

John sounded disgusted. "Who else?"

Now we could hear the car coming closer, and I could feel everything about my body tightening up.

Daddy said, "Just ignore them."

This time the car didn't whizz on by and they didn't throw anything. The car stopped with a great squealing skid and jamming on of brakes. It was a shabby-looking jalopy, and inside it was a gang of boys. John was right, as usual, but that didn't make me any happier. The left front door opened and the boy behind the steering wheel got out. He had on black tapered pants and a black leather jacket.

Daddy got up from the picnic table, speaking in low command. "Stay where you are. You, too, John."

I looked at Mother, sitting very still, her arm around Rob. I knew she was frightened because she was as motionless as a statue. I looked at Daddy walking unhurriedly down towards the boy.

Before Daddy said anything the boy snarled, and he sounded more like an animal than a human boy, "Ah believe you have one of our Cokes. We'd like it back."

Daddy is used to giving orders and he is used to being obeyed. He spoke very quietly, but his words were as cold and

46

sharp as ice. "Get in your car and get out of this campgrounds. At once. If we have any further trouble from you I shall report you to the police."

"Yea-uh?" the boy said. "Un-hunh?" His voice had a southern drawl, but it wasn't soft and it wasn't pretty. "Just you try, mistah. We'll go when we feel like it."

"You will go now," Daddy said, still very quiet.

"Yea-uh? Now just tell me why?"

Daddy spoke as though he were talking to Suzy and Rob when they were being disobedient. "Because I say so."

The boy moved slowly, insolently towards Daddy. I remembered a TV show about delinquents where a boy had deliberately tweaked a man's nose in order to humiliate him, and the man stood there and took it. I didn't think Daddy would. I held my breath. Before the boy could do anything Daddy reached out casually and gave a flip and the boy was over his back and lying sprawled on the soft, wet leaves.

I let my breath out.

Daddy was a black belt in Judo before any of us was ever born. We've always been proud of it, but as far as I know he's never had to use it before.

The boy got up and as soon as he was on his feet Daddy flipped him again. Then he picked him up by the scruff of his neck. "Get back in your car and go home."

The boy stood there in front of Daddy. The back door of the car opened, but nobody got out. Beside me on the picnic bench John stood up and started to walk down to Daddy.

Daddy looked levelly at the boy. "Get back in your car. This is a state campgrounds and you are certainly a very poor

47

representative of your state. Go home. And don't come back here again."

The boy looked at Daddy. Daddy looked back, stern and commanding. The boy dropped his gaze and turned, saying, "Aw, c'mon, let's get out of here." He got back in the car and started it so quickly that the wheels spun. They went careening down the road, taking the curve on two wheels.

Daddy and John came back to the picnic table. Suzy said in a shaky voice, "I don't think I like Tennessee." My hands were drenched in cold sweat, and I could see that Mother's hand, as she reached for her tin mug, was trembling.

John's voice was gratey, so I knew that he'd been scared, too. "Don't be a nut. It's just hoods anywhere. They're all the same. Tennessee, New York, the U.S.S.R."

"Not in *Thornhill*," Suzy protested.

"There're a couple in Thornhill, and a gang of them over at Regional. Vicky knows that."

Yes, he was right. I thought about some of the boys at home who had been grinning, freckle-faced kids just a couple of years ago and who were now hanging around the drugstore and smoking and thinking they were so darned big. I couldn't even talk to them any more. It was as though we spoke different languages. What was changing them? To what?

Suzy asked, "Daddy, weren't you scared?"

"I didn't like it," Daddy said, "but most hoodlums are cowards when it comes to a showdown. They're only brave when they think you're afraid of them. Now don't let this spoil our trip, and don't let it spoil Tennessee. John's quite right."

"Are we to be frightened by our teen-agers?" Mother asked bitterly. "Has it come to that?"

"Vicky and I are teen-agers," John said. "You can't blame teen-agers any more than you can Tennessee. There are dopey fringe elements in every group. I wrote a paper on it for Social Studies once."

Daddy finished his milk. "Okay, son, you stay here and take care of everybody. I'm going down to talk to the ranger."

"About those JDs?" Suzy asked.

"I doubt if they're really JDs," Daddy said, "but it's certainly a very poor idea to allow them in a state campgrounds. Come along with me, Rob. Girls, you help Mother with the dishes."

After we'd washed and dried the dishes and emptied out the rinse water Suzy remembered, "Hey, we haven't had dessert!" So Mother said just to roast some marshmallows. The fire had died down now and there was a lovely bed of glowing coals, just right for marshmallows. John likes to burn his, and Suzy likes hers raw, but what I like is to toast mine a lovely, puffy, golden brown, then eat off the toasted skin, hold it back over the embers and watch it puff up again, almost to full size, eat off the skin, toast it again, and go on until I'm almost down to nothing. Mother likes hers that way, too, and we had a contest to see who could make the marshmallows last for the most layers.

We were all very jumpy. Mother knew this, and maybe she was jumpy, too, I don't know. That's one trouble about parents; they always try to hide it from you when they're worried about something, and lots of times you'd feel a lot better if they'd just come out and tell you what was on their minds. I think Mother sometimes does tell John things. I suppose I'm too young. Too young to be told things properly like a grown-up, and too old to go clamoring to Mother for comfort. This is something Uncle Douglas understands. He talks to me as though I were twenty at least, but when he sees I'm upset he's apt to pick the biggest chair available and then pull me down into it with him, so that I feel protected and can have the pleasure of being treated like a baby with none of the problems.

"I don't like Tennessee," Suzy said again, looking at a marshmallow and deciding whether or not to toast it. "Where'll we be tomorrow night?"

"Tennessee again," Mother said. "It's a bigger state than I'd realized, and we're going diagonally across it, from the northeast corner to the southwest."

"Ugh."

Mother rumpled Suzy's curls. "Don't blame Tennessee for an unpleasant incident, Suzy. Daddy took care of it and nothing happened."

"But it might have," Suzy said. "I wish we had Rochester with us."

I went along with Suzy. Having Rochester around would have made me feel lots happier. "Mother, what would have happened if Daddy didn't know Judo?"

Mother laughed. "Judo was just a spectacular way of handling the situation. I think Daddy could have managed without."

Suzy made a face. "If we have to be in Tennessee again tomorrow I'm just as glad he knows it."

Mother held her marshmallow carefully over the embers. "Tennessee's a lot prettier a state so far than I'd expected. I love the rolling hills and winding roads. *And* the amazing and utterly unusable speed limit of sixty-five."

John laughed, "It made me feel kind of a square to be driving about fifteen miles under the speed limit all the time."

"And remember that wonderful house?" Mother said. "Oh, I guess it was still in Virginia—the one full of gables and painted every color of the rainbow."

"Red, orange, yellow, green, blue, indigo, violet," Suzy counted.

So we got to talking about the things we'd seen that day and began to forget the black leather jacketed hoods. Then we heard a car coming up the road, and Suzy called out happily, "There's Daddy and Rob."

John can identify all kinds of engines. "That's not our car. And it's going much too fast."

Five

I felt my skin raise up into goose pimples. If the hoods came back and Daddy wasn't there I wasn't at all sure of John's ability to take care of us, no matter how much Judo Daddy had taught him. But of course I didn't say this to John.

The car swished up the hill and into view, a shiny black gorgeously new station wagon with a tent trailer behind it, and a California license. It was obviously not the hoods' car, but there was a black jacketed boy at the wheel, and all I could think of was that he was one of the gang and they'd stolen the car.

It swooped all the way around the campgrounds, then returned and swooshed into the campsite next to ours. I started to get up, but Mother put a restraining hand on my arm. Then we saw that the only other people in the car besides the boy at the wheel were a man and woman, both quite a bit older than Mother and Daddy, I'd say, and sort of plump, wearing the kind of camping clothes you see in ads and not usually on people.

The sun was breaking through the clouds, now, and, though it was low on the horizon and the sky was turning pink, there was more light than there had been during dinner and when the hoods threw the Coke bottle.

The boy was about John's age, very thin and not a bit sun-tanned, so that he looked white in comparison to everybody else. Even his parents looked a lot browner than he, but maybe they'd been sitting around under sun lamps. They were the type. He had this velvety black hair that made him look even whiter, and he wore brand new blue jeans and a pink Ivy League–type shirt under the jacket. He was really pretty spectacular.

They began setting up camp and you've never seen such stuff; it would have filled a store. I couldn't keep my eyes off them. I kept wanting to see what they'd pull out next.

"They're had; they don't have," Mother murmured.

They went about unpacking without glancing our way or saying a word to us. With the entire campgrounds to choose from I don't know why they had to pick the site next to ours if they weren't going to be friendly.

The tent trailer when they unfolded it was easily large enough for all of us. It was filled with built-in gadgets and they'd added a lot of extra ones. There was a plywood base they'd obviously had made for it. Then the mother saw to it that the boy and the father laid down a linoleum carpet, clucking over them the whole time.

"I guess he's not one of those other kids after all," I murmured.

"*Him*," John grunted. "The poor sap'd probably faint if he ever saw that gang."

53

We heard the sound of another car, and John stated categorically, "That's Daddy," and our station wagon came up, looking very shabby in comparison with the shiny black new one, and backed in to our parking space and up to the tent so that we'd be able to fit the back flaps over the tail gate.

Daddy told us that he and Rob had met the ranger just about to come up and check on us. The kids who'd thrown the Coke bottle were a gang that had been causing trouble, and they'd slipped into the park while the ranger was out getting supplies. His wife hadn't dared stop them, but she'd called him in town to come right home. He was very apologetic, Daddy said, and he was going to keep the park gates locked from now on. The people in the next campsite had arrived to get their camping permit just as the ranger was telling Daddy all this; the mother was very upset and wanted to go to a hotel, but the boy insisted on coming up to the camp anyhow.

I realized that they were probably camping next to us because the mother was scared, but you'd still think they could have said hello.

Now the boy and the father were struggling to tie a plastic top over the entire tent. Daddy and John called over and asked if they could help.

"Thanks, it's very simple, we don't need any help," the father said, rather ungraciously.

Mother asked, "Just what is the plastic for?"

The plump mother replied, "So the top of our tent won't get dirty."

Mother smiled and said, "I think we're going to enjoy the battle scars on our tent. It'll make us feel that we've really traveled."

(Daddy said afterwards that that was not nice of Mother at all.)

The father paused in tying plastic and looked down his nose at our tent. "We had an outfit like yours last year. But we like to have the very best so we threw it out and got this. It only takes seven minutes to put up."

I didn't know which seven minutes he was referring to, because we saw them working at it for over half an hour. Daddy and John had already got our tent time down to eleven minutes, and figured that in a couple more weeks they could cut that.

Mother said in a low voice to Daddy, "What on earth are they doing on a camping trip? She'd look more at home at a bridge table than in a state park."

"She ought to know better than to wear plaid pants," Daddy said.

Right after Mother's remark about the bridge table we almost burst when the father pulled out a huge flat cardboard box, struggled with it, and extricated a brand new folding bridge table! Then came new folding chairs. A new and shiny cooler. Another big plastic cloth over their cooking equipment. Their own garbage can.

"Why are we being so snide about them?" Mother asked Daddy.

"Because they don't belong in a state park," Daddy said. "Come on, Robin, time you got ready for bed."

Rob collected his towel and toothbrush and started up the path to the lavs. When you're camping if you have lots of choice of campsites you try to set up not too close to the lavs, but not *too* far away in case it rains or you want to go in the middle of the night.

The rich family was getting dinner ready. Or, rather, the mother was. The father sat in a folding chair with a newspaper. Must've been the *Wall Street Journal*. The boy stood around with his hands in his pockets, whistling, a kind of pretty melody, and after a while he sauntered across the path and stood looking at John and me. When he spoke his voice was quite normal and friendly.

"Hi, I'm Zach. Zachary Grey. Who are you and where are you from?"

"John and Vicky Austin," John said. "Connecticut." He spoke rather shortly, and I could tell he didn't like the boy much.

"L.A.," the boy said, "but I just got kicked out of Hotchkiss so we decided to camp out on the way home." He spoke very gayly, as though being kicked out of school was what everybody did, but I had a feeling he didn't like it at all. He looked at Rob coming down from the lavs, and at Suzy emerging from the tent with her towel. "You're kind of a big family, aren't you?"

"We like it," John said. "You an only?"

"What else?" Zachary said. He turned towards me. "How about a spin down into town for a soda or something?"

"Now?" I asked. I guess I must have sounded foolish.

"Why not? I have my license and I do most of the driving."

"Well—I'd have to ask my parents."

"Still back in the Victorian age, are you?" Zachary said. "Okay. Go ahead and ask them." He started to whistle.

John hitched his thumbs into the belt of his jeans. "I can tell you right now they'll say no."

Zachary stopped whistling. "Give them a chance to say no for themselves, Daddy-O."

Mother and Daddy came out of the tent just then, so I asked them.

"No," Daddy said. "I think not, Vicky."

Zachary sounded very deferential. "But why, sir? I have my license and I'm a very good driver. Oh, I'm Zachary Grey, by the way."

"Sorry to say no, Zachary, but we're getting an early start in the morning, and we're all about ready to go to bed."

"Well, could she take a walk around the campgrounds with me, then?"

Daddy looked at Zachary sharply before replying, "As long as it's a short walk within the campgrounds, yes."

Zachary shrugged. "I'll have to settle for that, then. The old lady will want me to eat, anyhow. Come on, Vicky-O." He put his hand on my elbow and we started off. "The old man rules you with a rod of iron, doesn't he?"

"No, not really. He's pretty reasonable, as fathers go." Somehow I wasn't happy about the way Zachary was referring to Daddy.

"How old are you?"

". . . Sixteen."

"Gad! A mere infant! I'd have thought you were at least seventeen."

I was glad I hadn't told him the exact truth. He'd probably have dropped me like a hot coal if I'd admitted I was fourteen.

"How come you're on a camping trip?"

"We're moving to New York, so my father's taking the time off. How about you?"

"I told you. I got kicked out of Hotchkiss, so I told my parents I wanted to camp on the way home."

"They do anything you ask?"

"I have them pretty well under my thumb."

"Did they mind your getting kicked out of school?" That wasn't a polite question, but I'd asked it before I realized it.

"Wasn't much they could do about it after it'd happened," Zachary said. "Let's go this way."

"It's out of the campgrounds."

"So what?"

Now this may sound funny, but going for a walk with Zachary Grey was really what you might call my first date. I mean, I don't count school dances and stuff. I've known all those kids since they were in diapers, practically. Anyhow, going to dances in a station wagon full of other kids isn't a date. And I didn't want to foul this one up. Zachary had said he thought I was seventeen. I didn't want to act like a kid Suzy's age. But one reason Daddy and Mother say *yes* to most things, is that when they give a limitation, like staying within the campgrounds, they know I'll stick to it. But somehow I didn't want to explain all this to Zachary. It wasn't just that I thought he'd think me parent-ridden; I didn't think he'd even understand what I was talking about. So I said, "I don't want to go that way. I want to go this way."

"Scared?"

"Of what?"

"The old man."

Then I had an inspiration. "No," I said. "Of you."

That seemed to please him, and we kept on walking within the campgrounds. We could see down to the two campfires, ours and the Greys, ours down to nothing but a glow, theirs still burning brightly. I tried surreptitiously to look at Zachary so he wouldn't know I was looking. He was really very handsome, not in the least like John, but in a narrow, hawk-like sort of way. His brows and eyes were very dark, like his hair; his lashes were almost as long as Suzy's, which is spectacular on a boy, his face very pale. And yet he wasn't a bit sissy. I mean he was strictly terrific as far as looks went.

He led me to the picnic table at an empty campsite. "Let's sit." I noticed that he seemed a little out of breath. We sat with our backs to the table, and he leaned back, his elbows on the table, his legs stretched out, while dark fell quickly, coming much faster than it does at home. "Tell me about yourself," he demanded.

"I'd rather hear about you. Why did you want to go on a camping trip?"

He grinned. "I don't look the type, do I?"

"Not exactly."

"That's one reason. I like to play against type."

"Why else?"

"The old man thinks it's wholesome, though he'd rather do it up brown with a guide and stuff. Also my old lady hates it."

"What about you?"

"For a few weeks it's kind of fun. It's as interesting a way to get home as any."

"All this equipment just to get home?"

"Why not? We might use it again next summer. Unless Pop sees something new in an ad. Then he'll junk this and buy that. Next month I think we'll fly up to Alaska, but we'll stay at hotels there and charter a small plane to sightsee with."

"Money," I asked dryly, "is not a problem?"

"The old man's loaded. Spend it now, is my motto. You don't have a pocket in your shroud." He began to whistle, the same gay, pretty tune I'd heard him whistling before.

"What's that?"

He sang,

> *"They're rioting in Africa,*
> *They're starving in Spain,*
> *There's hurricanes in Florida,*
> *And Texas needs rain.*
> *The whole world is festering*
> *With unhappy souls.*
> *The French hate the Germans,*
> *The Germans hate the Poles.*
> *Italians hate Yugoslavs,*
> *South Africans hate the Dutch,*
> *And I don't like anybody*
> *Very much."*

He whistled the melody through, and I reacted as I might if it had been John, or one of the kids at school. "I think that's awful. It's ghoulish."

"Don't be naive, Vicky," he said, and sang:

"But we can be tranquil
And thankful and proud,
For man's been endowed
With the mushroom-shaped cloud.
And we know for certain
That some lovely day
Some one'll set the spark off
And we'll all be blown away.
They're rioting in Africa,
They're striking in Iran.
What nature doesn't do to us
Will be done by our fellow man."

He laughed gayly, the first real laugh I'd heard him give. "Cute, isn't it?"

I laughed, too, at the same time that I shuddered, the way you do when someone's supposed to have walked over where your grave's going to be. The melody was so pretty and gay and the words in such black contrast that I couldn't help thinking it funny at the same time that it scared me stiff. Sure, I was worried about war. We all were, even Rob, to the point of worrying about it in his God-bless. Who could help it, with parents listening to news reports, and current events and air raid drills at school, where you're taught how to hide under your desk to shield you from the worst effects of a nuclear blast? And all this stuff about building shelters or not building shelters. And do you stick a gun in your neighbor's face if he doesn't have a shelter and keep him out of yours? All that kind of business over and over until it runs out of your ears like mashed potatoes.

"So why not spend Pop's money now, eh, Vicky?" Zachary asked. "What're we waiting for? I have other reasons, too."

"What reasons?"

"Tell you some other time. So you're moving to New York? Stinking city. Can't stand it. What're you going to do there?"

"Oh, the usual, school and stuff," I said.

"What's your father?"

"He's a doctor."

"Specialist?"

"Internal medicine and research. But he was pretty much a G.P. in Thornhill. What does your father do?"

"Real estate. As for me, I'm studying law."

"You want to be a lawyer?"

"No, I don't want to be a lawyer, as you so naively put it, but I intend to be one. Therefore I suppose I'll have to pick up my high school diploma somewhere next year. It's a real bore having been booted, puts me back a stinking year. We live in a lousy world, Vicky-O, and the only way to get the better of the phonies who boss it is to outwit them, and law will help me do that. My old man's smart, but I'm going to be even smarter. If I know law I can protect myself. I can do pretty much anything I want and get away with it."

"What do you mean? Get away with what?" Zachary excited me, and he disturbed me. I kept wanting to let my fingers touch that velvety black hair.

"My dear child, if you have money and you know law, there are legal gimmicks for every situation. How do you think my old man's done so well? He's a smart cookie and he's got good lawyers. I intend to skip the middle man and be my own lawyer.

Then I don't have to pay out huge lawyers' fees like my old man does and I can get away with anything I want."

"But what do you want to do that you'd have to get *away* with?"

"My poor, innocent child. No wonder you're traveling in a cheap tent with practically no equipment." My skin bristled at that, but he went gaily on. "I suppose you're taught the golden rule. Can't get along that way any more, Vicky-O. That's outmoded. Got to be smart today. And that's what I'm going to be. Have what I want, do what I want, go where I want, get what I want. Don't let anybody kid you that money isn't everything. I've seen plenty and I've learned that if you have enough money you can buy all the things that money isn't."

"What about staying at Hotchkiss?" I asked. I knew it wasn't tactful, but I really wanted to know what he'd answer.

It didn't seem to bother him. "That was just a fluke. If I knew more about law I'd probably still be there. And money'll get me into another school next autumn I'd never make otherwise." He looked at his watch. "Your old man said you had to be right back. I suppose I'd better return you if I want to see you again. Where are you heading?"

"Out west."

"California?"

"Yes. We're going to stay with our uncle and aunt in Laguna Beach."

He raised his eyebrows, but all he said was, "Same trail. I'll be seeing you then. Where're you going to stop on the way?"

"I don't know. That's the fun of this trip. We just go."

"Haven't you *any* idea?"

"Well, Daddy said something about going to Mesa Verde and seeing the Pueblo remains."

"Culture vulture, eh? Maybe I'll see you there. I don't object to anthropology." He stood up. "Come on, Vicky-O. You're very refreshing for a change."

I didn't really think refreshing was what I wanted to be, but I didn't say anything. I thought of a very plain black sheath Mother sometimes wears with a string of pearls, and wondered how I'd look in it. I'm almost as tall as she is. For once I was glad I wasn't a golden girl like Suzy.

"You've got an interesting face, Vicky," Zachary said as we walked back towards our tent. "Not pretty-pretty, but there's something more. And a darned good figure. I'd say something other than darned only I might shock little unhatched you."

"I'm not so unhatched as all that."

"No?"

"No."

"I'll bet you that nothing's happened to you all your life long. Your meals have always been put in front of you and if you skin your little knee you can run crying to Mommie and Poppie and they'll kiss it and make everything all right."

Well, maybe I didn't have very much experience so far. But I was on my way to getting it. "Has so much happened to you?" I asked.

"I am as old as Methuselah, Victorinia. I am old beyond my time. Someday I shall tell you all. Don't want to shock you on first acquaintance."

We got back to the campsite and Mother and Daddy and John were sitting around the table drinking coffee. Zachary handed me over to them with a bow, making me feel about two years old. "Good as my word, sir," he said to Daddy. "Here's your daughter, safe, sound, and unsullied. See you tomorrow, Vicky-O. Good night, all." He waved, and bounded across the path and into their elegant tent.

"What'd you want to take a walk with that creep for?" John asked.

"I like him," I said, sitting down.

Mother looked at me. "I made some cocoa for you, Vicky." She poured me a cup, but didn't say anything else.

John went on. "For heaven's sake don't go getting interested in the jerk. It was from hunger as far as he was concerned. Nobody else here."

Mother said, "I hardly think you need worry about Vicky's getting interested in him, since she'll probably never see him again. And as to its being from hunger, John, Vicky's not Zachary's sister, and he sees her with perhaps fresher eyes."

John heaved a persecuted sigh. "I didn't mean that."

"I know perfectly well what you think of my looks, John," I said stiffly, "but in case you haven't bothered to notice, I've changed a lot in the past year."

"Hold it," John said. "Let's have no quibbling, sibling. You're a cute kid, and the trouble is I was just feeling protective about you." He got up, yawned, and stretched. "Before I get into any more trouble around here I'd better hit the hay."

"Let Vicky go first," Mother said. "Suzy's waiting for her to go up to the lavatory."

Even with our flashlights it was dark on the path when Suzy

and I went up to wash, and Suzy was sleepy, and cross because I'd gone off with Zachary and kept her waiting for so long. The lav itself was pretty well lit, not like the other camps where there hadn't been any lights at all, and we stood side by side brushing our teeth.

"For heaven's sake, Vicky," Suzy growled, "what were you doing all the time with that spazz. Making out?"

"We were talking," I said, stiffly.

"I bet," Suzy said, and spat. She was using chlorophyl toothpaste, so she spat green.

"When you're old enough to know what you're talking about you'll have more right to shoot your mouth off," I said.

Suzy spat greener and bigger.

I finished brushing my teeth, washed my face, and stared in the mirror. I contemplated putting my hair up, but I'd just washed and set it for the wedding, and it keeps its set pretty well between washings, so I was afraid I'd get too many comments.

"Quit staring at yourself and come along," Suzy said.

"I'm not ready yet."

"Then I'm going without you."

"Okay, go ahead." I didn't really think she'd go into that dark without me, but she swished on out in a huff, and left me there. I looked at myself in the mirror for a while longer, longer than I really felt like it, because I didn't want Suzy to think I was running after her. Then I left the bright wash-room and went out into the night. The path was tree-hooded and dark, and the trees still dripped when the wind blew them. The tent seemed much further off than it had when I'd walked up the path with

Suzy, and all my flashlight did was make the shadows move, and they were moving enough anyhow in the wind.

Suddenly, out of the corner of my eye, sort of beyond my left shoulder, I saw something dark moving towards me.

Six

At first I thought it was one of the hoods, but then I realized that it was an animal, and I wasn't sure which was worse. I stood still in a panic, then made myself swing around and turn my flashlight in the direction of whatever it was. Whatever it was hadn't waited for me, but was disappearing into the darkness of the woods. I pelted the rest of the way down the leafy path to the tent.

"Vicky, what on earth's the matter?" Mother asked as I plunged in and went sprawling onto John's sleeping bag.

"I saw a bear!"

"Nonsense," Daddy said.

"But I did!"

"It might have been a woodchuck or a raccoon." Daddy spoke in his most reasonable voice. "Not a bear."

"Woodchucks and raccoons don't stand on two legs, and they aren't as big as people. I thought it was one of those JDs at first, but it wasn't, it was an animal."

Rob sat up in his sleeping bag excitedly. "I want to see the bear! Where was it, Vicky?"

"Near the lavatories."

"It was not a bear," Daddy repeated. "Let's read our chapter and get to sleep, kids. Tomorrow we cross Tennessee."

Mother read to us, and then we said prayers. I kept my voice very low. I could imagine Zachary laughing.

Suzy and Rob went right to sleep as usual, but I was wide awake. I lay rolled up in my sleeping bag and thought about Zachary and the strange way he'd talked. He wasn't a bit like any of the boys I knew in Thornhill. In the first place he was older than the kids in my grade, the ones I knew really well from the time they were in short pants, and he wasn't in the least like any of John's friends, who never have anything to do with me anyhow, except to insult me in a friendly sort of way, or dance with me at school dances. I didn't think Zachary'd get on very well with the kids in Thornhill, but I was beginning to realize that Thornhill isn't the whole world. It used to be, for me.

Mother and Daddy had the lantern on between them, and were reading, Mother a paperback book, Daddy a medical magazine. I rolled over and sighed heavily. Mother looked at me over the book. "Still awake, Vicky?"

"Um hm. What're you reading?"

"*Anna Karenina*. I haven't read it since I was about your age."

"Would I like it?" I peered down over the tail gate.

"I remember enjoying it very much, but I obviously didn't get a lot of it. I think you might wait a couple of years."

Suzy gave a kind of mutter, and Mother said, "We'd better not talk any more or we'll wake Suzy and Rob. Good-night, honey."

69

Mother and Daddy turned out their light before I went to sleep, but right after that I drifted off, still thinking about Zachary, and if I was going to see him in the morning, maybe, and then I was deep dark asleep.

CRASH!

I was so sound asleep that I was still half in the middle of some dream, and I thought it was an atom bomb, I guess because of Zachary's stinky old song. Then I realized that Daddy and John were out of the tent with the lantern and Mother was standing in the door. I heard Zachary's voice, kind of cross.

Daddy and John came back.

"What *was* it?" I squeaked, sure the hoods had managed to sneak back in the park, locked gates or no.

Mother said, "Shh. Suzy and Rob are still asleep."

"It had nothing to do with those boys." Daddy said firmly in a low voice. "It was only the ice box. Evidently a coon or something knocked it off the bench onto the ground. I looked all around, but I couldn't see anything. So I put the ice box up on the table, right in the center. It ought to be okay now." We had the box of food in the front seat of the car, but had left the cooking things, and the ice box, which shuts tight, out by the table, so they'd be more convenient in the morning. "Go to sleep, Vicky."

I looked at my watch, and it was around midnight. I snuggled down in my sleeping bag and went to sleep.

CRASH!

I opened my eyes and struggled to wake up. John was crawling out of his sleeping bag, and Daddy was just going out of the tent with the lantern. This time I was pretty sure it was the ice box again, so I wasn't so scared. I heard Zachary's father sounding

sort of disagreeable, and Zachary saying, "For cripes sakes, Pop."
I looked at my watch and it was almost two. "I bet it's the bear," I
said to Mother, "the bear I saw when I went to brush my teeth."

Daddy stuck his head through the tent door. "It's the ice box
again. All the way down from the table and onto the ground. It
must be a coon."

"It's a pretty heavy ice box," Mother said. "Vicky thinks it's
a bear."

Daddy pooh-poohed that, put the ice box in the front of the
car, and we all went to sleep again.

I slept so soundly that I didn't hear anybody getting up in the
morning, and Mother let me sleep until breakfast was ready. When
I emerged Daddy came to me, grinning. "Look at this, Vicky." He
showed me a large paw mark on the tent, more paw marks on the
table and bench and on the ice box, and a big dent in the ice box.
"We measured the paw prints," he said, "just for future reference,
and they're exactly the size of Suzy's hand. I hate to admit it but I
think you were right. It may have been a bear after all."

I looked over at Zachary's fancy tent, but there wasn't a
sound, and when we sat down to breakfast Mother told us to be
quiet because the Greys were still asleep. We were packing the
car, still trying to be quiet, when the ranger came by in his green
truck and stopped.

"Sorry about those kids last night," the ranger said. He
looked where the Coke bottle had made the dent in the fender.
"That's not so good. You want to take action?"

"It would delay us too much," Daddy said. "But I hope it
won't happen again to someone else."

"Ah'll see that it doesn't," the ranger promised. "Ah've got something to go on, now." He had a nice kind of drawl, not snarly and nasty like the kid who asked for the Coke bottle back.

Daddy asked, "What kind of an animal might have been trying to get in our ice box last night?"

"A b'ar," the ranger answered without hesitation. "A black b'ar. They come around the campgrounds looking for food. Won't bother you if you leave 'em alone and don't try to feed 'em. Wall, hope yawl had a good night." He waved at us and drove off.

Seven

Nobody emerged from the Greys' tent, no matter how often I looked towards it, and I had to quit when John made a snide remark. We got going about eight-thirty and if it hadn't been for this funny feeling that I had about Zachary I'd have gone along with everybody else in being glad to get out, what with wind and weather and hoods and bears.

John and Mother were right about Tennessee. It's really a beautiful state, and everybody we talked to at filling stations and markets and places was lovely and drawly and friendly. Of course John had to go through Oak Ridge, which was fascinating but scary. I mean all that stuff about radiation and cancer and all. It's facts and we have to face it and it isn't any worse than the Black Plague and the Spanish Inquisition but that doesn't make me have to *like* it.

Well, that was Oak Ridge, and that isn't Tennessee any more than the JDs were. What was Tennessee if I look back on it with my mind instead of my feelings is roses, laurel, and rhododendron all in bloom, and birds flying across the road. Red earth and wind-ey roads and lots of mules, which the farmers at home don't have. And people wanting to help us and saying *Tinn*essee instead of *Tenn*essee. And stopping at a funny little store up in the hills to get gas and cash a traveler's check, and the little old lady who ran the store coming out in a gingham dress and an old-fashioned sun bonnet and a corncob pipe in her mouth and knowing all about credit cards but never having heard of a traveler's check!

Somewhere along in the early part of the afternoon a shiny black station wagon with a tent trailer whizzed past us on a curve, honking loudly. "That crazy kook," John said. "I'm glad he's not driving *us*. Just as well that's the last we'll see of *him*."

Montgomery Bell State Park all the way across Tennessee was one of the nicest state campgrounds we hit, with *hot showers* and laundry tubs, so we all got bathed and Mother and I washed out some of our drip dry clothes and hung them up on our laundry rope which John and Daddy strung for us between two trees. There was a ball park right by the camp, so as soon as John got his jobs done he was off and before long he was in the middle of a baseball game, with Suzy and Rob sitting on a fence with a group of other younger kids, watching. Meanwhile Mother and I started getting dinner ready and Daddy struggled with the fire. There must have been a heavy shower early in the afternoon, because all the firewood was sopping wet, and about all it did was smoke. So Mother said it was a good time to initiate Uncle Douglas's stove, the fancy one he got us from Abercrombie and Fitch. The thing wouldn't work. Big deal. So dinner was cooked exclusively over magazines Mother and Daddy had brought along, medical magazines, the *Saturday Review* (Daddy loves the Double Crostic puzzles in those and pulled out all the pages with the puzzles he hadn't done before putting the magazines in the fire), *Harper's,* science fiction magazines, *Life,* the *New Yorker, Scientific American*—oh, it was a real conglomeration.

"More paper, more paper," Daddy kept calling to Mother.

"But I've *given* you all the ones I've read."

"I have to have more," he said, "even if we get Reader's inDigestion," Daddy said. "Since it cooks your dinner you can digest it along with your food."

Mother groaned at this display of wit, and handed him some more pages.

We were through dinner; John, Suzy, and Rob had gone back to the baseball field, when there was the sound of a car being driven at high speed, and a black station wagon came roaring into the campgrounds, stopping with a squeal of brakes at our campsite. I'd quit thinking all cars being driven too fast belonged to hoods. That was one effect Zachary had.

He got out in his gorgeous black leather jacket and said, "Hi, Austins." His mother and father weren't with him, and the tent trailer wasn't hitched to the station wagon.

"My mother insisted on staying at a motel tonight," he said. "We've just finished a zuggy shrimp dinner. I'll probably upchuck it before morning. May I take Vicky in to town for a movie, sir? There's a good show on."

I could tell Daddy didn't think much of Zachary the way he said, "Sorry, Zach. We've got a six hundred mile drive ahead tomorrow. We're going to push on to stay with relatives in Oklahoma."

"Where do you go from there?" Zachary asked.

"I really don't know," Daddy said coldly. "We plan to stay in Oklahoma quite a while."

I got the message even if Zachary didn't. It was the first I'd heard of going all the way to Tulsa the next day, and what Daddy meant was that Zachary wouldn't be able to find us at the next camping place and that was just as well and it would also be just as well if we never saw him again. Usually Mother and Daddy have their arms out and the doors open to all our friends. There's almost always someone extra at our house for dinner, and, on week-ends, spending the night. But the welcome mat wasn't out for Zachary.

I looked at Mother and Daddy and kind of scowled. I didn't think Zachary was all that undesirable. John's brought home some pretty gooney characters and nobody's blown any gaskets.

They didn't ask Zachary to stay, but he obviously wasn't about to go. He leaned against the shiny black of his station wagon and talked Tennessee politics, about which he seemed to know a lot. After a while Mother and Daddy excused themselves and went to sit on a fallen tree that edged the brook behind our campsite.

Zachary grinned. "Finally smoked 'em out. You intrigue me, Vicky. Don't wonder that gang last night tried to pick you up."

This flattered me, even if it wasn't true. "They didn't," I said. "They were just a bunch of kooks looking for kicks."

"You think you're not a kick?" He kind of leered at me. Out of the corner of my eye I looked at Mother and Daddy sitting on the fallen tree. I didn't know whether I wanted them to be nearer or further away.

"When are you going to be in Laguna Beach?" he asked.

"I don't know exactly. Somewhere near the end of June."

"Who're you staying with there?"

"An uncle and aunt."

"What's their *name*, for crying out loud? How'm I going to look you *up*? Laguna's not too long a haul from L.A."

"That's where you live?"

"Yes. Now what's your uncle's name?"

"Douglas Austin." If my parents would have reservations about Zachary's looking me up, so did I. But somehow it seemed safer to have him look me up when we were in a house in a town in the middle of civilization than in the wilderness. I wasn't a hundred percent sure whether I wanted him whizzing into any more campgrounds.

"Who's keeping you all that time in Oklahoma?"

"Another uncle and aunt. They used to live in California, but now Uncle Nat has a church in Tulsa."

"Oh my aching back, a *church!* What's he doing with a church?"

"He's a minister," I said stiffly.

"Ick. Have fun."

"We will," I said. "We've got a lot of cousins there and Uncle Nat and Aunt Sue are marvelous and we're going to have a ball."

"I bet."

I was mad. I liked Zachary and he was different from anybody I'd ever known and I didn't want to scare him off by seeming pious or something, because after all I think I've made it quite clear that I'm not, but I wasn't going to have him thinking people like Grandfather or Uncle Nat were squares just because they were ministers. What's wrong with being a minister? It's not like having leprosy in the family. I looked Zachary fiercely in the eye and put all the disdain I could manage into my voice. "You don't have the faintest idea what you're talking about."

"Oh, no?"

"You think just because a person has a *church,* for heaven's sake, they can't have any fun."

Zachary's face kind of got whiter and little spots of pink showed just above his cheek bones. "What's fun got to do with it? Religious guys are *phonies,* that's all, *phonies,* every crumby one of them."

I stood up. "My *grand*father is a minister. My *uncle* is a minister. I bet you don't know any ministers half as well as I do. And they're not phonies. They're the realest people you'd ever want to meet. If they tell you anything you can trust them. One hundred percent."

Zachary reached out with one skinny hand and took my wrist. He had a lot more strength than I'd have expected and he took me by surprise. I sat down hard on the picnic bench. He stood leaning against the shiny black hood of his car (I bet they have that darned car washed and polished every other day) and talked with withering scorn. "My eye. Pie in the sky. The best of all possible worlds." He began whistling the tune he'd whistled the night before, then said with ferocious intensity,

> *"What nature doesn't do to us*
> *Will be done by our fellow man."*

"What's *that* got to do with anything?" I asked impatiently.

"They're our fellow man, aren't they? Ministers? What're

78

they doing about war and stuff except coming to your bedside in the hospital and praying over you and if you weren't going to die anyhow you'd do it right then and there with embarrassment."

"*Well*," I said, "we *ob*viously know *diff*erent kinds of ministers. Maybe they're like that in California, but they aren't at home."

"I thought you said your zuggy uncle used to *be* in California!"

Now. Take my mother. She's the daughter of a minister and all. But when she and Aunt Elena were in boarding school in Switzerland (that was when Grandfather was in Africa and Mother got sick and had to be sent out of the climate) the worse thing anyone could be was pi. Pious. You know. The kind who pray loudly on the street corner instead of quietly in their closet, the way it says in the Bible. People who don't really mean it. It's all on the outside. Whited sepulchers.

If there's anything I'm *not* it's pious. I'm *proud* of not being pious. But it got me, the way Zachary talked. I didn't like it. So I said, "What're you so *scared* of ministers for? What do you think they're going to *do* to you? You sound as though you thought they were some kind of *witch* doctor just waiting to surround you, muttering evil incantations, and if they can close the circle you'll turn into a handful of *dust* with a small puff."

"You're a card, Vicky," he said. "You really are. That's cool."

I thought he was being sarcastic, but he reached over and patted my knee, and I saw he really meant it.

He said, "If I had somebody like you around maybe I wouldn't go getting kicked out of schools all the time."

"Why do you?"

He shrugged. "Oh, you know. The usual reasons. I get bored, so I goof off on a couple of subjects. Or I get caught smoking. Or trying a new kind of cheating on exams. If I *needed* to cheat of course I wouldn't do it. I mean that kind of cheating's phony. I do it because it's an art, and the teachers are all squares. Most of them. There's usually one or two who come close to being human beings."

"I know what you mean about teachers," I said. I was feeling more relaxed, now that Zachary hadn't had a spazz attack over what I said about ministers. "Lots of them are muffins. But it isn't just teachers. It's people."

"Muffins?" He sounded kind of interested.

"Well, at home we have this kind of club. The anti-muffin club. Very exclusive. I mean you have to be really *un*muffiny to belong."

"Yah?"

"You know my little brother, Rob? He really started it. It was about a year ago, and Uncle Douglas was up for the weekend."

"He a minister, too?"

"He's an *art*ist. He came up that weekend without a girl, but the weekend before he came up *with* a girl. He wasn't married, then, and he used to bring his girls up for us sort of to look over. We used to like some of them, but this one was a real stinker. I mean a real snob, asking questions about the family, I mean Mother's and Daddy's families. You know, wanting to know all about grandparents and things." I started to laugh.

"What's so funny?" Zachary wanted to know.

"It's Rob. The way he goofs up on words. The more syllables they have the more he likes them. He's really bright, but he gets all tangled up in words. And this girl kept talking about her ancestors and Rob went up to Mother and said, 'Her aunt must have had an awful lot of sisters.'" Zachary looked blank, so I said, "Aunt's sisters. Ancestors. Get it?" He gave a kind of grin, and I realized the only time I'd ever heard him really laugh was over that ghoulish song. It must be awful never to laugh. I felt sorry for him, and at the same time curious. I didn't think the reason he never laughed was that he didn't have a sense of humor, even though he'd been kind of slow about the joke about aunt's sisters.

"I still don't know about your lousy old muffins," Zachary said. But he didn't really sound sore.

So I explained.

What happened was that Uncle Douglas came back the next weekend and told Mother and Daddy—and all of us—that he and the girl were through. And then he gave us a lecture, as though *we* were the ones, about how we shouldn't worry about where people were born, or what kind of people they came from, whether they had important families or lots of money; you should like them or dislike them for themselves. He said that people like his ex-girl thought that where people were born made them what they were. He said it loud and clear.

Well, that afternoon Prunewhip, our sort of funny-looking, mottled-brown cat, had kittens. We knew she was going to have kittens, and Mother had fixed her up a nice place in the cellar to have them in. So when Prunewhip didn't come around for supper we were sure she'd gone to have her kittens, and we ran down in the cellar to her bed, but she wasn't there, so we looked in the garage and under all the beds and in the closets and everywhere we could think of. Then, when Mother was making muffins for breakfast (she usually makes them the night before) she noticed that the oven door was part way open, and she opened it all the way, and there was Prunewhip with five kittens! We'd had kittens all over the place, but never in the oven before.

Prunewhip looked very pleased with herself, and Mother said, well, we'd have to do without the oven for a while.

Rob asked, "Mother, would Uncle Douglas' ex-girl think the kittens were muffins because they were born in the oven?"

So that's how our muffin club got started.

Zachary thought it was all very funny. He almost laughed, and you could see the idea really appealed to him. He didn't even ask what was the point to the club or anything. I mean, he got that it wasn't just being born in an oven, but you shouldn't go around wanting to be like all the other muffins in the pan, either.

Mother and Daddy came strolling back around then, and John and Suzy and Rob came up from the ball field, so Zachary said good night. As he drove off he leaned out the window and yelled, "See you in Laguna Beach, Vicky-O."

"I wish he wouldn't call you Vicky-O," Suzy said in an annoyed sort of way.

"Anyhow he *won't* see us in Laguna Beach," John said. "He wouldn't have the faintest idea how to find us."

I kept my mouth shut.

By the time we were in our sleeping bags and Mother and Daddy had switched out the lantern it began to pour, a real cloudburst with great flashes of lightning and crashes of thunder. Rob wiggled his sleeping bag very close to John's, and Suzy and I held hands for a while, but the tent stood up to the storm nobly and didn't leak a bit.

The next day was sunny and clear and all our laundry that had got soaked by the storm was dry. We got up about half an hour earlier than usual in order to get going as soon as possible.

It was by *far* the longest drive of our whole trip. I suppose we'd have done it anyhow even if I hadn't had the feeling we were sort of fleeing Zachary, because Daddy said Aunt Sue and Uncle Nat were expecting us, and it wasn't as though we'd have to set up camp when we arrived, there'd be beds and food waiting for us. More thunderstorms kept being forecast, too, and we were kind of tired of wet wood to cook dinner on.

We all got pooped, and it got hotter and hotter, and we just kept on and on and on, with Mother and Daddy and John switching the driving. Once Suzy said, while John was at the wheel, "Hey, John, couldn't you just tesser us there?"

It would have been nice if he could have, like Meg and Charles Wallace Murry, but that, as Kipling would say, is another story.

Arkansas was flat and hot and had long stretches of wet rice fields, which took me completely by surprise. I'm sure I must have learned in Social Studies some time or other that Arkansas produces rice, but in my imagination I saw rice growing only in the Far East, with people in coolie hats paddling about.

Oklahoma was gently rolling hills with lots of groves of trees. Clean, white cities, because everything is heated by oil. And of course there were the oil wells, which particularly fascinated Rob. We were there over a week, in order to avoid the Memorial Day week-end traffic, and our only disappointment the whole time we were there was that we never saw an Indian.

I was right about Oklahoma: we had a ball. We hadn't seen Aunt Sue or Uncle Nat for years, but they were just the way I remembered them, and not the way Zachary would have thought at all. As for the cousins, they were completely different. I knew they'd have gone on growing up along with us, but I kept seeing them in my mind's eye as little kids, but the youngest, Sukey, was Suzy's age, and Pete was half way through college. They knew a lot of kids, and especially one family with a swimming pool; we were over there every day, and to other places for barbecues and stuff, and all the girls went mad over John. I've mentioned me and boys, but I've never mentioned John and girls. At home in Thornhill John usually dates Izzy Jenkins, my best friend Nanny Jenkins' older sister, but he could have his pick of any girl in the county. John can't see a thing without his glasses, he's very near-sighted but he's tall and good looking and he has this wonderful dark red hair, like Uncle Douglas. None of the rest of us has it. Suzy and Rob are blonde, and my hair's just plain brown, though lately it seems to me there have been kind of reddish lights, and it's a prettier sort of brown than it used to be. John doesn't have that dug-out-from-under-a-rock complexion that some red-heads have, either, and he's terrifically intelligent, but not a bit of a grind. I mean he just comes home from school and sits down and gets his homework done in half the time it takes me to do mine. He's good at sports, too, the kind you can do with glasses on, like basketball and track. As far as I can see he's good at just about everything. I'm proud of him, sure, but sometimes I feel, well, just sort of sad, because I can't ever hope to be the kind of person John is. I don't even know what I want to *be* yet, and Suzy's always been a beauty and known she was going to be a doctor. That's *always* what she's wanted to be, ever since she could speak. I don't know what I'd do if it weren't for Rob.

Anyhow, we had a blast in Tulsa, and then we spent a couple of nights in Oklahoma City with some people we'd met in Tulsa but who lived in Oklahoma City and insisted we come visit them there.

Then it was back to the camping routine again, and a trek across Texas. Just the way I don't think I'll ever forget Tennessee, I'm not likely to forget Texas, either. None of us is. It's such a big state that we really didn't see very much of it. Just a corner. But we'll always remember that corner.

Eight

We drove mile after mile over absolutely flat, treeless land that stretched out and out to the horizon. Every once in a while we'd come to enormous white granaries. The granaries looked like skyscrapers in the distance, stuck way out in nothing, but they shrank when you came up to them. In those great open spaces perspective was all off and we couldn't tell where anything was or what size it was going to be till we came right up to it. Granaries, water towers, towns, seen on the horizon, seemed much closer than they actually were. Sometimes we would try to guess at the mileage, and we were always way off. One rather unusual thing we passed, and certainly something that didn't seem to belong in Texas, was a convoy of *naval* trucks, yet, bearing missiles. I thought of Zachary's awful song and shivered, but the others were all excited and talking about space probes and sending a manned rocket to the moon and if a space war was really possible or not. It just scared me plain stiff. I wonder if I'm developing a tendency to be morbid?

But I kept looking at that enormous sweep of land, stretching out to eternity so you couldn't stay afraid because fears were so small they just lost themselves. The only other place I know where you can see that far and makes you feel the same way is the ocean, which is why I went down to the beach the day of the wedding. In Texas one thing that seemed to make the distance look even distanter was the telephone poles, stretching out and out and out; the only reason you couldn't go on seeing them forever was that they got so tiny in the distance they finally got too small to see and just merged in with the land. That's perspective, Uncle Douglas says. It seems very mysterious to me.

Every once in a while we would see tumbleweed rolling across the road. At first I thought it was birds, but Daddy explained that it's a plant that seeds itself by being blown by the lightest breeze across wide sweeps of land. It was really fascinating, and if you looked at it up close it was almost like something you might see by the ocean. Daddy and Mother knew an old song about it, "Tumbling along with the tumbling tumbleweed," and we all learned it.

We were heading for Palo Duro State Park, which Daddy said was in a canyon. When we reached it the canyon came as a complete shock, appearing abruptly in the middle of the flat lands. The canyon is eroded, I mean it's really ancient, so it's all worn away from wind and weather, and it's *striped* in color, lots of reds and yellows and pinks, and even bluish stripes. It's really spectacular.

When we stopped at the ranger's place to get our pass he

looked at our license and said, "Yawl from Connecticut? One of these young ladies Miss Victoria Austin by any chance?"

You could have knocked me over with a feather, but he handed me a note. Everybody was very excited and kept asking me who it was from and everything. I had a very good idea who it was from, but I wasn't saying, and I wasn't going to open it with Suzy breathing down my neck.

"Let Vicky alone," Mother said. "After all, it's her note."

"Who else but that California crumb," John growled in disgust. "Is he going to turn up *here*?"

But there wasn't any black station wagon down in the campgrounds. We had to drive all the way down into the canyon to get there. It was by far the most beautiful and by far the worst kept place we'd been to so far. The camping area and the picnic grounds weren't separated, the way they'd been in the other camps, and picnickers are evidently slobs, not clean like campers.

"Litter bugs!" Suzy said, and it sounded like swearing, as we went around picking up literally hundreds of bottle caps in order to clear enough ground to set up the tent. It burned me up because I wanted to get camp set up and go off somewhere private to read Zachary's note. It was the dustiest camp we'd been in, too. Our sandalled feet were filthy in two minutes. The fireplaces had been all mutilated and the grills stolen, so cooking wasn't as easy as it had been, though we *could* have used Uncle Douglas's stove, which Daddy had fixed in Oklahoma by pushing a thin wire through the feed lines to clear them.

As soon as we finished setting up camp Mother and Daddy dragged us back up the canyon to take a ride on a narrow gauge railway. I said I didn't want to go but they made me. Normally I might have enjoyed it, but I wanted to read Zachary's letter. Anyhow, let's face it, the ride wasn't really very exciting to anybody except Rob. He was so thrilled that I didn't mind it as much as I would have otherwise, and the scenery was kind of interesting, like something out of TV or a book, and not like anything I'd ever really expected to see. There was lots of flowering cactus, and the man who drove the train showed us mesquite trees. I'd read about them, of course, and they weren't a bit as I'd imagined them, but sort of like prehistoric, overgrown ferns. There were juniper trees, which we'd never seen before either; but when you keep on seeing things you've never seen before, one right on top of the other, they begin to lose their excitement, particularly if you have a letter you want to read in your pocket. Suzy had her notebook out and kept putting down birds. The canyon was just loaded with birds, all kinds of birds, especially red, red cardinals which looked beautiful against the reds of the canyon walls. There were also mosquitoes and flies, but Suzy didn't mark those down.

Just as we got back to the little station, all scratching our legs and arms, we saw two wild turkeys, and then the guide, quite excited, shushed us up and pointed to a largish bird with a very straight, moving tail, like something in Geometry. He said it was a Road Runner and he'd never seen one so close to the station before. So Suzy had two more birds for her book.

While we were cooking dinner a whole bunch of girl scouts with very Texan accents arrived for a cook-out and an overnight. Boy, were they noisy! They'd evidently expected to have the whole place to themselves, but they put up their tents quite a way away from us, close to the lavs and the playgrounds. We'd deliberately camped far from the Palo Duro lavs because they were an inch deep in muddy water and stank, even though they had flush toilets. It made me think a lot more of the two camps in Tennessee.

The scouts were making so much noise I couldn't stand it, so I started off, up the side of the canyon near our campsite. It wasn't just that I wanted to read Zachary's note. It was about time for me to be alone for a while. On a camping trip you're falling over each other twenty-four hours a day. Most of the time it's fine, but every so often you need to get out. You have to go off by yourself or you just stop being you, and after all I was just beginning to be me. Sometimes, like that evening at Palo Duro with the scouts yelling back and forth as if they owned the place and nobody else had a right to be there, I felt that doing nothing but be with the family was making me muffiny, though we're not a muffiny family. So that's not really what I mean. I guess what I mean is, I felt they were sort of holding me back, keeping me from growing up and being myself.

I only went a little way up the side of the canyon. I wasn't even all the way out of sight and if anybody'd wanted to yell for me and remind me that I hadn't finished my jobs they could have. But nobody bothered to.

I pulled Zachary's letter out of my pocket and read it: "Dear Victoria," (it sounded formal and kind of unlike Zachary) "I'm playing a game of hares and hounds with you and leaving notes at campgrounds all the way across the United States. Only I'm the one who's hounding you, and it's the hares who're supposed to leave the trail. I'll catch up with you in Laguna Beach if not before, or you'll catch up with me, whichever way you want to look at it. We'll sit on the beach and chew the fat and you can even talk your corny religion stuff if you want to. I forgive you. SWAK. ZACH."

It wasn't exactly what you might call a love letter, but it was nice and I liked it.

I was happy about Zachary's leaving notes for me at campgrounds all across the country, and at the same time I felt so lonely I could have put my head down on my knees and bawled. It wasn't the kind of loneliness that would have got any better if I'd gone back to the family; it would have just been worse. It was that kind. I wonder if John ever feels that way? John always seem so secure. If I had everything to be secure about that John has maybe I'd feel secure, too. On the other hand, maybe he doesn't. He's too darned bright really to feel secure all the time. And Suzy. Well, she's just a kid, still. I never used to feel lonely this way when I was a kid in Thornhill. Thornhill was the whole world, and our big house on the hill was the top of the world, and that was all that mattered. Now I knew about rioting in Africa and strikes in Iran and Thornhill wasn't even going to be home any more.

Suddenly I froze. There was something coming towards me along the little shelf on the canyon's side where I was sitting. It wasn't a hood and it wasn't a bear. It was a skunk. He minced along, his tail straight up and swishing, his pretty little striped body moving closer and closer to me. I hardly breathed. If I was lonely sitting there on the side of the canyon you can imagine the kind of lonely I'd have been if I'd gone home sprayed with skunk juice. Mr. Rochester got squirted by a skunk once, and we had to buy gallons, literally gallons of tomato juice to bathe him in, and in rainy weather he still smelled for months. I could image just how popular I'd be with Zachary in Laguna if I smelled of skunk when my hair got wet.

The skunk swished right by me, practically stepping on my toes, as casual as though I were just something growing in the canyon. I waited till he was safely gone by me and had disappeared into the scrub. Then I high-tailed it back to camp.

Nobody seemed very pleased to see me. I might just as well have been sprayed. Why hadn't I finished my job before wandering off like that? And why didn't I tell anybody I was going, and where? That sort of stuff. From everybody, separately and all together.

Daddy said, "This camping trip's a family affair, Vicky."

John said, "If anybody goofs off it messes everything all up."

I drew circles with my toe in the dusty sand of the camp ground. "I didn't mean to goof off, but I'm not so hot on all this togetherness stuff any more." I went over to the picnic table, took a tomato out of the food box, washed it, and started slicing it into the middle-sized pot where Mother'd been making the salad.

"I already have a tomato in the salad, Vicky," Mother said. That was all she said, but she said it as though I'd stabbed her or something.

Daddy looked at me as though I were a patient and not one of his own children. "If this is the way Zachary affects you it's just as well you're not likely to see him again."

"What's Zachary got to do with it?" I shouted. I had to shout in order not to burst into tears. "I've been deteriorating all year, according to you."

Mother came around the table then and put her arms around me, and then I just started to howl. Noisily. I couldn't help it. Everybody came around and started patting me on the back and telling me it was all right, I was all right, I was a good kid, and I wished they'd just go away and leave me with Mother.

"Let's eat," Daddy said in a very casual voice. "Come on, Vicky, blow your nose and put some dinner inside you and you'll feel better. Everybody loves you."

Suzy stuck a hankie into my hand. I blew my nose and we were just about to sit down to dinner when I heard a squeak from Rob and a "shh" from Suzy and turned to see a young deer coming up to us. Suzy held out her hand and the deer nuzzled it; Suzy really has a way with animals. Then it started wandering around our picnic table looking for food. It was so delicate and so tame that it seemed like an animal out of a picture book instead of a real live animal in a canyon in Texas. As soon as I saw the deer I stopped feeling lonely and sad. You can't feel that way when a beautiful young deer is trying to share your dinner. Suzy fed it lettuce and bread, and it nuzzled Rob's shoulder and my ear and then kind of nibbled at Suzy to tell her it wanted something more to eat.

"Daddy!" Suzy cried. "Look! The deer loves me!" She held out her hand again and the deer delicately nibbled at a leaf of lettuce.

"She's certainly tame," Daddy said. "She must be used to being fed by campers and picnickers."

Suzy's face fell. "Do you think she's this way with *everybody*?"

"Probably," Daddy said. "I think animals feel pretty safe around campers."

Suzy got a stubborn look. We all know that look. "Daddy, she's just a young deer. She hasn't had *time* to get to know lots of campers. And she loves us. Couldn't we keep her?"

We all know Suzy well enough to know that the worst thing to do when she makes a request like this is to laugh. Daddy answered perfectly seriously, "How would you suggest doing that, Sue?"

"She could sit with me in the car. She wouldn't be any trouble. Really she wouldn't."

"You know, Suzy," Daddy explained, "a wild deer isn't house-broken."

"I could housebreak her. I know I could."

"Look at it from her point of view," Daddy suggested. "I think she'd be terribly unhappy being shut up in a car day after day after day."

"But Daddy—"

"Think, honey. We're just at the beginning of our trip. Think about it from the deer's point of view."

"Let's eat dinner while it's still hot," Mother said. "Wash your hands, Suzy."

Suzy went draggingly to the bowl of hot soapy water Mother keeps ready for handwashing.

"And no feeding the deer while we're eating," Daddy added.

Suzy washed her hands and sat down, looking longingly at the deer. The deer butted her gently to ask for food, but Daddy said firmly, "Not at the table, Suzy," and after a few moments the deer wandered off in the direction of the girl scouts. I could see Suzy's eyes fill with tears of disappointment, and her chest got all heave-ey, and she ate ferociously to control herself.

Just at that moment, the right moment, Rob called out, "A skunk! A skunk!" And there my skunk was, I'm sure it was my skunk, strolling nonchalantly right by us, its lovely bushy tail erect, its stripe white against its dark body, paying no more attention to us than it had to me. We might not have been sitting there eating stew. I didn't freeze quite as solid as I had on the side of the canyon, but we all sat very still (even Suzy had no inclination to rush out to cuddle it) until it had disappeared in the bushes on the hill above the water spigot.

Shortly after we'd gone to bed a thunderstorm came up. We were pretty used to them by this time, and we'd been very lucky in having them come either before time to set up camp, or after we'd gone to bed, and got quite accustomed to having high winds batting at the tent. But this was the worst storm we'd had, with thunder reverberating from cliff wall to cliff wall, back and forth against the sides of the canyon, echoing and re-echoing, with a much noisier crashing than it would have made anywhere else. Under cover of all the sound and fury Suzy whispered to me, "Whatever did you go making that crack for, and hurting Mother and Daddy and all?"

"What crack?" I whispered back. I didn't know what in thunder she was talking about.

"About Togetherness. Jeepers, Vicky! We've never gone on about Togetherness. Because we *are* together. We don't have to make a *Thing* about it. We just *are,* and we always *will* be, just the way Mother and Grandfather are, even if they don't see each other for months and months and months, and the way we are about Uncle Douglas and all."

"You're too young to understand," I said.

Suzy's three years younger than I am, and if there's anything she hates, it's being reminded of it. But all she said was, "All I know is that you hurt Mother and Daddy, and I think it was cheap."

I began to get riled up. "If you don't know what I mean, what about the way you and Maggy always used to yell *get out of our room* if I even stuck my toe across the doorsill?"

"That's not the same thing at all. It didn't hurt your feelings or anything, and you did the same thing if we tried to come in to Rob's and your room. If Rob wasn't around. *He* didn't mind. Anyhow I think what you said was *cheap,* that's all. Good night." She rolled over, thunderstorm or no thunderstorm, and went to sleep. She could always do that. It made me furious.

Everybody else seemed to have gone to sleep, too, but the storm kept on keeping me awake and I was too hot. Not just around the collar. One thing about sleeping bags, it's difficult to adjust their temperature. You have to have them either open or closed, on you or off, and that night it was too hot with them up and too cool with them down, though I knew we'd need them by morning.

I got to sleep at last, though, and was dreaming that I was out in a tiny boat in the very middle of the ocean, and that a blindingly bright sun was rising, when I realized that the lantern was on and shining against my eyes. I pulled myself out of sleep to see Mother sitting up in the sleeping bag, and Daddy standing in the tent door talking to someone. I had no idea how long we had been asleep, whether it was in the middle of the night or almost morning.

I heard a voice with a Texan accent drawl, "How long does it take you to break camp? In a hurry?"

Nine

"A little over half an hour," Daddy said.

"Kin you manage by yourselves? I got to help evacuate the scouts."

"We can manage," Daddy said.

I leaned over the tailboard of the car. "What's the matter?"

"Get dressed, Vicky," Mother told me. "Quickly. It's the storm and the ranger's afraid of flooding. There've been hail-stones and roofs ripped off houses a couple of miles from here." She started shaking Suzy to wake her up. "As soon as you're dressed, Vicky, help me get things back in the car."

Daddy pulled on his jeans and sweatshirt right over his paja-mas, and John must have done the same because Suzy and I weren't quite dressed, moving in a daze of sleep, before Daddy and John started clearing out the tent. Rob was already in the car, and Daddy told Suzy to get in with him and finish dressing there.

I shoved my feet into my sandals and Mother and I grabbed

everything up off the tent floor, rammed pajamas, towels, flash-lights into the suitcase, and then I shoved it over the tailgate into the car. Then I ran splashing across the wet ground to the picnic table for the ice box, which was heavy because we had fresh ice in it.

"Can you carry it alone, Vicky?" Mother was taking down the laundry and the line.

I grunted in assent, and when I got back to the car Suzy and Rob helped me lift the ice box in. My clothes were soaking wet; my hair was dripping (of course I'd washed and set it the night before); and when I ran back to Mother I realized that I was no longer just splashing along on wet ground. The water was up to my ankles.

I forgot about just having set my hair.

Daddy and John had the tent rolled up. Mother had let the air out of the mattresses and bundled up the sleeping bags. We'd done everything so hurriedly that it all took up twice as much room as usual, but nobody was bothering about that.

"Everybody in," Daddy said. "I'll get you up out of the canyon and then John and I'll come back and help with the scouts."

John and I, dripping, climbed in. Suzy and Rob were sitting wide-eyed and quiet, which is of course very abnormal for both of them. They're chattery kids. At any rate they were dry. Suzy rooted around and found a towel and handed it to me silently. It's things like this that make me feel that Suzy will really end up being a doctor. I mopped at my hair so that water stopped trickling down my neck and gave the towel to John. Suzy found another one for Mother.

Daddy got in. The car wouldn't start. We all sat there, tense and not saying anything, until the motor caught. The headlights poured across the rain, and great silver drops seemed to rush and quiver along the shafts of golden light. The bushes on the canyon side were bent down under the onslaught of wind and rain. The floor of the canyon had disappeared, covered with a wrinkled carpet of water. I wondered how fast it was rising, and sat a little closer to Suzy than usual. I didn't like the idea that John and Daddy would be going back down into the canyon again. But we could hear shrieks from the scouts, and they would be climbing up the canyon on foot; they were little kids, only Suzy's age, so I knew, I understood, that Daddy and John would have to go back down.

The station wagon splashed forwards; we could hear water swirling behind the wheels. Then we began to climb, and we pulled up out of the water. There was still a swishing sound as we hairpinned up the side of the canyon, but it was only the sound of wheels on wet ground, of rain and wind belting against the car; we had left the flooding campgrounds behind us. Daddy drove quickly, not speaking. His jaw was tight, and he held the steering wheel so that his knuckles showed white in the light from the dashboard. Mother sat beside him, absolutely still, looking ahead through the streaming windshield. The windshield wipers groaned as they tried to keep up with the rain.

The station to the little railway came before the ranger's quarters. The station building where they sold postcards and soft drinks was shut and dark, but there was a shed-like roof over the platform, and in the center of the platform were benches which were still fairly dry.

Daddy stopped. "Everybody out. We'll empty the car. Pile everything in the center of the platform."

It didn't take us long to get the junk out. Since Suzy and Rob were dry, Daddy had them stay under the shed, and we shoved things at them to pull in out of the wet.

"Okay," Daddy said, "Mother and Vicky, put on coats so you won't get cold in your wet things. John and I'll be back as soon as we can." He swung the car around. The light streamed over us, picking out Suzy and Rob sitting on the bulky pile of tent and sleeping bags, glinted silver against the railroad tracks, against the windows of the darkened station building, then pointed down the canyon. The platform seemed dark and wet and cold. I shivered and looked after the red tail lights as they moved down, down, further away from us. Then I felt my raincoat being draped around my shoulders.

"Let's sing while we wait," Mother said. "It won't be long now till it gets light."

I looked at my watch. It was almost five o'clock. Mother started to sing, and I joined in with her rather feebly.

Mother laughed. "What a pathetic noise! Where's my guitar? I want to check that it's not under the tent or getting soaked, anyhow." We found the guitar between the ice box and the wooden food box, fortunately not crushed, and Mother took it out of the case. "Okay, what'll it be? You choose, Suzy."

"I don't feel like singing," Suzy said in a tense voice. "I want to go back down to help Daddy and John."

"So do we all, Suzy," Mother said, "but we'd be more of a hindrance than a help. I imagine they want all the room in the car they can get."

"But they may need medical help!" Suzy said desperately.

Mother laughed, but kind of *with* Suzy, not *at* her. "I think Daddy can take care of that, don't you?"

I remembered something Daddy had said once when we were criticizing Maggy: most of us don't believe that anybody close to us, anybody we love, can really die. We know that it *can* happen, but it happens to other people, not to us. But it *had* happened to Maggy, both her mother and father were dead, and this had come close enough to us so that all parents were forevermore in danger, and I knew that Suzy was thinking about this while Daddy and John were going back down into the flooding canyon. If they were going to be in danger she wanted to be there, too. Somehow you think that if you can just be there, you'll make the danger go away. I know that's how I felt.

Mother spoke quietly, reassuringly. "There isn't anything to be worried about, children. The ranger's evacuating the camp just as a precaution, be*fore* it has a chance to get dangerous. And it'll be a lot easier to get those girl scouts out in the car than on foot. Now. It'll make waiting a lot pleasanter if we play games or sing, and I choose to start with singing. Rob? Something gay."

"'Eddystone Light,'" Rob said promptly.

So Mother started, and we all joined in,

"My father was the keeper of the Eddystone light.
He married a mermaid one fine night.
Of this union there came three,
A porpoise and a porgy and the other was me.
Yo ho HO! the wind blows free.
Oh, for a life on the rolling sea!"

Mother kept us going from one song to another. But we missed Daddy's and John's nice, deep, masculine voices. We were used to having the bass stronger than the melody, and while we were singing I kept straining to look down the road for the first glimpse of light pushing through the rain ahead of the car, to listen through our voices and Mother's guitar for the sound of the motor. I forgot all about not thinking so much of togetherness. All I wanted in the world was for the family to be together again.

Finally it came, the headlights steaming through the rain, the chugging of the station wagon almost drowned by the shrill voices of the scouts. Daddy stopped by the platform, and he and John had really packed that car! The scouts started pouring out, and they kept on and on coming until it looked like one of those little cars in the circus that look as though they wouldn't hold more than two people at the most and seem to go on disgorging clowns forever. Daddy told us that John and the ranger and the scout leaders and the rest of the scouts were already up on high ground; there wasn't anything more to worry about; and the rain was beginning to let up, anyhow. We'd have got our feet good and wet if we'd stayed down in the canyon, but we wouldn't have drowned.

Daddy turned the car around and headed down the canyon again. The sky began to get white around the edges, and the rain stopped as suddenly as if had begun. While we were waiting for the rest of the scouts we played games to try to get everybody dry, and soon the kids were over their scare and all laughing and having a wonderful time. When the second batch arrived and were reasonably dry and warm we all sat down on the platform and sang. I guess scouts sing the same songs everywhere, though we each taught the other group a couple of new ones. The scouts all said it was the most exciting Overnight they'd ever had, and, when summoned by the ranger, the school bus which had brought them to the canyon came to pick them up, they didn't want to leave. Their leaders and the ranger and Daddy herded them all in, and they drove off, their heads and arms out the windows, calling and waving good-bye.

We repacked everything in the car, a little more tidily this time, though it still took up more room than usual, and drove to the ranger's headquarters. He had an old-fashioned black combination coal and kerosene stove, and he made an enormous pot of coffee, and even Rob drank some, with lots of milk in it. The ranger got flour and eggs down from a cupboard and Mother made pancakes for everybody, and while we gobbled them the ranger told us stories. The sun was quite high and bright and hot when we left. We certainly felt as though we'd been there more than one night, and it seemed that the ranger was an old, old friend. We promised him that we'd come visit him if ever we were back in Texas, and he was full of plans to come stay with us if ever he came east. We all shook hands solemnly with him, and he gave John a snakeskin belt as a token of thanks for helping with the scouts. The belt is one of John's greatest treasures, and he never wears anything else. I mean that he never wears any other *belt*.

Daddy said we'd have to stop early that afternoon in order to get the tent thoroughly dried out. We left Texas and drove into New Mexico, which was very different country. It was much wilder, and we saw our first buttes, which are cones and peaks of stone sticking up out of the desert. It was also lots more touristy than any place we'd been, with strings of motels and gift shops and snake farms. Suzy wanted to go into one of these, but Daddy said they were just expensive tourist traps, and she'd have to find her snakes in their natural habitat.

In Santa Fe we did our marketing and drove around a little, but couldn't really get out and sightsee because it was starting to storm again. We felt we'd really had our quota of wind and weather, but the skies didn't seem to agree with us. Santa Fe, with its Indian and Spanish atmosphere, was fascinating, but I won't describe it because anybody can look it up in the *National Geographic* or the encyclopaedia or someplace.

New Mexico was gorgeous, though, and at the same time a little depressing because, except for Santa Fe, it seemed so *poor*. At home in Thornhill nobody is really poor, and it was awful to see the shacks and shanties and the poor, foreign-looking people along the roadside. No wonder D. H. Lawrence wasn't really happy in New Mexico. The non-people part of it was wonderful, though. Mostly the mountains. I do love mountains. There were mountains of all shapes and sizes. In color everything was mostly tan, spotted with the darkness of juniper. I had never seen tan mountains before, or even realized that there *could* be tan mountains. At home at this time of year everything would be a soft, young green, with occasional touches of red or yellow from the early leafing of the maples. There would be a sense of birth, of gentle and fragile newness, so that, looking at the faintly wrinkled leaf of a spring maple as it slowly unfurled, I would touch it almost as timidly as I did Rob's cheek and soft, fuzzy head when Mother first brought him home from the hospital. But in New Mexico there was no sense of spring. Everything seemed ancient, pre-historic. Or maybe I mean post-historic.

This was the kind of landscape, austere and terrible, that I could imagine on a dying planet.

Once Daddy pointed to a river bed coursing with turbulent brown water, with waves seeming to go in every direction. The water wasn't more than three feet deep, I don't think, but it was rushing so wildly that no one could possibly have stood up in it; they'd have been thrown down and sucked under and drowned. This, Daddy explained, was a flash flood, and was what the ranger had been afraid of the night before down in the canyon. Looking at that wild water, I didn't wonder he'd been scared. In this untamed country a river bed can be caked, dry mud one minute and a thunderstorm later it can be a raging torrent. As we looked at the mad waters we understood why campers were warned never, never to set up their tents in dry river beds.

That day we got our first glimpse of snow-capped mountains, the first we had ever seen, mountains whose peaks stay white all year round. At home we are anxious, each spring, to have all the snow go from the shadowy places in the orchard, because then we knew that spring is really there. I suppose if you lived in New Mexico all year round you'd have ways of telling spring, but I had a feeling only of great tumult and great age. I felt very far from home, and that these mountains must have been formed very differently from our gentle Litchfield Hills, with wild, flaming upheavings.

Then, suddenly, as we got into Colorado ("Two states!" we always yelled as we crossed the line) the face of the earth changed. The mountains were less wild and more like those at home. And then we saw fresh green trees leafing, and lilac in full bloom, and the wildness of the sky changed to a soft, pearly gray, from which came a gentle spring rain.

"I think we'll stop at a motel tonight," Daddy said. "We've done enough battling with the elements to last us quite a while, and we need a good night's sleep and a chance to dry the tent. My only complaint about sleeping bags is that they're a little bit short for Mother and me."

"I think we've had *quite* enough weather for some time," Mother said firmly.

Rob asked, "If we didn't have weather, what would we have instead?"

The next day we just had a morning's drive to get to Mesa Verde. Zachary had said maybe he'd see me in Mesa Verde. I knew enough not to *say* anything, but I couldn't help *think*ing.

Ten

The drive to Mesa Verde, with Zachary lurking in the corners of my mind, was through terrifically mountainous country, one staggering view after another. Colorado is completely unlike New Mexico, and I'd never realized before how each state differs from the other in terrain, flora, and fauna, to be scientific-sounding about it. In New Mexico the mountains are bare, and suddenly in Colorado they're green. It's like two different worlds. We didn't see any animals for Suzy's notebook in New Mexico except lizards, but in Colorado there were lots of sheep. One lovely thing about having started our trip so early in the season was all the adorable babies: lambs, ponies, piglets, fledglings. One funny thing was that every day we would see at least one white horse, starting with the one Rob won Animal Rummy with the first day. It began to be a good luck sign with us, to see a white horse, though I think I took it more seriously than the others, dope that I am. I wish I didn't worry so much about omens and things. I don't do it aloud because Suzy and John are both scientific and they think I'm nuts. If we hadn't seen a white horse by near to camping time I'd begin to peer anxiously out the window, pretending I was just looking at scenery, but we always found one, and Suzy would jot it down in her book.

The road up to the Mesa Verde campgrounds was a hairpin job that made the road in Palo Duro seem like the infant's section in a playground. They were working on the darned road, too, and there were sheer drops at the side going down into forever, and I found that looking down gave me a very uncomfortable feeling in the pit of my stomach. Mother said this was called acrophobia, or fear of heights, and that I was too young to have it bother me. But Daddy reminded her that the only instinctive fear in a newborn baby is that of falling, so perhaps I wasn't growing into acrophobia but just had to learn to grow out of it.

When we signed in at the Park Headquarters the ranger must have seen that we had a Connecticut license, but he didn't say anything about a note for me, and I certainly didn't ask. Maybe Zachary was just leading me on when he said he was playing hares and hounds with me all over the United States.

This was by far the most crowded camp we'd been at, and already, so early in the day, a lot of the campsites were occupied. We found a nice one, though, set up, and had lunch.

While we were eating there was a familiar sweesh of tires, and then the black station wagon swooping on by us. Then its brakes were jammed on, it was backed up, and there was Zachary, standing by our picnic table and grinning. I grinned back but nobody else looked terribly happy to see him. John looked as though a scorpion had just come prancing up to our campsite. I could have swatted him one.

Zachary was all very polite about speaking to everybody,

though there was a general freeze when he said "hi" to John. It was obvious those two were never going to hit it off. He told us that they were staying in one of the lodges because his mother really didn't feel like camping and wanted to spend the afternoon resting. "So if you're going to go on one of those guided hikes to the Pueblo cliff dwellings this afternoon I wonder if I could string along with you? I'd honestly try not to be in the way."

"We'd be glad to have you, Zachary," Daddy said, though rather coolly, "if you really think you want to come."

"Oh, I really do, sir. Anthropology's one of my *Things*."

I knew that Zachary meant what he said, but I think Daddy thought there was an edge of mockery to the words, though all he said was, "We'll be leaving in about half an hour."

"Thank you, sir. I'll be ready. May Vicky come for a walk with me till then?"

"Sorry. She has jobs to do."

"Oh. I see. Very well, sir. I'll just sit in the car and read Ruth Benedict's *Patterns of Culture* till you're ready."

I guess he *was* showing off then. I mean, *Patterns of Culture* is about American Indians and all, but he didn't have to *say* it. I thought John was really going to let loose, but all he did was turn to Daddy and mutter, "Why'd you say he could come with us, Dad?"

"What'd you want me to do, John? Turn him down?"

"Oh—I suppose not. As long as he doesn't hang around me."

"I don't think he has any intention of hanging around you."

We got things tidied up and organized, and I sneaked off to the lavs to put some lipstick on. Suzy followed me. Well, maybe she had to come to the lav herself, but she stood and looked at me putting on lipstick, and said, "What on earth are you *doing*, Vicky?"

As if she didn't know. "I got a piece of bacon caught in my teeth."

"Bacon, hah. It's that dumb Zach. I suppose you'll be wanting to make out with him next. What've you got all that lipstick plastered all over your face for?"

I tried to answer with dignity. "In the first place it isn't plastered all over my face. I happen to have put a small amount on my lips. In case you've forgotten, Mother told me to use it when we were in New Mexico so my lips wouldn't get so dried out. They were cracking."

"Yah, real hot and dry here. I heard the weather report and it's supposed to turn *cold* tonight."

"So if I want to put on lipstick it's my own business. I'm older than you and I started wearing it when I went to Regional."

Suzy scowled. "I agree with John. He's a jerk."

I stalked out of the lav and went back to the tent.

At Mesa Verde there are quite a few rangers instead of the single one we'd got used to at other camps, and bulletin boards with lectures and hikes posted. We chose a hike with a lecture that took us on a climb right down the cliff side, down sheer precipices with narrow steps cut in the rock, down wooden ladders that dropped straight over nothing. While we were climbing I couldn't think of Zachary, who was behind me. All I could think of was not getting acrophobia and getting down in one piece. It was a descent that no elderly person could possibly have managed. About half way down, as we were trotting along a narrow path that for a few yards was almost level, John

111

mentioned this, and Rob asked anxiously, "What about Mother and Daddy?"

Daddy assured him that they weren't quite that elderly yet. But I couldn't help wondering what some of the elderly school teachers or people like that who went camping, or even stayed in the cabins or the hotel, would do. It would be an awful shame to miss the Pueblo remains. After all, they're the *reason* for coming to Mesa Verde. I was sure Zachary's parents couldn't manage it, and wondered what they were doing. Zachary didn't seem to pay much attention to them.

As I reached the bottom, just behind John, I let out a "Phew!" of relief, and turned around to Zachary. His smile was somehow very tight, and I thought he seemed even whiter than usual. Also I caught Daddy giving him a sharp kind of look.

When Zachary spoke he sounded even more winded than I felt. "Let's stop and talk for a few minutes, hunh, Vicky? We'll catch up during the lecture. I can tell you anything the ranger can, anyhow."

He talked gaspingly and Daddy looked at him again, saying, "Stay with Zach, Vicky. You can come along when you get your breaths." He and Mother and the others went with the ranger. There were about a dozen people on the hike, all asking the ranger questions about the Pueblo remains. Zachary squatted down on a rock, and I sat by him. He just sat there, sort of panting, and I felt a little funny about it, but I thought it would be best if I didn't say anything, or seem to be worried, so I looked over at the cliff houses.

We were on a level now with the cliff dwellings themselves, and Zachary began to talk to me about them, at first breathless, then seeming to relax. Boy, did he ever know about those Pueblo

Indians! Maybe he was putting on side when he talked about Ruth Benedict, but I'm sure he really *was* reading her, and I bet he's read everything Margaret Mead's written, too.

"Look at that honeycomb of buildings," he was saying. "It was built for about five hundred Indians and it's as complicated as a New York skyscraper, only everybody in the cliff dwellings knew everybody else, and what you see here was built into a natural cave in the side of the mountain. See, I told you New York was zuggy."

"What do you want me to do, go back a couple of thousand years and be an Indian? Anyhow, why don't you be an anthropologist instead of a lawyer?"

"It's all right for a hobby, but there's no money in it."

"Ruth Benedict and Margaret Mead did all right."

"They're dames, and anyhow they didn't make the kind of moola I'm thinking about. Look at this place, Vicky. *Look* at it. You know what you're doing? You're *see*ing it. You're not just *read*ing about it in some zuggy school. You know what these Indians were that lived in these caves? They were *peop*le. People like us. I can just see one of those Indian braves, sitting right here on this rock, with his quiver of arrows and his bow beside him, sitting here and snowing some Indian girl. Only she'd have shiny black hair, coarse as corn silk, instead of soft silky browny stuff like you. You've got very pretty hair, Vicky-O. Whyn't you let it grow so I can run barefoot through it some moonlight night?"

He kind of snuck his arm around me then, and I said, "Well, I don't know much about anthropology, but I do know the Pueblos haven't lived here for ages. I mean, it wasn't us moving out west a hundred years ago or anything. It didn't have anything to do with Americans, the cliff dwellers were history way back then."

"*They*'re the Americans, we're not. We're just thieving, murdering, genocidal upstarts."

"Yah, I know, but why did they stop living here?"

"It was drought, Vicky-O, a long and terrible drought that drove them out of their caves." When he told me this Zachary sounded as sad as though he were talking about people he really knew. He cared more about those dead Indians than he did about anybody alive today. He looked straight at me as though it were my fault. "They prayed for rain in their songs and dances and rain didn't come, and the crops up on the mesa withered up and there wasn't enough to eat, and finally they had to leave their homes, the land and the cliffs and the caves that had been theirs for generations, and go find another place to live."

When he talked about the Indians Zachary was completely different from when he talked about anything else, that awful song, for instance, and what he had to say scared me, almost as much as the song did. People lived here and had families here and were happy here, just the way we were in Thornhill, and suddenly they were gone, and we were gone from Thornhill, too. Though of course everybody else would be there. It was just *us* who were being like the Pueblo Indians, driven from our homes.

"I was talking to a friend of mine who's an Indian last night," Zachary said, "and he's afraid that a new drought, as bad as the one that drove the Pueblos from their homes, might be starting now. All the omens point to it. The funny thing, no, it really isn't funny, is that some of the meteorologists are afraid so, too. You want to go join those other dopes now?"

"We'd better."

When we got to the others they were looking down into a sort of circular room. The ranger was saying that they knew that

114

only men were allowed in the round rooms, but I didn't hear *how* they knew it because I missed the beginning of the lecture.

"What'd they *do* in the round rooms?" I whispered to Zachary.

"It was something to do with their religion; they even had *religion* and all, the goons. That ranger's a pretty good guy. He teaches trig or something at some university in the winter."

One man, standing near our family, asked the ranger, "You say this was all around 600 A.D.?"

"That's right," the ranger said.

"How come you know so little about them, then?"

The ranger turned to John. "What was happening in Europe about six hundred A.D. fella?"

"Well, it was the Dark Ages, sir," John answered. "It was monks, wasn't it, who were keeping civilization alive?"

"Tell me, don't ask me," the ranger said.

"It *was* the monks, then," John said. "And feudalism was beginning. Let's see, the Visigoths and the Vandals were the four hundreds, Theodoric of the Ostrogoths was five hundreds, and, oh, yes, it was Frankish kings of Gaul in the six hundreds, but there wasn't any strong central government. And wasn't it in the six hundreds that Jerusalem was taken over by the Mohammedans?"

"Right you are. The point is, that we know more about the monks in their cells in Europe than we do about the Indians right here in our own country. Why?"

A woman who turned out to be a first grade teacher called out, "Because of the way we treated them."

The ranger nodded. "Nevertheless we *do* know that the Pueblo were advanced enough in their civilization to paint the insides of their windows white. Why?" He looked at John again.

"To reflect light," John answered. I had a feeling that it

annoyed Zachary like anything to have John know the answers to the ranger's questions.

"Right you are," the ranger said again. "We know a few material things about them, but very little else. We don't know anything about the religious rites that must have gone on in these round rooms, or what kind of a God they worshipped. They built elaborate storage rooms and ventilating systems, and yet they left no written language, and they dumped both their garbage and their dead over the edge of the cliff. Thank you, people. You've been very patient. We'd better get moving now because I can see that the next group is close on our heels."

Rob was standing right in front of the ranger, and he asked, very earnestly, "They're all gone? Nobody lives here any more?"

"No, son. Not for hundreds and hundreds of years."

"They're all dead?"

"Long, long ago."

Rob looked very seriously at the ranger, as though the two of them were there all alone in the Pueblo remains, as though there weren't anybody else standing around to listen. "I don't want to die."

"Nobody does, son."

"Do you?"

"No."

"But people get old, and then they get wore out because they're so old, and then they have to die."

"That's about the long and short of it, son. Come along, let's us lead the way."

That's one reason I love Rob so much. The same kind of things bother him that do me, and he's really only a baby.

We started the long climb *up* the cliff, Zachary and I right

116

behind Daddy, the rest of the family ahead. We went up steep stone steps, up stony paths, up ladders, and Zachary's steps got slower and slower and he looked very white. I slowed down, too, and let a group of people go past us, and then I saw that Daddy had stopped and was looking at Zachary.

"You'd better stop, Zach."

"It's all right, sir. I can make it."

"Not without a rest," Daddy said.

"No, sir. I want to go on. Please." That *please* sounded funny, coming from Zachary, and all of a sudden it made me want to cry.

"Sorry," Daddy said. "When you elected to come with us this afternoon you put yourself under my supervision, and I tell you to stop and rest. Then we'll take the rest of the climb in easy stages. What's your problem? Rheumatic fever a few years ago?"

Zachary's eyes seemed enormous in his white face. "How did you know? I didn't tell Vicky—"

"I'm a doctor. Rheumatic fever's my specialty, so I made a guess. Sit down and get your breath."

"I'm all right now," Zachary said. "I'd rather go on."

Everybody had pushed on past us, now, some looking curiously at us standing there at the edge of the path, just barely able to make room for them to get by.

Daddy looked at Zachary. "Do you make a habit of doing things you know you oughtn't to do?"

"Why not?" Zachary stood up as though to start climbing again.

"If you want to kill yourself on your own time there's not much I can do to stop you," Daddy said. "When you're with me you'll do as I say. Sit down."

Zachary swallowed. I could see his Adam's apple move. "Yes, sir."

"Vicky, go on and catch up with the others. Zachary and I'll be along in a few minutes."

"I'll wait with you," I said.

"Vicky, I asked you to go."

"But—"

"Nobody's going to wait for anyone, for crying out loud!" Zachary said. I thought he was going to burst into tears. He got up and started to scramble up the stone steps cut in the side of the cliff. Daddy reached out and caught his wrist.

"Zach."

Zachary tried to pull away. "You don't really think you can stop me, do you?" He gave a nasty grin.

Daddy's a lot stronger than Zachary. He didn't need to do any judo on him. "Is this the way you behave with your parents?"

"My parents know better than to order me about. When I don't get what I want I have hysterics. They're very effective."

Daddy sat down on the stone steps just above Zachary, blocking the path completely. Our group was out of sight above. The next group was clustered down below us. Daddy said, "The acoustics ought to be excellent here." Then he noticed that I was still standing just above him. "Go on, Vicky."

If I had hysterics instead of obeying Daddy when he uses that tone of voice I don't think it would work very well. I went on up. The family was waiting at the top of the path. The ranger and the rest of the group had gone on.

"Where's Daddy?" Mother asked.

"With Zach." I didn't want her to ask any more questions. I didn't want to have to tell about Zachary in front of John and

Suzy. But Mother is often very good about knowing when not to ask questions, and she didn't say anything more, and we went to look at a place where Indians had lived more recently, though still hundreds of years ago, just above the path. There were signs and all telling us about it, which John had to read word for word. Somehow I wasn't very interested any more.

It seemed a long time before Zachary and Daddy came up the last steps of the ascent. Zachary still looked very white, but he wasn't panting the way he had been. Daddy must have made him take it very, very slowly.

He asked Daddy if I could go off to the commissary and have a soda with him, and Daddy said yes.

We walked, side by side, along the dusty path, and Zachary asked, "Are you leaving tomorrow?"

"Yes."

"Where're you going?"

"I don't know where we'll be tomorrow night, but we're heading for Grand Canyon."

"It's kind of spectacular in its own way," Zachary said. "Spaniards from Coronado's expedition discovered it in 1540."

He sounded as though he were trying to get back at John for having known so much. "Yes, I know. Daddy told us."

"Daddy knows everything, doesn't he?" Zachary sneered as we went into the cool darkness of the commissary.

"He knows a lot."

"So do I. Grand Canyon is twenty one and a half miles long, from four to eighteen miles wide, and over a mile deep."

"It's in our camping book, too," I said tactlessly, climbing up on the high stool next to Zachary. "Are you going?"

"Again? Not even for you, Vicky-O. I think we'll head for

home. I suppose you heard your father say I'd had rheumatic fever?"

"Yes. I don't know much about it, though."

"What'll you have, Vicky? Two lemon Cokes, please. Sometimes it leaves you with a heart condition."

"Oh."

"It did me. I might drop dead at any time. It's a very useful weapon. If people don't do just as I like I might have a heart attack."

I didn't say anything. Because Daddy had made Zachary stop on the climb up to the top of the cliff I knew that it was probably true, what Zachary had just said. But the way he was speaking, it didn't seem as though it ought to be true. It seemed as made up as the plays we put on up in the attic at home, with costumes out of Mother's costume trunk.

"Are you sorry for me?" he asked.

I think there must be something terribly wrong with me. I ought to have been all flooding with pity for Zachary and I wasn't. Just the way I wasn't properly sorry for Maggy when she first came to stay with us. Is it that I'm frozen-hearted, like the boy with the splinter of ice in his heart in Andersen's story? I don't think so. If we see a squirrel or even a skunk that's been killed by a car and is lying flung by the side of the road I feel horrible. I can't bear it that its little life has been cut off. So why wasn't I sorry for Zachary?

"Are you sorry for me?" he asked again.

I wasn't sorry for him, and somehow I didn't want to lie to him, so I just said bluntly, "No."

"Anh-*hanh!*" he said. "I knew I was right when I saw you and decided you were a girl I wanted to know. I knew there was something about you. Why aren't you sorry for me?"

"Well—that song the other night in Tennessee."

"What about it?"

"About blowing ourselves to bits and stuff. I mean, when our parents were growing up, they could count on a future. Now nobody can. Not just you. Nobody." As I said these words I faced them for the first time, and I began to shiver.

"Do you believe that?" Zachary asked. "Do you really believe it?"

"No, of course I don't believe it!" I cried, so loudly that other people sitting at the counter turned to look at me. I lowered my voice. "But it's there. It's a possibility."

"Only a possibility," Zachary said. "It probably won't happen for a long time and it may never happen. But my heart condition is more than a possibility. It's there."

"Then why do you keep doing things you shouldn't do?"

"Oh, what's the use, Vicky?" He sounded very tired, sitting there with his hands around the coolness of his Coke. "What's there worth living for?"

I felt as though I were being drawn down into a dark, deep hole. The sunlight was outside. It was shadowy at the counter, and the blades of the fans whirring around seemed to suck me deeper and deeper into the hole. I wanted to leave Zachary and run out into the blazing sunlight, run pelting down the dusty path to our campsite, to get hot and sweaty from the bright heat of the day, to be part of light and joy again. I said, too loudly, "*Life*'s worth living for! Just being alive! I love it! I love every minute of it!"

Zachary could change without batting an eyelash. He turned on me fiercely. "You think I don't, too?"

We finished our Cokes and he walked me back to the tent and then turned on his heel and left without saying a word about ever seeing me again.

I hoped he never did.

Eleven

That night at dinner I was sort of quiet, and John said, very kindly for John, "Don't let it get you down, Vicky."

"What?"

"That boy. He's just an oddball."

Mother gave John another helping of hash. "It ought to teach us not to make snap judgments. They really annoyed me with their fancy equipment. But that poor, silly boy. With parents who don't have the faintest idea how to handle him."

"More hash, too, please, Mother," Suzy said.

Mother heaped her plate. "I wish we had this lovely firewood at every campsite. Dinner was a joy to cook tonight. Come on, kids, eat up. We don't want to be late for the campfire program."

This was the first campgrounds we'd been to that had evening programs, but all the National Parks we went to later had them, and quite a lot of the state parks, too. But the setting at

Mesa Verde was the most gorgeous of them all. It was a natural amphitheater cut out of rock, a half circle of stone benches looking way across the canyon. I don't suppose you'd have this feeling of great space in ancient Rome but that's where it made me think of. The moon was rising, seeming almost to leap up out of the canyon. I was sitting there, half dozing, not really thinking about anything, just being contented, when suddenly somebody plunked down beside me.

Who but Zachary?

I was glad when he left me that afternoon. I couldn't wait to get back to our campsite. But now I was just as glad to see him. I didn't understand my own feelings at all, but that's been nothing new for about a year now.

"Hi, everybody," he said. "Destry rides again." He turned and murmured in my ear, as though it were something very important and for me alone, "The old man and woman hate these lectures. They wanted me to go for a walk with them and then have a game of bridge, but I told them I had a pain in my chest and had better just sit this evening."

"Do you?" I asked.

"No, but I might have if I went for a walk. I can always get a pain without too much trouble, but I don't do it if I can get my own way without."

The ranger who was to give the evening talk came out just then and lit the kindling under a big teepee of logs, so Zachary put his arm around my waist and leaned back as though he owned the place. He seemed to be fascinated by the lecture, which was on how ruins and civilizations are dated, but I must admit that most of it was beyond me, and anyhow I didn't pay as much attention as I should have. I was too aware of Zachary's arm around me, and then the flickering of the firelight made me sleepy. Rob climbed over John and sat on my other side, and right after the beginning of the lecture he put his head down in my lap and went sound asleep, so all I remember is that you can find out something about when civilizations flourished by tree rings and carbon decay.

After the ranger had finished his talk he told us that some Navajo Indians who worked in the park were going to come do some dances for us. He warned us that if anybody had a dog they'd better take it back to the car, because if a dog barks during a dance it's very bad luck, and they'd just quit and refuse to dance. Or if anybody irritated or disturbed them in any way they'd stop and go home.

I'd never seen an Indian dance before, and I woke Rob up for it, but I must admit that I was very disappointed. It wasn't at all the wild leaping about the fire that I'd imagined, but just a slow, rhythmic shuffling around in a circle. In one dance they shook gourds, in another they patted a drum, and always they sang a rather sinister, high-pitched melody, each melody starting with a high "hau!"

I whispered something to Zachary about this, and he whispered back, "It's a re*lig*ious dance for Pete's sake. They take it very seriously. What'd you expect? A fertility orgy?"

After the Indians had danced for a few minutes one of them came around the stone benches passing a hat, and everybody put some coins in. Then, without a word, they stalked off into the darkness.

I heard Daddy whisper to Mother, "I don't think they were satisfied with the take. Most people didn't put in very much."

With the departure of the Indians the program was over and everybody started straggling back to tents, cabins, or hotel. Zachary took my hand and pulled me back so that we were walking behind everybody else, alone on the path, with only the beams from our flashlights to light our way. The nicest thing we saw was a sleepy little bunny rabbit at the edge of the path, blinking at our flashlights, and I hoped Suzy and Rob had seen him, too. But I couldn't get those Indians out of my mind, nor their looks as they'd stalked off into the night.

"Those Indians," I said to Zachary. "I don't think they liked us. I think they resented us."

"Do you blame them?" Zachary sounded quite violent. "We've taken their country, we've misused them, and here they are, paid laborers in their own land. Wouldn't you burn if you were in their place?" We were silent then until he said, "I don't think your father likes my having followed you."

"I don't think he thought you were following me or anything," I said awkwardly. "I mean lots of people come to Mesa Verde. It's kind of a logical place to come to."

"Logic doesn't have anything to do with it," he said. "And I was following you, Vicky-O. Have no doubt about it." His voice was low and intimate, though everybody else was so far ahead of us on the path now that nobody could have heard him. "You've got something, Vicky. Of course you're not the beauty of the family. That yellow, curly-haired little sister of yours is going to be miles ahead of you in looks. She's filled with S.A., as our parents used to say in their youth. Or sex appeal, in case you don't remember their bygone prattle."

"I know what sex appeal is," I said stiffly.

126

"Now you. You're different."

"I know I am. You needn't rub it in." There it was again, the old difference between Suzy and me, which I'd been beginning to forget this past year. When we were little, and Mother would take us shopping, people would stop in the street and say what an adorable little girl Suzy was, and they didn't even seem to see me, and it wasn't just because I was three years older. Mother used to say that Suzy was pretty and I was distinguished, but nobody ever coos over anybody looking distinguished. And when you get older nobody makes passes over you being distinguished, either. It's a heck of a lot worse than wearing glasses.

"My dear girl," Zachary said, "I'm not rubbing anything in. I picked you, didn't I? Not your sister."

I shone my flashlight down on the pebbles of the path. "There's the little matter of age."

"Age!" His black eyebrows shot up. "You're years younger than that golden-haired kid. You're an innocent little babe in the woods. Hey, I know what, let's lie down and cover ourselves with leaves and let the robins bring us berries like in the song."

"Are you a babe in the woods?"

"You got me there. Guess we can't do it. Anyhow what I really had in mind was something else again." He turned around there on the path between the amphitheater and the campgrounds and kissed me. My heart began to pound as though I were the one with the heart condition. I wasn't sure I wanted my first real kiss to be from Zachary. But he gave it—or took it—without so much as a by-your-leave and there wasn't a thing I could do about it.

"Well!" he said. "That was very nice. I think you're going to

127

be okay, Vicky-O. *Very* okay." He took my hand and we walked slowly along the path again. He intoned,

> *"I grow old, I grow old,*
> *I shall wear the bottoms of my trousers rolled.*

T. S. Eliot. I don't suppose you've ever heard of him."

"We did *Murder in the Cathedral* in church," I said.

He stopped and kissed me again. Longer, this time. "You're a funny kid," he said afterwards, "a mixture of goody-goody little Miss Prunes, and quite a gal. I look forward to knowing you in five years."

—*You're* a funny kid, I could have said right back at him, but I didn't. One minute he was talking about dropping dead any day, and the next he was making plans into an indefinite future.

"Here we are, Victorinia," he said. "I brought you safely home. I won't see you again till Laguna. But expect me there, sweetheart. Expect me there!" He called out good night to everybody and walked off down the path, whistling that darned melody.

We were in bed a little after nine, and it was cool enough so that the sleeping bags felt very comfortable. I was just about to drift off to sleep when I heard the Indians singing again from wherever it was they sleep. It scared me. It sounded raw and primitive and I felt that they hated us and it wouldn't take much to make them work themselves up to the point where they'd take their tomahawks (did Navajo's use tomahawks?) and come around to the tents and scalp all the audience that had displeased them that evening.

They must have sung for half an hour, this weird, high singing with its strange "hau!" and they got me thoroughly waked up. Maybe it was partly Zachary, too. And getting kissed. Anyhow, I kept bouncing about in my sleeping bag, getting wider and wider awake every minute. I let some air out of the mattress but that didn't help and I decided I'd let *too* much air out, but there wasn't anything I could do about that, except be uncomfortable.

So finally I decided to play my alphabet game to get to sleep. Grandfather taught it to me. He plays it when he can't sleep, but most of his are prayers and psalms and stuff like that, and most of mine aren't. What you do is think of a song or poem for each letter of the alphabet, and you never get to XYZ without falling asleep first. So I've learned all kinds of things. Most of them I've learned during sermons. I write what I want to learn on a slip of paper and then stick it in my hymnal at church. Our minister at home is a very kindly person, but he preaches long and dull sermons. He's nothing like Grandfather. Grandfather is short and to the point and exciting and you can't *help* listening to him.

I had a perfect A for a camping trip, Walt Whitman's "Song of the Open Road."

"*Afoot and light-hearted I take to the open road,*
Healthy, free, the world before me,
The long brown path before me leading wherever I choose. . . ."

Maybe that was true for our family, for me. But it wasn't for Zachary. I went on to B. My favourite B is "The Blessed Damozel." I love that one. It's all mysterious and golden and like music.

> *"The blessed damozel leaned out*
> > *From the golden bar of heaven;*
> *Her eyes were deeper than the depth*
> > *Of waters stilled at even;*
> *She had three lilies in her hand,*
> > *And the stars in her hair were seven. . . ."*

It's about this beautiful girl who's in heaven, but heaven doesn't mean a thing to her because her lover is still on earth, and even though she's in heaven she can't keep from weeping for him.

Well, that didn't put me to sleep, even though it's quite long. I went on and on and still I was wide awake and scared, which doesn't usually happen. I got up to I, and I'm usually asleep long before then. There are quite a lot of nice ones for I. There's "In the Bleak Midwinter," which is best for around Christmas. And there's the poem painted on the wall of the loft at Grandfather's. But this night for some reason I used "I will lift up mine eyes." I guess I used it because of the hills around me, and because I thought it would be comforting. I said it slowly, trying to relax into its promises.

> *"I will lift up mine eyes unto the hills*
> *From whence cometh my help.*
> *My help cometh from the Lord*
> *Which made heaven and earth."*

Oh, it's a very comforting thing, that, particularly at the end, where it says,

"The Lord is thy shade upon thy right hand.
The sun shall not smite thee by day,
Nor the moon by night.
The Lord shall preserve thee from all evil;
He shall preserve thy soul.
The Lord shall preserve thy going out and thy coming in
From this time forth, and even forevermore."

The moonlight had been beating against our tent and coming in through the windows, but now as I said these words it didn't seem to be smiting, it was just silver and beautiful. I didn't even get to my J, but drifted down deep into sleep.

About three thirty I was wakened by a loud, barking wail. It kept on and on, and I didn't know what on earth it could be, because it didn't sound like anything I knew. But I was still too sleepy and comfortable to get nervous again, and I went back to sleep. In the morning the campers in the tent next to us told us that it was a coyote.

"If I'd heard it I'd have recognized it from TV," Suzy said, pulling out her notebook. "Do you think it's fair if I write it down if I didn't hear it?"

We didn't see Zachary that morning, and I didn't really expect to, the way he'd said good-bye the night before. John made a couple of cracks about losing my boy friend, but Mother shut him up.

When we left Mesa Verde we had to go back through a corner of New Mexico to get to Arizona. As we neared the New Mexico border we went into a Ute Indian reservation, and again the whole face of the earth changed completely and spectacularly. John has a book, *The Conquest of Space,* with illustrations by Chesley Bonestell, of what scientists think other planets and satellites must look like, and this Ute reservation was like one of these illustrations. I began to feel that after we'd finished seeing America no land anywhere would have any surprises for us, even if we should go to Mars or the moon or the slushy frozen ammonia snows of Jupiter. The Ute Indians' land was dry and tan with dusty-looking grey vegetation. In the background were high cliffs with flat tops and eroded sides. As we drove along, strange, fairy-tale rock formations appeared out of nowhere. Daddy said they were volcanic monoliths. It gave me the feeling of absolutely tremendous age, as though this land had been made so long ago that the Pueblo civilization was only yesterday. It seemed that we could almost reach out and hold hands across time with the people in the cliff dwellings, but this Indian reservation reached so far back into the distant past that there was no way of bridging those hundreds of thousands of years. Were the Indians in the reservation part of that past? Zachary would probably know. How could they, how could *anybody* live there?

Arizona. Another state. (Rob finally did it first this time. "Two states!" he cried triumphantly.) A*nother* world.

It was really staggering. I mean, when your whole world has been a little village like Thornhill you can't help getting amazed when you see things you never realized even existed. I kept thinking that all these differences couldn't keep on, that we must have seen *everything* and the rest of it'd just be more of something we already knew, and then we'd round a bend and there'd be a kind of landscape I'd never even dreamed of before. How can *people* in all these places be the same when where they live is so completely different? Well, Zachary lived in a different place, and *he* wasn't like anybody else I'd ever known before.

"There should be Bug-Eyed Monsters here, or Little Blue Men," John said as we drove into Painted Desert.

Hot, hot it was, and dry. We stopped at a filling station and bought a desert bag, a canvas bag that you fill with water and then hang outside the car. The water in the bag, even when you're driving in blistering sunlight, keeps cool because of evaporation. I don't understand this, even though Daddy and John and Suzy all tried to explain it to me. The main thing is, it works.

The desert was yellow, as though it had soaked up the color of the sun, with red, lava-like cones and pyramids that looked almost as though they had been made by people instead of being something nature dreamed up. The shadows were purple and blue and looked as though they were things in themselves, so that they'd be there, lying on the hot sand, even if there were nothing to cast them. There was a feeling of eternity about it, of being outside time, that must have affected even Rob, because suddenly he asked,

"Mother, do numbers have any end?"

"No, Rob."

"If I counted all day and night would I come to an end?"

"No, Rob. You could go on counting forever."

"But if *everybody* counted wouldn't there have to be an end?"

After a while the road started to get ugly and touristy again. We went across bridge after bridge over dry rivers, but now we knew how quickly those cracked river beds that looked as though they'd been empty for centuries could become raging torrents. Sometimes at the side of the road we would see Indians with impassive, closed-in faces. They looked unfriendly. It was nothing as active as hate. It was just stolid dislike. I thought of the things Zachary'd said about Indians and I couldn't blame them. But it still made me uncomfortable.

Every once in a while Daddy pointed out small dust twisters moving across the barren land. I leaned over the front seat towards Mother. "I don't think I want to live in Arizona."

"We haven't seen much of it yet," she said. "Some people think it's a paradise."

Towards the end of the day's drive we began to climb. We'd been seeing hazy mountains in the distance for a long time, and as we finally reached them the blast of hot air began to get cooler, and at last we *did* see some green, the light green of grass and the darker green of pines, and then Daddy pulled in to Townsend Campsite, which is near Flagstaff, Arizona. It was by far the most primitive campsite we'd had, not much bigger than the roadside picnic areas at home. No lavatories. Only dirty, fly-inhabited privies. Suzy decided they were highly unsanitary and announced that she wasn't going to use them, but Daddy told her that she had no alternative, and when she had to go badly enough she'd use the privy, flies or no flies.

The only thing to remember about Flagstaff, Arizona, is beautiful tall pines at the campgrounds, and strawberry jam.

There were a lot of kids there around Suzy's age, and while Mother and I were getting dinner everybody else played baseball, even Rob, who still isn't very good at it, but John pitched when he was at bat.

When Mother called out that dinner was ready Suzy came rushing back. The big green box of food was on the picnic bench and she bumped against it and knocked it off the bench with a re-sounding crash.

Mother just looked at Suzy, and Suzy cried, "I didn't mean to!"

Daddy picked up the box and set it on the table. Mother looked in and said, "Oh, no."

I looked. We had just bought a brand new king size jar of strawberry jam. It was broken. Very broken. Jam was all over everything in the box.

Suzy offered quickly, "I'll clean it up."

"No," Mother said. "Thank you, Suzy. But no." She pulled out the jar of mustard and it was covered with strawberry jam. Still holding the gooey mustard bottle Mother closed her mouth tight and walked around the table. Then she walked around the tent and the car. Then she came back to the table. "Suzy and Rob, get me water. Lots and lots of water." She took a paper towel and wiped off the mustard jar. Then she reached in the box and pulled out a handful of broken glass and strawberry jam. "The sugar jar is broken, too."

"Be careful of broken glass," Daddy said, and took out the salt container, though you couldn't tell what was in the container for strawberry jam. The paper napkins were covered with straw-berry jam. The English muffins for breakfast were covered with strawberry jam.

Mother moaned, "Why did I ever think I liked strawberry jam?" and then giggled.

Suzy and Rob came back with one small pot of water.

"What's this?" Daddy asked.

"The man wouldn't let us get any more," Suzy said. "He says there's a water shortage."

"He didn't like us," Rob said. "He sounded mad."

There wasn't a ranger at this campground, just an old and rather crochety man. Daddy said, "I'd better explain that we have a slight emergency. Come along, kids."

We used up a whole roll of paper towels on the strawberry jam, putting the dirty towels in the fireplace until the fire smelled of burned sugar and strawberries.

Suzy, Rob, and Daddy came back with water, which, Daddy said, the man had been very loath to give them, even with explanations, and Suzy asked, and she wasn't being funny, "What are we going to have on the English muffins tomorrow morning?"

John said, "Suzy, people have lost their necks for less than that. If you'll take my advice you'll just be very, very quiet."

The next day was Grand Canyon and we got there around noon. The only trouble with Grand Canyon was that we were already so saturated with beauty that we looked at it and said, "Oh. Pretty." Which is hardly the word for Grand Canyon. But it just didn't mean to us what it would have meant if we'd come straight to it from Thornhill without all the other things in between.

Also, Grand Canyon was crowded and commercial, and it's a place you should see without any people at all.

Anybody can read all about Grand Canyon, so there's no point in describing it. We took a two night stopover there and had a lot of fun. There was a nuclear physicist and his family across from us so another baseball game got started and kept on going, on and off, for two days, with new kids joining in all the time till we had two full teams. John and I were the oldest. Not many teen-agers seem to go camping.

We went on some guided hikes, went to the campfire lectures, and took hot showers which you had to *pay* for at Grand Canyon—twenty-five cents.

We were there over Sunday so we went to the church service, and I'm sorry to say it was the dullest of all the ones we went to, held in a hall instead of outdoors like at lots of other parks. If there was ever a place to have church outdoors Grand Canyon was it. Suzy wriggled and Rob went to sleep and fell off his chair with a thud in the middle of the sermon. We had a terrible time not giggling, and I let out a loud, disgraceful snort, and that sent Suzy off, and it was a relief when it was over. Mother and Daddy were not pleased.

From Grand Canyon we went to Zion Canyon. Each day we kept thinking that we couldn't see anything more beautiful than the day before, but the drive to Zion was one of the most strange and beautiful of all. Along the roadside were high grey sand-dunes, only they weren't made of sand, they were solid and hard. John and I thought maybe they were petrified, but Daddy said no. The desert was spotted with sage and bounded by eroded red cliffs. It was terribly hot and Suzy was whiney and Rob's chest and back got spotted with heat rash, and Daddy let us have water from the desert bag quite often. Suddenly we climbed into a great and beautiful pine woods, and the air seemed to stretch out, so that it was light and clear. Then, climbing down, the desert lay spread out before us, every shade possible of rose and mauve and blue. This part of Arizona was wild and beautiful and *again* unlike anything we'd ever experienced or expected. I kept thinking of strange planets in distant solar systems.

"Turn your space ship around and come down from the stars," Mother said. "Don't you realize you're home?"

When Mother said "home" I had a vision of our white house with its orderly green lawn, of our elms and maples, of the tree house John built, and the rambler roses coming into bloom on the fence. "Home?" I asked stupidly.

"This is your country, Vicky," Mother said. "This is America. A New England village isn't your only heritage. This is part of it, too."

Daddy added, "Your great-great-grandparents came out this way in a covered wagon. They didn't have road maps or even roads, and they weren't sure that the desert would ever end or that they'd eventually reach green and fertile land again. When we send our astronauts up, every possible precaution is made to bring them safely home, and the whole nation watches and prays. Your great-great-grandparents were on their own. They lost one child on the way with fever. Their oldest boy was captured by Indians, and they never knew what happened to him. Crossing our own unchartered land took as much courage and imagination as a trip to the moon."

I must have been listening with a rather set expression, and Daddy must have seen me in the rear-view mirror, because he laughed and said, "Vicky, I can just see you thinking, 'Mother and Daddy are sermonizing again.' Well, we're going to go on preaching, and," Daddy's voice grew more serious, "I expect you to listen."

"I'm listening," I kind of muttered.

Mother turned around and grinned at me. "I think it was Mark Twain who said, 'When I was seventeen I thought my father was

138

the stupidest man I'd ever met. When I was twenty-one it was amazing how much the old man had learned in those four years.'"

When we crossed into Utah the countryside *again* took on a character of its own. The earth was pinkish sand, with many more green things growing in it than in Arizona, and we saw river beds that actually had water in them. The rocks were eroded in graceful whorls and swirls, as though the wind had been dancing by, instead of blasting in from the Equator as it had seemed to do in the Arizona desert.

The campgrounds at Zion were down in the canyon, the way they were at Palo Duro, instead of up on the rim, like Grand Canyon, and it was very hot, up in the nineties. The campgrounds were in a grove of cottonwood trees, and around us we could see the great red cliffs with their strange formations rising up two thousand feet on each side. It was one of the nicest campsites we'd had, with good fireplaces with proper grates, and there were tiled bathrooms with cold showers—free ones. The showers were icily, shiveringly cold, and on that blazing hot day they felt marvelous.

For some reason we liked Zion Canyon better than Grand Canyon, partly, I suppose, because the campgrounds themselves were so much more beautiful. Grand Canyon was a desert canyon, pines the only trees. In Utah things were much greener; up on the mesas we actually saw green fields, and in Zion there were lots of trees, and there were lovely wild hanging gardens growing out of the rocks. And birds! The birds were singing like mad (on our whole trip the birds were a beautiful and persistent accompaniment). The birds and animals around the camp-grounds seemed very secure and not a bit shy, like my skunk and

Suzy's deer at Palo Duro, and I loved seeing them, even though I didn't give a hoot about collecting species, like Suzy. I guess I'm just an enjoyer. Maybe I'll end up a beachcomber, since I don't seem to have any talents.

Not far from us was a lovely little river, and after we'd got our jobs done, and Mother had spaghetti sauce simmering over a fire, we went for a swim. The water was shallow, but quite swift. Rob kept getting thrown about and having to be rescued, but he wasn't a bit frightened and had a wonderful time. He's a very brave little boy.

The people in the campsite next to us were an elderly couple in a small trailer. While Mother and I were getting dinner ready Daddy and John went exploring about the canyon, and Suzy and Rob made friends with the lady and gentleman in the trailer, and brought them over to talk to Mother and me. Their name was Williams, and they told us that they were planning to stay in Zion for two weeks, which was as long as the dollar permit entitled them to. Then they would go on, maybe to Bryce Canyon, and stay there for a while. Mr. Williams was retired, their children were grown and married, and they spent most of the year wandering from one beautiful place to another, following the weather around.

When Mrs. Williams realized that Mother was out of oregano for the spaghetti sauce, she insisted on going back into the trailer and getting some. After the campfire movie and lecture she invited us over for lemonade and showed us through the trailer. We'd never been in a trailer before, and we were thrilled. It was more like a doll's house than anything else, everything tiny and compact and in its own place, little nooks for beds, a miniature kitchen, a corner for a tiny dining table and two benches. There was even a little cupboard with a toilet in it, but Mrs. Williams said they couldn't use it in Zion because it wasn't a trailer camp and didn't have outlets for plumbing and electricity.

We were going to spend two nights in Zion because we were all still quite tired. Daddy said he thought we'd been feeling the altitude. So we slept late, and after a leisurely breakfast we went exploring. There were several guided hikes and these were fun and beautiful, if not as difficult as the ones at Mesa Verde and Grand Canyon. The ranger kept pointing out new insects and birds for Suzy, and told us how things manage to grow on the canyon walls: lichen forms on the rocks, and the lichen produces enough soil for ferns and grass, and so on, and all this is aided by occasional streams trickling out of the rocks. There's one rock that's even called Weeping Rock because it's always dripping water.

In the late afternoon we went back to the brook for a swim. Mother had a headache; she thought it was just too much sun and altitude, so she decided to stay in the tent and have a nap. We had a wonderful swim, came racing back through the campgrounds, and Suzy dashed into the tent to be the first to get dressed. In a second she backed out, finger to her lips, looking absolutely white.

Twelve

"What gives?" John called as he ran to catch up.

Suzy is seldom at a loss for words, but all she could do was croak, "D-d-daddy—" and point at the tent.

"'Smatter, Sue?" Daddy asked.

"In the t-tent," Suzy gasped. "M-mother—"

All I could think of was that something terrible had happened to Mother, and I grabbed John's arm.

Rob ducked into the tent under Daddy's elbow, and I heard him give an excited shout. "Mother's had a baby!"

Daddy's voice came, low and startled, "Wha—a-at?"

And we heard Mother say sleepily, "Wallace?"

As John and I headed for the tent Suzy's tongue was released. "There's a baby in there with Mother!"

"Hunh?"

"I went in, and Mother was on the sleeping bag sound asleep, and there was a baby sleeping right beside her!"

We heard Rob asking, "Is it ours?"

Now we were all sticking our heads in the tent. Mother was sitting up on the sleeping bag, and right beside her was a baby, sleeping all through the sound and fury, its tiny thumb loosely in its mouth.

"Where did you get the baby?" Mother asked Daddy.

"That's what I was just about to ask you," Daddy said.

Mother looked down at the baby, couldn't help smiling at it, then said, "Wallace, is this your idea of a joke?"

Daddy often looks dead serious when he's joking, but there wasn't a hidden twinkle anywhere this time. "Victoria, I've never seen this baby before in my life."

"Is it ours?" Rob asked again.

Mother looked at all of us clustered in the doorway of the tent. "Where did you get the baby?"

Nobody answered.

"Who put the baby in the tent with me?"

Silence.

Mother started, "Now look, fun's fun, but—"

Daddy broke in. "Victoria, we've all been swimming together. We haven't been separated for a moment. Suzy ran ahead and into the tent, but she certainly didn't have time to pick up a baby on the way."

"Suzy?" Mother asked.

Suzy still sounded a little shaky, but now she was perfectly able to gabble. "I ran in to the tent, and there you were, sound asleep, and the baby right with you."

"Then it *must* be ours," Rob said.

The baby waked up and began to cry. Mother picked it up

and patted its little bottom; it gave a hiccup and put its head on Mother's shoulder.

Daddy stood looking down at them. "One thing's certain. It's too small to have got here by itself. Clear out for a minute, kids. I want to have a look at it."

We stood huddled outside the tent until Daddy came out, announcing, "He's a fine, healthy boy, about five or six months old. The first thing to do is ask at the tents and trailers around us if anybody's lost a baby. It's a little difficult to imagine anyone putting a baby in the wrong tent by mistake, but it's possible. John, you and Rob go together, and Vicky and Suzy. John, that way. Vicky, over here. I'll take this section across the road. Mother'll stay in the tent with the baby in case anybody comes looking for him."

Suzy and I got back before the others. Nobody knew anything about a baby, and they looked at us as though we were kookie or trying to play some kind of trick on them. We went back to our tent and there was the baby lying on his back, cooing, gurgling, laughing, and trying to catch a dusty shaft of light that came in through the tent window and was shaken tantalizingly by tree shadows.

Suzy is almost as good with little children as she is with animals, so she sat down by the baby and began to play with it. It was really pretty to watch.

When the others came back they hadn't had any luck in finding anyone who'd lost a baby, either.

"The poor mother must be frantic," Mother said.

Daddy raised his eyebrows in an odd sort of way.

Suzy had the baby up on her shoulder. "Oh, Daddy, he's

adorable! What are we going to do? He's going to get hungry soon, and we don't have a bottle or formula or anything." As though on cue the baby began to cry, and Suzy said, "See? He's hungry. There's a family with quite a small baby across the campgrounds, and I bet they'd lend us a bottle if we explained."

"Hold it, Suzy," Daddy warned. "This is a baby, not a kitten, and the next step is for me to go to the Ranger Headquarters. Try to keep the baby happy while I'm gone. Want to come, Rob? John, get the fire going, please. Vicky, you help Mother start dinner." Daddy and Rob got in the station wagon and drove off, with Rob calling out, "Suzy! Play Elephant's Child for the baby!"

Suzy took the baby and sat on the picnic bench so he could watch John start the fire. Mr. and Mrs. Williams came out of their trailer and came over and clucked at him, and Mrs. Williams tch-tched, "How could any mother go off and leave her child that way?"

Suzy looked horrified. "You mean you think she left him on *pur*pose?"

"Well, it looks that way, doesn't it?" Mrs. Williams asked, tickling the baby under his chin. "Poor little tyke."

"You mean you think his mother just *dumped* him? You mean she wanted to get *rid* of him?"

Suddenly I realized why Daddy had raised his eyebrows when Mother had talked about the baby's mother being frantic. Mother was looking into the ice box, bringing out lettuce and tomatoes. Suzy asked passionately, "If his mother doesn't want him couldn't we keep him? Please? Please?"

Mother shut the ice box lid carefully. "Suzy, darling, this isn't like the deer at Palo Duro."

"I know, Mother, that's exactly the *point*. It doesn't *mat*ter if a *ba*by isn't housebroken. He wears *dia*pers. And he wouldn't be unhappy in the car. When Rob was a baby you know he always stopped crying whenever we took him for a ride—"

"Suzy!" Mother said. "Hold everything! Babies aren't like stray animals, even when they appear unexpectedly in tents."

"But—"

"Let me finish, please, Suzy. Children can't just be disposed of by a whim. A home for a child is a very serious matter, both for the child and the people who take the child."

I looked at Suzy and thought of Maggy. I guess it wasn't just a whim that sent Maggy to us for two years. Maybe it's because I wasn't in on the arrangements, the talks with Maggy's grandfather and the lawyers and Aunt Elena and all, that it seems so sort of casual to me. Certainly there wasn't anything planned about Uncle Hal's and Maggy's father's plane exploding in the middle of the air, and that's what started it all. After that, finding a strange baby sleeping beside our mother in the tent didn't seem so extraordinary, and it was going to take a lot to convince Suzy, being Suzy, that it wouldn't be perfectly simple to add the baby to our family. I really don't think that Suzy sees much difference between babies and animals, and after all our Mr. Rochester, beautiful Great Dane though he is, was a stray, and Suzy's always coming home with a new kitten in her pocket. Mother and Daddy may fling up their hands in horror, but they usually end up by letting her keep them.

"In the first place, Suzy," Mother went on, "the baby's mother may not have abandoned him. This could perfectly well be some kind of mistake, and the poor mother may be looking frantically for her child. And even if she *did* abandon him we would never be allowed to keep him. He'd be made a ward of the state, and the court would assign him to foster parents or a children's home. This is the law, Suzy."

"But it's *cruel*," Suzy protested passionately, holding the baby closely to her. "Babies need to be *loved*. What do states or courts know about that! If you're lost it's better to be a *kit*ten than a *baby*, for crying out loud! At least someone can bring a *kit*ten in and give it milk and *cud*dle it. It doesn't have to worry about states and courts."

John was squatting by the fire, poking in little kindling twigs. "Look at all the kittens who aren't found and rescued by Suzy Austin," he said. "The kittens who're put in a bag with a stone and drowned, or just left to fend for themselves. The law's to protect babies, Suzy, not harm them."

Suzy wasn't going to give up that easily. "It's not *fair*," she muttered, brushing her lips gently against the soft fuzz on the baby's head.

Mother said, "Enjoy him for these few minutes, Suzy. Come on, Vicky, let's get dinner ready. It's so hot I think we'll just have tuna and vegetable salad. We'll only need to heat water for the dishes, so don't worry too much about the fire, John."

I sat at the table and diced celery and made carrot sticks, and Suzy bounced the baby until he was laughing happily and forgetting that he was hungry and away from his mother. But Suzy had tears in her eyes, and Suzy does not cry easily. She's much the most spartan of all of us. Except where babies or animals are concerned.

The Williams went back to their trailer and the baby grew

drowsy, so Mother took him back to the tent and put him down on one of the sleeping bags. "He's really a very good baby," she said as she came out. "I wound up Elephant's Child and it put him right to sleep. Do you kids want to eat so you can go on over to the campfire program?"

Suzy said immediately, "I want to wait and see what's going to happen about the baby."

"Vic? John?"

We decided to stay, though John made Suzy furious by saying the only reason he was staying was to make sure we weren't stuck with a sniveling brat. We had enough kids in the family already.

Suzy flounced away from John and turned to Mother. "Okay if I go in now and look at the baby?"

"Not now, Suzy. I don't want him disturbed."

"But I'll be very quiet."

"No, Suzy. Wait till he wakes up."

The Williams' said good bye and went off to the evening program, and we could see almost all the families from the tents and trailers strolling off in the direction of the amphitheater. The last of the sunlight shone against the red canyon walls. Then, as the sun went, the cliffs seemed to hold its glow, and then, very slowly, to fade.

The baby slept. Mother and John and I read. Suzy just sat and looked unhappy, until we heard the sound of motors, and up came a green Park truck, followed by our car. A ranger and a woman got out of the truck, and Daddy and Rob from the car. The woman had funny-colored red hair, a flowered silk dress, too short, and black patent leather pumps with high heels. The pumps were all run down and dirty and cracked, as though she'd been walking in strange places with them, and all in all it was a very peculiar costume for a campground. Her eyes looked red, as though she'd been crying, and she ran up to Mother, sort of limping.

"Where is he? What did you do with him?"

"He's in the tent, asleep," Mother said quietly.

The woman rushed over to the tent, fumbled at the entrance and didn't seem to know how to get in. Mother unzipped the door for her, and the woman half fell in, and we could hear her cooing and crying and laughing over the baby.

Mother turned back towards the ranger questioningly, and he said, "She managed to get into the canyon by one of the back roads, and then climbed down a good mile of cliff. How she did it with the baby and in that costume I'll never know. Her feet are a mass of blisters as is."

"How did you find her?" Mother asked.

"She evidently couldn't face another climb—can't say I blame her—and the ranger on duty at the gate was a little suspicious of her and called in just as I was talking to your husband, here."

Suzy looked anxiously at the ranger. "She doesn't really want the baby, then, does she? Can't we keep him? Please?" Her voice quivered a little and she blinked hard to keep tears back.

The ranger was a very nice man (most rangers are) because he didn't laugh at Suzy but answered her perfectly seriously. "She's changed her mind about the baby, honey. She's decided she does want him after all."

"Why did she try to give him away, then?"

The ranger still answered her directly, and very kindly. "Life's pretty rough for some people, honey. She doesn't have a job, and she doesn't have a husband, and she thought maybe the baby would be better off without her."

"But she's changed her mind?"

"That's right."

John asked, "But what happens—what does she do now?"

"We'll put her in touch with some people at an agency where she can get help."

The woman came out of the tent, then, holding the baby closely. She limped up to Mother. "I'm sorry if I caused you any trouble."

"It wasn't any trouble," Mother said. "He's a darling baby."

"He's never been a minute's trouble," the woman's eyes filled. "He's always been as good as gold. I just thought—" Her voice filled, and she swallowed hard several times the way you do when you're trying hard not to cry in front of somebody.

The ranger put his hand on her shoulder. "Come along. I'll take you to a place where you can spend the night."

"May we say good-bye to the baby?" Suzy asked. She went up to the woman and put her finger gently against the baby's cheek. Then she looked seriously at the woman. "Why did you pick *us*?"

The woman gave a shaky laugh. "You looked so kind. I saw you at lunch. You said grace, and I liked that, and then you were laughing so much. You looked like good people. Oh, I don't know, hon. I didn't hardly know what I was doing." She turned back to Mother. "Anyhow, I'm sorry. And thanks for taking care of him." She gave us all a sort of floppy wave and then ran, stumbling, to the ranger's bus.

Thirteen

The next morning we were a little late getting off because Daddy and John had a terrible time getting the tent pegs out, and several of the pegs got quite bent from being whacked at with hammer, pliers, screw driver, hatchet, almost every tool we had with us. The pegs had been a little hard to pound in, but not unusually so, and we never did find out what there was about the canyon ground that made them so hard to get out.

So the sun was already high in the sky when we started on what turned out to be the hottest drive of the whole trip. Every time we stopped at a gas station we filled the desert bag and water jug, but even so we kept on being dry and parched. I felt like a left-over, wrung-out tea bag.

At Las Vegas we marketed, had trouble getting a traveler's check cashed (what did they think Daddy was? A crook or something?), and drove up and down the Strip a couple of times. The Strip is the avenue in Las Vegas that has all the great gambling places on it, some as huge and elegant as palaces, some just like fancy motels. Then there were the wedding chapels, and I can't think of anything more gruesome than getting married in one of them, but evidently thousands of people do. Thank heavens Uncle Douglas and Aunt Elena got married properly on the Island with Grandfather. There was one chapel that was shaped like a wedding bell, and these phony chimes came pealing out over a loudspeaker. Another had a false front like a New England church and it looked about as out of place there as a roulette wheel would on the Thornhill green. Then, right between two wedding chapels, called SWEET MYSTERY OF LIFE and FORGET-ME-NOT, WEDDINGS AND DIVORCES, was a funeral parlor called ROCK OF AGES. You pays your money and you takes your choice. We all howled with laughter, but at the same time it was all so phony it made me want to puke. I wondered what Zachary would have to say about it all.

We were just as glad to leave the Strip and go off to find the campgrounds at Lake Mead. Lake Mead's a huge, man-made lake created when Hoover Dam was built.

If somebody was going to make a movie of hell, and if he could reproduce the heat as well as the scenery, what we saw of Nevada would be the perfect setting. Maybe this isn't being fair to Nevada, because after all we didn't see very much of it, but what we did see was perfect for hell: dry, burning ground with practically nothing growing on it. What little *did* grow was sort of scruffy-looking, not green, but browney-olive fungusy-looking stuff. The mountains were bare, crumbling stone, and the sky was searing. It was so hot the sky wasn't even a proper blue. Even the Strip in Las Vegas seemed like something in the underworld, and I could imagine a hairy devil presiding at a big gambling table and swishing his tail with annoyance when somebody won.

We'd thought that when we got to Lake Mead for sure there'd be trees and green things growing around it, but instead there it was, a great dark body of water that engineers had just plunked down in the barren land. It *looked* like a gigantic do-it-yourself lake, not like something real at all. Then we thought that when we got to the campgrounds there'd surely be trees and shade and relief from the scorching sun. But the campgrounds were so bare that we went right on by and had to turn around and go back. Well, sure, there were a few trees, kind of twisted, skimpy ones. And the place was crowded, not with tents, but with picnickers come to get away from the heat of Las Vegas. We drove around and around and every spot was filled.

"I'm wet with sweatperation," Rob said.

"What're we going to *do?*" Suzy wailed. We knew there wasn't another campground anywhere around, and our next stop was Laguna Beach, and that was too far off. Anyhow, to get there we had to cross the Mojave Desert, and Daddy said there wasn't any question of doing that before the cool of the next morning. Friends had told us of having to dip towels in their water jug and hang them up in the car in order to survive the desert heat. It made me feel like Lawrence of Arabia, and I'd just as soon have gone on. Partly, I've got to admit, because I hoped maybe there'd be a message from Zachary. Now that I hadn't seen him for some time I forgot how he sometimes scared and depressed me and I was dying to see him again. Whatever else he was, he was different, and he was exciting. He was, you might say, an education, and everybody keeps talking about how you ought to get all the education you can.

Suzy was half-crying, but that was partly because she was still upset over the baby.

"Let's have a drink of water," Daddy said, "and then we'll have another look for a campsite." While Mother was filling our cups from the desert bag a man came up to Daddy and told him that he and his family were there only for a picnic, and would be gone in an hour. Daddy asked if we could leave our gear there to reserve the spot, and then we'd go off to Hoover Dam and wouldn't bother them till they were through.

Hoover Dam's in all the encyclopaedias, and engineering doesn't send me the way it does John. The enormous hunks of machinery were scary, but the main thing was that lots of the tour was underground and it was heavenly cool. We went down into the bowels of the earth, jammed with dozens of people into an elevator. We were jammed so tight you couldn't move, and I didn't care for it. Maybe it's because there aren't any elevators in Thornhill and I wasn't very used to them.

When we got back to our campsite the picnickers were gone, so we set up camp, drinking quantities of water every few minutes. It gave me great admiration for camels, I mean being able to store up enough water in themselves to take them across the desert. Rob kept refilling the desert bag and water jug for us; we evidently couldn't store for more than a few minutes in that climate.

"Mother, I'm so Thursday," Rob said over and over again.

About the only time we weren't thirsty was when we went swimming. It was a long hot walk from the campgrounds to the lake, and there were no trees, no shelter of any kind from the great, brazen sun. The lake itself was marvelously cold. I don't mean cool, I mean *cold*. I don't know how it stayed so cold, out there in the middle of the desert. John and I were having underwater races when we noticed a sort of commotion and came up. Mother and the little kids were all laughing at Daddy, and Daddy had a very funny look.

" 'Smatter?" John asked.

"Split my trunks," Daddy said. "And but split! I might as well not have anything on."

We hadn't bothered to bring towels down to the lake with us because it was so hot. John looked from the lake across the long bare stretch to the campgrounds. Then he looked at Daddy and they both raised their eyebrows.

Daddy said, "I'll just stay submerged till we're ready to go in. Then you will all surround me very closely."

When Daddy called Time it became obvious that he hadn't exaggerated the state of his trunks. We all huddled about him, making a fairly good screen. The trouble was that we were all laughing so hard we could barely move, and the more we laughed the more peculiar we must have looked. Daddy didn't get back to the tent in one piece, but he got there, and we had something good to tease him about for the rest of the trip.

That night for dinner we used Uncle Douglas's little stove instead of building a fire because it didn't give out as much heat. During dinner we got to talking with the family picnicking at the next table, mother, father, and twelve year old daughter. Their name was Newton, and they told us that the temperature, around 104°, was perfectly normal, nothing unusual, and that they often came out to the lake for picnics. If it had been a week-end we wouldn't have had a chance in the world of finding a campsite because of the picnickers.

Karen Newton had never been in a tent, so we took her into ours, and told ghost stories. It wasn't just that she'd never been in a tent, but I don't think she knew many kids, because she hadn't heard any of our ghost stories, and she got so scared at one I was telling that she started to cry. So we switched to funny ones, and then got her talking about herself. Her father had a rug-cleaning business and the funny thing was that he had to keep it open twenty-four hours a day; nothing ever closes for the night, because there really isn't any night or day there; everything is all topsy turvy. Her school hours were the only regular hours in her family's life. It sounded very weird to us, but I guess our ordered life in Thornhill would have seemed as strange to her as living at the gates of hell seemed to us.

After the Newtons left, and they stayed quite late to catch every tiny breath of cool air from the lake, and the breaths of air were *very* tiny and few and far between, we all lay on our sleeping bags and panted. After a while Suzy and I pulled ours off the tail gate of the car and out of the tent, and even so it was too hot to sleep, and it seemed to me all I did was doze, the kind where you're not really quite asleep and you're not really quite awake and you're not really dreaming, but your thoughts sort of drift around and you don't really control them because they're more dreaming than thinking. I was walking down the strip with Zachary, and he was deciding whether to take me into SWEET MYSTERY OF LIFE or ROCK OF AGES for a Coke.

Daddy had set the alarm for five thirty so we could drive

across the desert before the hottest part of the day. It seemed like the middle of the night when people interrupted my walk with Zachary by slamming car doors, packing up, and driving off with a lot of noise. I felt Mother's hand on my shoulder and she said, "It's only four thirty, but Daddy thinks we might as well get up and go, because it's too hot to sleep. Try to be quiet and not wake anybody who's sleeping."

"Those other people weren't quiet." I sounded kind of cross.

"Do you want to be like them?"

"No."

"Well, then."

We ate just cold cereal and some sweet buns for breakfast, and Mother and Daddy made coffee on Uncle Douglas's stove. We left camp before six and suddenly it was really *cool*, and what do you know, the dreaded drive across the Mojave was a more nothing, not nearly so hot as the drive from Zion the day before.

Now for Laguna Beach:

I don't really know where to start, because it was both wonderful and terrible as far as I was concerned. I guess everybody else had a ball, what with going to Disneyland and the zoo in San Diego and Knott's Berry Farm and swimming every day. I did all those things, too. It wasn't any of that. It was Zachary.

Uncle Douglas and Aunt Elena and Maggy have a scrumptious house, all redwood and windows, with a big terrace overlooking the Pacific. Suzy and I slept in with Maggy; John and Rob had foldaway beds in the dining room (we ate out on the terrace all the time, anyhow); and Mother and Daddy had the guest room.

We unpacked and got settled and I thought maybe Zachary would have left a note for me or something, but nobody said anything, and with the way everybody felt about Zachary I just kept my mouth shut and waited. Uncle Douglas asked me if I had something on my mind, and I don't think I convinced him that I hadn't; Uncle Douglas always knows when I'm bothered. But he let it drop when he saw that I didn't feel like talking.

After lunch we all had a short snooze, though Maggy kept whispering to Suzy. She'd grown taller and seemed older than when we last saw her, but she talked as much as ever. When she saw that Suzy had turned her back on her and gone to sleep as usual, she tried to talk to me, but I closed my eyes and pretended to be asleep. It wasn't that I didn't want to talk to Maggy; but we hadn't had much sleep the night before and I was tired. And I was disappointed because there wasn't any word from Zachary. Somehow I had more than expected it, I had counted on it.

In the late afternoon we went down to the beach for a swim. It's about a ten minute walk straight downhill from the house, and the beach was wild and rocky and completely unlike the long, level sweep of Atlantic we knew from Grandfather's. Another difference was that on Grandfather's Island there aren't many people; there are great gorgeous stretches of deserted beach where you can walk and walk and not see a house or another human being. California was crowded, with one town running right into another so that you couldn't really tell where one ended and another began, and the beaches always had a lot of people on them. Swimming in the Pacific, at Laguna Beach at any rate, is completely different from swimming in the Atlantic, not because of the people, so much: it's just that the Pacific is lots wilder. The land tumbles precipitously down to the sea, and the beach itself slopes rapidly into the ocean and is uneven and has rocks for you to stub your toes on if you don't watch out. Mother is always saying, *comparisons are odious* (that's a quote from John Donne, John Fortescue, *and* Christopher Marlowe), but I'm not making that kind of comparison, just explaining differences. For instance, on our swim that first afternoon it was a calm, sunny day, but the waves were much rougher than the slow, gentle swells of the Atlantic on a quiet day. The push of the waves and the pull of the tide were stronger than we were used to, too. John and I had fun going out and riding in on the breakers, but it was too rough for the little ones (how Suzy and Maggy hate being called the "little ones"!). They stayed close to shore, where they had plenty of rolling and tumbling by the waves. The water was warmer than at Lake Mead the day before, but the air was cool. I guess one thing you can't beat about Laguna Beach is the climate.

That night after dinner Mother and Aunt Elena played two piano music. Rob, Suzy, and Maggy went to bed, but John and I sprawled on the couches in the living room and listened, half asleep ourselves. After a while Mother said, "Oh, Elena, I'm so rusty I can't make my fingers do a thing. You play for us."

Aunt Elena played and suddenly I realized that I'd missed this kind of music. At home I never think much about it. It's always there in the background. Mother'd never get any housework done if she didn't play records, LOUD, to drown it out. And if I *did* think about it at home, it was to feel that it was longhair stuff, dull, nothing I liked much. But listening to Aunt Elena playing, the music from her big grand piano filling the house, I began to feel happy all over without really knowing why. It was as though a hunger I didn't even realize existed had been satisfied.

Three days at Laguna and never a word from Zachary. I kept thinking maybe he'd called while we were out, because we were off on trips or at the beach most of the day. But he could have called in the evening, couldn't he? It wasn't like Zach to give up on something like that. And what about a letter? There's always mail. We had letters from some of the kids in Thornhill, and we wrote everybody postcards. But not a squawk from Zachary. I came to the sad conclusion that once he'd got back to Los Angeles and all the sophisticated, rich girls there, he didn't care any more about a doctor's kid from New England.

Then the fourth afternoon when we were walking up from the beach there was a red convertible parked by the house, and Zachary was sitting on the terrace steps, smoking a pipe. My hair was all wet and dripping, but I did have on a good-looking bathing suit, a hand-me-down from Aunt Elena, and Zachary himself had said my figure is okay. Uncle Douglas looked at Zachary and then he looked at me, and then his eyebrows went up in the same way that Daddy's do.

Zachary got up from the steps and came down and introduced himself to Uncle Douglas and Aunt Elena and said hello to the rest of us. He couldn't have been more polite or charming, but I thought there was a kind of glint behind it all, as though it didn't come really from inside him, but was some kind of an act. It's difficult to explain. It wasn't that he was phony. Zachary is lots of things, but phony is one thing he is *not*. It was just that there was somehow more to it than met the eye. He asked if he could take me out to dinner, but Uncle Douglas and Aunt Elena invited him to dinner instead. Mother and Daddy didn't say anything. They looked at each other. I didn't like it.

After dinner Aunt Elena and Mother played two piano, and then Aunt Elena played, and it turned out that Zachary knew a lot about music, he really did, and you could see that Aunt Elena thought he was just wonderful. At least *some*body besides me appreciated him.

After he'd left and I was ready for bed and went to say good night to Uncle Douglas, where he and Daddy were sitting out on the terrace, Uncle Douglas pulled me to him and said, "That's quite a boy you picked up, Vicky."

"I didn't pick him up," I said. "He picked me up."

"You don't think he's too old for you?"

"He's not that old. And I'm not that young any longer, Uncle Douglas."

"He's an appealing kid," Uncle Douglas said. "I'd like to paint him. Those planes to his face are a painter's joy. But do your old Uncle a favor and watch it, Vicky, will you?"

Zachary'd invited me to go to the theater with him the next night, where some group he knew was giving a performance of *The Diary of Anne Frank*. Aunt Elena invited him to come over in time for a swim and dinner. He looked very thin and white in his swimming trunks. Here he was living in California and he didn't have any tan at all.

The waves were rougher than usual that day, and Daddy just looked at Zach and said, "No swimming for you, Zachary, please." The please was just courtesy.

Zachary scowled as though he were about to argue, but then he said, "I'm just going to sit on a rock for ten minutes and dangle my feet. I don't want to get brown. Come sit with me, Vicky. Don't be a muffin with a sun fetish like everybody else."

You get a better sun tan if you're wet; also I didn't want to seem in too much of a hurry to do exactly what he wanted me to do, so I gave myself a good dunking, rode in once on the breakers, got tumbled around and a mouth full of pebbles for my hurry, and went to sit on the rock with Zachary.

We sat there silently, and then he asked me, sort of formally, as though we'd just met instead of having had all those talks in Tennessee and Colorado, and as though he'd never kissed me the way he did, "How d'you like California?"

"I like it."

"I've got a couple of your aunt's records. Didn't know you had celebrities in the family."

I suppose Aunt Elena *is* a celebrity if you know a lot about music. "Uncle Douglas says he'd like to paint you," I said. I didn't want Uncle Douglas being left out.

Sitting there on the rock Zachary gave a little bow, still all very formal. "I'd be honored."

We sat there and then we didn't say anything. It was very uncomfortable. I knew I ought to be able to think of lots of things to say, but I couldn't. And Zachary, who'd always kept the conversation going before, just wasn't talking.

Finally I said, "I don't think the Pacific looks as big as the Atlantic, but John says it's bigger."

He just nodded.

I'd started, so I had to go on. "Well, you see, the thing is, it doesn't *look* bigger. It looks smaller. The Pacific does. And I've figured out why. The reason it looks so small is that it doesn't go on stretching out and out to the horizon the way the Atlantic does."

Zachary turned to me as though I were some kind of moron. "What're you talking about? Sure it does."

I was stuck with it. "*No*," I said. I guess I sounded kind of desperate. "You know how gently the Atlantic goes out to the sky? You can walk and walk and you're still not even knee deep. But here you take a few steps and you're practically over your head. The land just drops instead of reaching out. So when you look out to sea there's less of it to see."

Zachary laughed loudly. A rude laugh. "Oh, grow up, Victoria. The shape of the earth is the same everywhere."

"But—"

He didn't even let me begin. He said, quite violently, "Sooner or later you're going to have to face *facts*. The Pacific's bigger than the Atlantic."

I said right back, "That's not the *point*—"

Zachary cut in. "Give up, Vicky. I'm not interested."

I suppose you could call it a quarrel. I felt awful. I put my head down on my knees and let my fingers trail in a small puddle in a depression in the rock. I didn't want to go to the theater with Zachary that night. I didn't ever want to see him again. He was different in California. I hated him.

Then I felt fingers gentle at the back of my neck. "Vicky. I'm sorry. It's not you. It doesn't have anything to do with you. I've been in a filthy mood. Get me out of my mood." His voice was soft, cajoling.

"Why're you in a filthy mood?"

"Just one of the times I hate everybody. Except you. Don't let me drive you away, Vicky. I have a way of doing that. Driving away anybody I happen to love. Stick by me, Vicky, will you?"

What do you do when somebody speaks to you like that, particularly if that somebody is Zachary? Sure I'd stick by him. I'd do anything he wanted me to do.

"Let's go back up to the house," Zachary said. "I don't want to get too much sun. And if we sit here much longer your father'll start bossing me around again. I saw enough of doctors when I was sick. I haven't seen one since in spite of my parents' yammering. I refuse ever to see a doctor again. I've had enough of their inept mucking about. C'mon."

We started up the long, steep flight of steps that led from the beach to the street. I saw Daddy looking at Zachary, but Zachary took it very slowly, stopping every once in a while as though just to talk. But I knew it was to catch his breath.

"I guess everything seems pretty crowded here after New England, doesn't it?" he asked. I nodded. "All these expensive houses sitting on their little plots of ground. Pretty nice gardens, though. Nothing like these flowers in Connecticut. Nothing exotic about Connecticut." We went up to the top of the steps and he stopped again.

"You don't want every place to be alike," I said. "I like Connecticut, too."

"When I get over my mad at Hotchkiss I'll probably agree with you. I'm going to Choate next year. We managed to wangle it. All kinds of recommendations from Hotchkiss about how I ought to be given another chance and all. I'm bright enough, they're quite right about that. If I put my mind to it I can pass any exam they care to fling at me. The point is, most of the time what's the point?"

"There's lots of point," I said. I was glad he didn't ask me to explain what the point was. Maybe he was too winded.

When we got back to the house I fixed us a couple of Cokes, first picking an enormous lemon off the tree. *That* was something you couldn't do in Thornhill. We sat in the kitchen, because I thought I might as well help get the dinner going. Aunt Elena and Mother'd already fixed fried chicken and potato salad, so really all I had to do was make salad dressing and throw in the greens and tomatoes and all. Aunt Elena has quite a kitchen, redwood and stainless steel and a built in oven and the burners sunk into one of the countertops, all terribly modern and tidy and completely unlike our wandery old kitchen in Thornhill. For instance, in Aunt Elena's kitchen you push a button and out comes a mixer and a blender. I wondered that Maggy hadn't broken it. She's always fiddling with things like that.

When I'd finished with the salad I made iced tea, and everything was very silent between Zachary and me again. I just went about my business, and he sat and drank his Coke and looked out the kitchen windows across the banana tree to the Pacific.

"Would you marry somebody if you knew he might die at any time?" Zachary asked me in a casual way.

At that point the others all came tumbling in to the house, and Aunt Elena was thanking me for fixing things, and people were taking showers, and Mother put the *Emperor Concerto* on the phonograph, and Aunt Elena sat down at the piano and began playing along with it, it was her own recording, anyhow, and everybody was noisy and usual.

After dinner Zachary drove me to the theater. It wasn't in Laguna, but a couple of towns further south. It was a gorgeous, modern little theater, and everybody in the cast was professional, Zachary said. He was very gay, and whistling that darned melody when he wasn't talking, but at least he wasn't the way he was before dinner.

I have to tell about the play, *The Diary of Anne Frank,* not just because it was a marvelous play, but because it got all tied in with the way Zachary had been that afternoon. I guess everybody knows Anne Frank, but anyhow the play's about this young girl and her family who were in Holland during the Second World War. They had to go into hiding because of the Nazi persecution of the Jews, and they spent two years up in an attic above the place where her father had been in business. During the day when people were downstairs working in the business offices Anne and her family couldn't talk or laugh or make any noise at all. They couldn't even flush the toilet.

You know how it is, in a book or a movie, or a play, when you suddenly *are* the person it's about? Well, all during that play I *was* Anne Frank. I felt that I understood everything about her, the way she kept getting into trouble with her family and the way she was right in the middle of growing up, not a child and not an adult, so she kept doing things all wrong, just like me. And then there was this boy, and the actor who played him looked like Zachary. And there they were, Anne Frank and the boy, hiding from the Nazis and everything, and discovering each other. But nobody really understood how she felt about the boy because they didn't think she was grown up enough yet.

One evening the family had their Hannukah festival. This is a little bit like our Christmas, because it's a time of love, and everybody gives presents. Of course there weren't any presents when they were in hiding, but Anne had managed somehow to make something for everybody. Some of the presents were funny, and everybody was gay, and they were all laughing, and almost able to forget they were unhappy.

Every Christmas Eve in Thornhill we have a special candle-light service, and Mother always sings the solo part of "Lullay My Liking" and when we get home there are certain carols we always sing and Daddy reads *The Night Before Christmas* and *St. Luke* while we hang up our stockings. Well, the Hanukkah festival has traditions like that, candles in an eight-branched candelabra, and as part of the ritual the mother of the family says, "I will lift up mine eyes unto the hills," and everybody is full of joy and peace. Just the way we always are at Christmastime.

But then, when everybody is relaxed and happy, they hear a terrible crash downstairs. They don't know what it is, and they're terrified, because they're afraid it may be the Nazis come to take them away. The father goes down to investigate, knowing that he may be going to his death, and Anne knows this, too, and it was as though Daddy were going, and I knew he might be shot at any moment. While they're waiting the mother falls to her knees, and her voice is shaking, and she says, very quickly, and it is a terrible cry for help,

> *I will lift up mine eyes unto the hills*
> *From whence cometh my help.*
> *My help cometh from the Lord*
> *Which made heaven and earth.*
> *He will not suffer thy foot to be moved;*
> *He that keepeth thee will not slumber.*
> *Behold, he that keepth Israel*
> *Shall neither slumber nor sleep.*
> *The Lord is thy keeper;*
> *The Lord is thy shade upon thy right hand.*

167

The sun shall not smite thee by day,
Nor the moon by night.
The Lord shall preserve thee from all evil;
He shall preserve thy soul.
The Lord shall preserve thy going out and thy coming in
From this time forth, and even for evermore.

Anne's mother got down on her knees and she said these words, which Mother has said to us so often, which we've said together, which I've said to myself because they hold so much security and comfort. But the Lord *did*n't preserve the Franks from evil. He *must* have slumbered and slept. Because the Nazis found them, they were captured, all of them who had hidden there in the attic for two years; they were sent to a concentration camp, and they died there, all except the father. The mother who had said those words died there. Anne Frank died there. She believed in the goodness of human beings, and I think that she must have believed that God would preserve her going out and her coming in. But He didn't. She died in a concentration camp. Before she had time to live. When she was just beginning.

Usually I cry like anything when a play or a movie is sad. As I said, Suzy doesn't like to sit next to me, I embarrass her so. At Anne Frank I couldn't cry. I was shaken too deep.

Zachary had asked permission to take me out for a soda after the show, so nobody expected us home right away. He took the car and drove to the beach. "Come on, Vic. Let's skip the soda and just sit out on a rock and talk."

We sat on a rock overlooking the ocean and I started to shiver. "Cold?" he asked.

I nodded. I couldn't explain that I was cold inside and not outside. He took off his jacket and put it over my shoulders. "What about *you?*" I asked.

"I wish everybody'd stop worrying about me. I'm fine. How'd you like the play? Pretty good, wasn't it?" I just nodded, and he said, "Well, didn't you like it? I thought it was terrific."

It would be rude if I said I wished he'd never taken me to it. I thought, well, if he doesn't understand the way I feel there's no point my ever seeing him again, so I said, "I guess I've lived a kind of sheltered life and all. I mean I knew about concentration camps, but it never hit me before."

"It's about time you woke up, Victoria," Zachary said. "Life's been too darned easy for you. It's about time you learned it isn't all peaches and cream."

"I never thought that."

"But you've never had to worry about people being cooked down, and made into soap, have you? That's the kind of thing they did to people like Anne Frank. And they made lampshades out of their skins. Don't they teach you anything at school? Haven't you ever read any modern history?"

Now I was having a hard time not crying. I just shook my head and stared out at the darkness of ocean so the tears would stay in my eyes and not overflow. I pressed my knuckles against my lips to try to stop them from trembling.

"You're just like that little dope, Anne Frank," Zachary said. "All innocent and trusting. Life's going to be *hell* for you when you stop being protected, absolute *hell*."

I just kept shaking my head.

"You still believe in God, don't you?" he asked. "Look what

he did to your precious Anne Frank. Maybe he'll do something like that to you, someday. Look what he's done to me. I'm probably going to die, and what for? Why?"

I spoke in a very trembly voice, but he didn't even seem to notice. "If you took better care of yourself—"

"Why the hell should I take better care of myself? What for? For the kind of stinking world we're living in? So I'll get blown up by a nuclear bomb? Or die of radiation sickness? No, thanks. I'd rather die of a nice, quiet heart attack. And then nice quiet nothing. No pie in the sky, Vicky. No burning in hell fires either. Just nice, quiet nothing."

"No!" I shouted. I didn't even try to stop from crying, now. The tears streamed down my cheeks and I hardly noticed.

Zachary shouted back. "What's the point of believing in God when nothing makes any sense? Nothing makes *sense,* Vicky! Anne Frank doesn't make sense and Pop fleecing other people to make his millions doesn't make sense, but it makes about the best kind of sense there is. You're so darned *good,* Vicky, you dope! Don't you know it doesn't make any sense to be good?" I gave a kind of sob, and then his arms went around me and he was kissing me. "Ah, Vicky," he murmured, "why do I *do* this to you? What makes me *do* it? You're such a *good* kid, why do I want to hurt you?" He held my wet face in his hands. "I only want to hurt people I love, Vicky." Then he kissed me again.

Fourteen

Right after Zachary kissed me again we went back to the car and he drove me home. We didn't talk much, but this time it wasn't a bad silence. You could leave it alone. You didn't have to fill it.

When we got back to the house he took me in. Just before we opened the door he touched my cheek with the back of his hand, but he didn't kiss me again. Then he said, "I won't see you tomorrow, Vicky-O, but we'll do something in a couple of days. I'll call you."

Uncle Douglas was the only one still up, and he was in his pajamas. He said good-night to Zachary, then took me by the arm and led me out to the balcony. "Sit with me and have a glass of ginger ale. I'll fix it for you."

How did Uncle Douglas know that I didn't want to go right to bed, that the one thing in the world I wanted was to stay with him for a few minutes? I didn't want to talk, to tell him about

Zachary or getting all upset or anything. I just wanted to be with him. He gave me the ginger ale and sat down, then opened his arms wide. "Come on, sweetheart. You're not too big for Uncle Douglas's lap, are you?"

I wasn't. How did he know I needed it? The white wooden chair was big enough for both of us, and I sat there, my head against his blue and white striped pajamas, hearing the strong thud-thud of his heart against my ear. It was beautiful sitting with Uncle Douglas looking out over the night Pacific. It wasn't only that you could see the ocean and all the lights of the towns along the coastline, but you could see all kinds of airplanes going by overhead, and often you couldn't tell which was a plane and which was a star until you could decide whether or not it was moving.

We just sat there and sat there and the distant rhythmic sound of the ocean and the slow rise and fall of Uncle Douglas's chest began to untense me. At last he said, "Drink up your ginger ale, puddin'. Everybody else is sound asleep and if we want to drive over the border into Mexico tomorrow you've got to get *some* sleep. Did you have a nice time with your young man?"

I tried to keep my voice as quiet as Uncle Douglas's had been. "I'm not sure 'nice' is the right adjective."

"What adjective *would* you use?" Uncle Douglas wasn't prying. He never does. He's just interested in words. I thought. There didn't seem to be any one word you could use as an adjective for that evening. Terrifying. Horrible. Glorious. Then I more or less got it, though it wasn't a real adjective. "I guess you might call it a growing-up kind of evening."

"Aren't trying to grow up too fast, are you?" Uncle Douglas asked.

"Uncle Douglas, I'm re*tard*ed."

"I've never noticed it."

"You're just *used* to me. You're just used to having me a little kid. The way it's sort of hard for me to realize we can't treat Rob like a baby any more. We have to let him grow up. I have to grow up, too."

"Of course you do, Vicky. But it's something that takes time. And it's a process that never ends. It isn't a point you attain so you can say, *Hooray, I'm grown up*. Some people never grow up. And nobody ever finishes growing. Or shouldn't. If you stop you might as well quit. What I have to tell you, Vicky sweet, is that it never gets any easier. It goes right on being rough forever. But nothing that's easy is worth anything. You ought to have learned that by now. What happens as you keep on growing is that all of a sudden you realize that it's more exciting and beautiful than scarey and awful."

I reached up to his chin, forgetting that he'd shaved off his beard a couple of months before he and Aunt Elena got married. His chin felt scratchy and sort of comforting. "*Why* did you shave off your beard?" I asked. I was beginning to get sleepy.

"Mostly for Elena's sake. Also when I first had my beard it was all right for an artist to have a beard because nobody else did. But now all kinds of people have beards. It isn't anything special any more."

"You mean like beatniks and everything."

"Yes. People who think things come easy in this life. People who sit around and wait for inspiration to descend upon them from the blue. Who think they can create with genius alone. Instead of with a background of work harder than any laborer's.

Am I philosophizing you to sleep, Vicky? That's my intention." I nodded. "Then go on to bed, sweetheart. It's getting late and you want to have fun tomorrow."

I didn't sleep well. I kept having dreams and waking up and not remembering what I'd dreamed. I just waked up because the dream had scared me awake, and then my conscious mind swatted at the dream and it went away before I could catch on to what it was and what had frightened me.

In the morning I had a headache and I felt the way you do when you're coming down with 'flu but I knew I wasn't. I decided maybe you got chills and fever with growing up as well as with 'flu. I tried to act as though nothing were wrong, but everybody noticed I wasn't talking as much as usual. But since I'd been acting more or less that way off and on for about a year they just left me alone, except for Maggy, who kept asking me what was wrong with me, until finally I had to snap at her.

When we went to bed that night Daddy put his hand against my cheek, and then he took my temperature, but I didn't have any.

I went to bed and tossed. And *why?* What did I have to be unhappy about? Nothing had happened to *me*. But that didn't seem to matter. That *any*body could be betrayed and killed by her own fellow men, like Anne Frank. That *any*body could die. Maybe somebody I knew. Maybe Zachary. That Zachary could say the things he did and feel the way he did. That he could feel that there wasn't any sense to anything, and make me feel that way, too. That he could maybe be going to die, feeling that way. I'd never known a kid to die. I knew it happened, but I'd never come close to it. I didn't want to come close to it. I didn't want to be involved in Zachary's dying, or in Anne Frank's death.

And I felt *guilty*. Can you understand that? I felt guilty because I wasn't fifteen yet and nothing had happened to me, while all over the world, in Asia and Africa and places, people my age had already had more than a lifetime's worth of suffering and horror. A woman right in Utah could be so desperate that she tried to give her baby away. And I wasn't doing anything about it at all. I was just going on a camping trip and letting it happen.

The next day everybody spent down at the beach, except Uncle Douglas, Aunt Elena and me. Daddy told me to stay home, sit around and take it easy. Aunt Elena said she had to practice. Uncle Douglas said he wanted to paint. After the others had put on their bathing suits and gone down to the beach Aunt Elena sat at the piano and worked on finger exercises, the same thing over and over again. When someone can play the way Aunt Elena does you never think about hours and hours on finger exercises.

Uncle Douglas came into the room where I was lying on the bed, not reading or anything, just lying there. Vicky's moping again, Suzy would say. "How about letting me do a few sketches of you, Vicky? Come on into the studio."

I sat with my arms on the back of a chair and my head down on my arms and Uncle Douglas began sketching me. I don't know how long it was with me just sitting and Uncle Douglas working before he said, "What's up, Vicky?"

I shrugged. When I shrug it infuriates the family, but Uncle Douglas doesn't get enough of it to have it bother him. We don't see him that often, and when we do I'm usually at my best instead of my worst. This was his first real dose of what I suppose you'd call my worst.

He asked, very gently, "Want to tell me about it, Vic?"

"I want to," I said. "But I don't think I can."

"Try."

"If I try it'll just sound dopey. I mean, I know everybody thinks it's something that happened with Zachary. But it isn't that. It's sort of everything. Uncle Douglas, *why* did Anne Frank have to die?"

"Because the Nazis put her in a concentration camp," he answered in a reasonable way.

"But it wasn't *right*."

"No. It was terribly wrong. But it happened."

"But it wasn't *fair!*"

Uncle Douglas just nodded slowly, as though to himself, and went on sketching me. Finally he said, "It's a bit of a shock, isn't it, when you realize that things aren't fair in life? It comes particularly hard to you, Vicky, because your parents are eminently fair. It comes hard because of your grandfather. But it was your grandfather who once recited a little poem to me. Want to hear it?"

"Sure," I said without much enthusiasm. I expected something religious and *comforting*, and the whole point was that the *comforting* things were what *scared* me most, because Zachary was right; they didn't make sense.

"The rain is raining all around,"

Uncle Douglas quoted,

> *"It rains on both the just and the unjust fellow.*
> *But more, it seems on the just than on the unjust,*
> *For the unjust hath the just's umbrella.*

176

All I'm trying to get at, Vicky, is that life isn't fair, and your grandfather, who is one of the greatest human beings I've ever known, is quite aware of it. He doesn't have anything to do with pie in the sky." (Pie in the sky again. It almost sounded as though Uncle Douglas could read people's minds.) "Your grandfather knows that the wicked flourish and the innocent suffer. But it doesn't destroy him, Vicky. He still believes, with a wonderful and certain calm, that God is our kind and loving father."

"But how can he!" I cried. "If God lets things be unfair, if He lets things like Anne Frank happen, then I don't love Him, I hate Him!"

Uncle Douglas didn't look shocked. He just looked thoughtful. "Tilt your head a little to the right, Vicky. That's better. Hold it." Then he said, "I guess you know I'm the heathen of the family."

"You're not a heathen."

"Thanks, dear. Happily your grandfather doesn't think so, either. Nor that I'm a heretic, bless him, though I have some pretty unorthodox ideas. I get mad at God, too, Vicky. I've gone out alone and bellowed in rage at God at the top of my lungs. But the fact that I bellow at him I suppose proves that I think he's there, doesn't it? Go ahead and be mad at God if you feel like it, Vicky. I happen to agree with your Grandfather that the greatest sin against God is indifference. But remember when you're yelling at God, what you're doing is saying, *Do it MY way, God, not YOUR way, MY way.*"

"How can things like Anne Frank be God's way? I don't want God if things like that are His way. It's a cockeyed kind of way. Look at Maggy. Both her mother and father died and she was too *young*. And the most cockeyed part of it is that she's probably turned out a much nicer kid than if they *hadn't* died the way she was being brought up and everything. Does *that* make sense? It's *crazy*. What kind of a God does things like that!"

"Do you mind if I give you a little lecture?" Uncle Douglas asked. "Your mother says that you've been very resistant to parental preaching lately. Do you mind a little avuncular philosophy?"

"Go ahead," I said stiffly.

"As I told you, sweetheart, I'm the heathen of the family. This is nothing to be proud of. It's just a fact we have to face. But if you go on the assumption—and I do—that man has freedom of choice, then you have to assume responsibility for your own actions. You can't go on passing the buck to God." I must have looked blank, because Uncle Douglas wriggled his eyebrows. "How can I explain it to you? Look, Vicky, you remember your bike accident, don't you?"

"How could I forget it?"

"Why did you have the accident? Because you exercised freedom of choice to do something you knew perfectly well you oughtn't to do. When you went on the back road in the dark you did wrong and you knew you were doing wrong, and when you were in the hospital afterwards you didn't whine around saying, *Why did God do this to me?* You accepted the responsibility for your own actions."

"But Anne Frank didn't do anything wrong. She didn't do anything to put her in a concentration camp."

"When you had your bike accident do you think you were the only one who suffered? Everyone in your family was hurt. And what you had done was not so terribly wrong, after all. But when the Germans set up concentration camps that was a very big wrong, and certainly many millions of people suffered because of it. Man exercised the freedom of choice to do wrong, and innocent people paid for it, but I don't think you can go around blaming God for it."

"He could have stopped it," I said stubbornly.

"If he interferes every time we do wrong where's our freedom of choice?"

"But it wasn't *fair*. It wasn't *right*," I persisted.

Uncle Douglas sighed. For a while he worked on his sketch of me. Then he sighed and said, "One of the biggest facts you have to face, Vicky, is that if there *is* a God he's infinite, and we're finite, and therefore we can't ever understand him. The minute anybody starts telling you what God thinks, or exactly why he does such and such, beware. People should never try to make God in man's image, and that's what they're constantly doing. Not your grandfather. But he's extraordinary. So in my heathen way, Vicky, when I wasn't much older than you, I decided that God, a kind and loving God, could never be proved. In fact there are, as you've been seeing lately, a lot of arguments *against* him. But there isn't any point to life without him. Without him we're just a skin disease on the face of the earth, and I feel too strongly about the human spirit to be able to settle for that. So what I did for a long time was to live life *as though* I believed in God. And eventually I found out that the *as though* had turned into a reality. I think the thing that did it for me was a jigsaw puzzle."

"A *jig*saw puzzle?"

"A jigsaw puzzle. Hold still. Chin a little higher. You know those puzzles with hundreds of tiny pieces? You take one of those pieces all by itself and it doesn't make sense, does it? You look at one piece and it doesn't seem to be part of a picture. But you put all the pieces together and you see the meaning of it all. Well, what I, in my heathenish way, Vicky, feel about life, and unfairness, is that we find it hard to realize that there *is* a completed puzzle. We jump to conclusions and decide that the one little piece we have in our hand is all there is and that it doesn't make sense. We find it almost impossible to *think* about infinity, much less comprehend it. But life only makes sense if you see it in infinite terms. If the one piece of the puzzle that is this life were all, then everything would be horrible and unfair and I wouldn't want much to do with God, either. But there are all the other pieces, too, the pieces that make up the whole picture. Now I'm just going to slap some water color on this. Can you hold it a while longer? Maybe when I'm done I'll cut it up into tiny pieces and put them in an envelope and give them to you to fit together. So you can find out what Vicky is. The jigsaw puzzle is a nice, stretchable metaphor. You can use it for almost anything. Now let's stop talking abstractions and get down to specifics. Did Zachary do anything to you that he shouldn't have done?"

I started to shake my head, then remembered that Uncle Douglas was painting me. "You mean did he make out too much and stuff?"

"And stuff," Uncle Douglas said.

"No stuff," I said. I don't know why I wasn't furious with Uncle Douglas. I would have been if it had been Mother or Daddy.

"Then. . . ." He left it up in the air.

"You *guessed* it," I said. "It was all the stuff you were talking about. Did Daddy tell you about Zachary's rheumatic fever and his heart and all?"

"Yes."

"Does Daddy think Zachary's going to die?"

"Why don't you ask him? Your father hasn't examined Zachary, so he can't really tell. But he says, on a superficial guess, it looks more as though Zachary were trying to kill himself than as though he really had to die young. I don't honestly think he's a very healthy person for you to see, Vicky."

"Nobody likes him," I said bitterly. "Nobody's even bothered to know him."

"You like him?"

"I don't know."

"We're not trying to interfere, Vicky. And we're not trying to keep you from growing up. We'd just like to try to make it as easy as possible, because we love you."

"But you said that nothing that was worth anything was easy."

"Touché. But it doesn't need to be quite as difficult as you can make it if you insist on going at it completely alone. After all, the only way man has gone as far as he has is by benefitting from other people's experience."

Aunt Elena'd finally switched from her finger exercises which had been sort of boring into our subconscious like a drill, and gone into a Bach fugue.

"It's like a fugue, too," Uncle Douglas said, as Aunt Elena started the fugue over again. "Elena and I are lucky ones. She has music and I have painting. They give form and shape to everything we do. It was music that kept Elena from being destroyed

181

when Hal died. You'll be better off when you know what you want to be, Vicky."

"But I haven't any talents," I said, "the way John and Suzy do."

"I think the trouble is that you have too *many* talents. There are all kinds of directions you could go. You're an artist of some kind. That I'm sure of. It's the roughest of all lives, and the most rewarding. There. That's all I'm going to do today. Want to see it?"

I got up and looked at the painting. "I'd just as soon you didn't cut it up into little pieces."

"Like it? So do I. You're on your way to being a real beauty, child, but it's all in what's *behind* your face. Right now everything's promise. I'm not going to let you have this because I like it, too. As a matter of fact it's one of the best darned things I've ever done. Let's go show it to Elena."

"But she's practicing."

"Right. And I never interrupt her except for something special. Bless you, Vicky, my darling!" His voice soared happily. "I've finally broken through to something I've been reaching for for weeks and was beginning to despair about. Come on! Hi, Elena! Vicky and I've done it!" He grabbed me by the hand and pulled me in to Aunt Elena, and he was so happy that I completely forgot that I was miserable.

Fifteen

I didn't see Zachary again while we were at Laguna Beach. He came down with a bad cold, and he had to go to bed, though he wouldn't see a doctor. But he called me and tried to get our itinerary.

"I don't *know* what it is. That's one of the whole points of this trip, for Daddy not to have to do anything on schedule or make any definite plans."

"But you must have some vague, general idea where you're going."

"We're going up the coast. All the way into Canada. We're going to stay with friends in Victoria, and I think we're going to Banff, and Glacier, and Yellowstone. Those are the only specific places Daddy's mentioned."

"That's enough to go on," Zachary said. "Give me your address in Victoria, so I can write you." I did, and he said, "I won't see you there, but later on I'll find you."

"But I thought you were going to Alaska."

"I've changed my mind. We can't leave things just up in the air like this. If I want to ask you to a school dance or something next year I'll have to win your family over. Right now they view me about as kindly as they would a king cobra. Have you got a radio in your car?"

"Yes. Why?" A radio didn't seem to have much to do with Zachary's winning Mother and Daddy. *And* John. John took the dimmest view of Zachary of all.

"You'll discover California radio stations are full of *doom*. They'll remind you of me, and I don't want them to remind you in the wrong way."

"I've had enough doom lately," I said. "I won't listen."

"You can't help it. *Keep your car full of gas at all times in case of an enemy attack.* Where the bleeding blossoms do they think you can go? *Keep refilling gallon jugs of water. Have a two weeks supply of canned food on hand at all times.* Nobody ever bothers to say that if people ever get insane enough to start a nuclear war *every*thing will get blown to bits and two weeks of canned corned beef won't save anybody. The thing to go on about is not remembering to keep your car full of gas, but to keep a nuclear war from starting. That's *one* reason I'm going to Choate next year. That's *one* reason I'm going to be a lawyer. Not just what I said. That's what I want you to remember when the radio starts talking doom and you think of me. With which untypical words I shall hang up. Here's a kiss." I heard the sound of a kiss and then he hung up with a clack.

Going up the coast, and knowing I wouldn't see Zachary for a while, I began to un-tense. I managed not to listen to the doom parts of the radio. After all, there's always been doom. What about teen-agers growing up during the Black Plague times when nine out of every ten people died? I mean we're not the only ones to have it rough.

Pismo Beach in California we loved, because there were great enormous sand-dunes, and it seemed much more like a real beach than Laguna. Uncle Douglas had told us that some of the desert scenes for movies were shot there at Pismo, and you could very easily imagine a camel appearing over the crest of a dune. Most of the people there were settled down for a two weeks vacation, lots of them to go fishing. It was too cold for swimming, but we had a marvelous time being Arabs on the dunes with a whole gang of other kids. I really threw myself into it as though I were Rob's age.

One thing we loved, especially Suzy, on the way up the coast, was the seals on the Seventeen Mile Drive, just beyond Carmel. We stood at the water's edge and looked out at the off-shore rocks, really not very far from us, and there, cavorting out in the water, or lying sunning on the rocks, were dozens and dozens of seals. One quite large rock was entirely covered with seals and cormorants. We'd never seen them out of a zoo before, and we could hardly tear Rob and Suzy away.

San Francisco; Humboldt State Park in the midst of the enormous redwoods; a big lumber mill in Scotia, Oregon; the Bumble Bee tuna and salmon factory in Astoria, Oregon, and John Jacob Astor's tower; it was all fascinating, if not violently exciting. In Oregon we saw our first *green* hills since we hit desert country way back in Arizona, but in Oregon also was the worst devastation from forest fires. It was very frightening to see the great, gaunt, blackened bones of trees. We drove along a beautiful, wild, winding coast line, with sheep grazing right by the road. We passed lots of trucks carrying redwood logs. Occasionally there'd be a log so huge it would be an entire truckload. Just *one* log, imagine! The average load we figured was three. There were fishing boats out in the Pacific, and one night we had fresh salmon for dinner, the best we ever tasted.

In Mt. Olympic National Park we had our first real rain, but we expected it, because it has the highest annual rainfall in the continental United States. The funny thing is that there's a place quite nearby, spelled Sequim, but pronounced Squim, which is so dry by contrast that they have to irrigate.

On Mt. Olympic it was easy to believe in the almost continual rainfall, because the campgrounds were in the kind of luxuriant forest that only comes with a lot of moisture; tall, lush green trees, many of the trunks almost covered with moss; grass that is constantly wet—and wet firewood, too, the first we'd had to struggle with since Tennessee. The leaves were so thick over our heads that although it drizzled the whole time we didn't get nearly as wet as you might have thought.

The next day to get to Victoria, in British Columbia, we had to take a ferry across the Straits of Juan de Fuca. Isn't that a beautiful sound, *the Straits of Juan de Fuca?* Like something out of a song. I wonder what kind of a song Zachary would make out of it?

Victoria seemed much more like really being in a foreign country than our few hours in Mexico had. It's a beautiful place, very English, with baskets of flowers hanging from the lamp posts, and the houses of Parliament outlined in lights at night like something out of fairyland. If Mother and Daddy had told us that we were all going to live in Victoria I don't think any of us would have minded it one bit.

We stayed with friends of Mother's and Daddy's, and we stayed in elegance, which we wouldn't have done if we lived there. These friends must have been as rich as Zachary's parents. They had a huge house, I mean but enormous, and I had a room completely to myself for the first time in my life. It was absolutely super and made me feel like royalty. There was a cook and a butler and stuff so we didn't even have to help with the dishes. We just sat back and got waited on. It was very nice for a change.

We washed hair and took baths and did laundry and Mother and Daddy had slews of mail and we had quite a lot of notes from the kids at home and we sent dozens of postcards back to them.

And I had a letter from Zachary.

> "Dear Victoria,
> They're rioting in Africa,
> They're starving in Spain.
> When will I see
> My Vicky-bird again?
> The whole world is festering
> With sadness and sorrow.
> I wish I could kiss
> My Vicky-bird tomorrow,
> Italians hate Yugoslavs,
> South Africans hate the Dutch,
> But I like Victoria
> Very much.
> And I'd deeply appreciate it

If you'd write back.
Love and hugs and doom and stuff.
Zach."

It wasn't exactly my idea of a love poem. But it'd do. It was just fine. The reason I knew it was just fine was I sang the whole time I was in the shower washing my hair, sang at the top of my lungs.

Mother came in and said, "That sounded good, Vicky. I haven't heard you sing like that for a long time. Put on your dress, darling, we're going to the Beach Hotel for dinner."

After an elegant dinner we went to the Butchart Gardens, in the dark, in a gently falling rain. It reminded me of Am-Lowell's poem, "Patterns."

> *And the plashing of waterdrops*
> *In the marble fountain*
> *Comes down the garden paths.*
> *The dripping never stops.*

The lover of the girl in the poem gets killed, and it's very sad, and she's terrifically brave and all. If she weren't so brave the poem wouldn't make you choke up the way it does.

I moved a little away from the others and walked on the soft wet lawn with the misty rain gentle against my cheeks, with lighted flowers gleaming on every side, and pretended that I was walking with Zachary, and that he wasn't being doom-ey and scarey, but gentle and strong. And that he took me into the flowers and kissed me. Anyhow, at least I'd never be sweet sixteen

188

and never been kissed even if another boy never looked at me be-tween now and then. At least I'd got *that* far in growing up.

We did a lot of sightseeing in Victoria. Mother's and Daddy's friends said it really was supposed to be very like England, and that the climate is similar, too, lots of rain, and never very cold in winter nor very hot in summer. We drove around the Lieu-tenant General's mansion and gardens and ate in a real fish and chips place. After church on Sunday morning, we drove out to a wonderful place at Shawnigan Lake where there was a gang of kids and we all went swimming and saw a mink sitting on a rock by the water. We were warned not to go near it because minks bite, but it was another new animal for Suzy.

From Victoria we went to Vancouver where we stayed with friends again. These friends had a tiny apartment, and Mother and Daddy slept on pull-out couches in the living room, with the rest of us in our sleeping bags wherever we could find a space on the floor. John and I put our sleeping bags under the piano, which took up most of the room, anyhow.

After we left Vancouver we spent almost a week wandering through British Columbia which is the most beautiful place I have ever seen in the world. As Mother says John Fortescue says etcetera, comparisons are odious, and we saw so many beautiful places you couldn't really choose between them, but British Co-lumbia was the most *happily* beautiful place we saw on the whole trip, maybe because nothing exciting happened. Unless you count having a snowball fight in July exciting. The weather was gorgeous, the scenery was gorgeous, for a change I wasn't feel-ing moody, and I think maybe part of it all was that everything was so unutterably beautiful that nobody could be unhappy there for long. If a place can remind you of a person, British Columbia reminded me of Grandfather.

The campsites were very clean but quite primitive. There were nice fireplaces, but no water, except from the rushing streams or lakes we camped by, so that we had to boil all the drinking water. No lavs, only small outhouses. But these were cleaner and less smelly than some of the lavs with full electrical equipment. It was the way you'd imagine the Norwegian fjords, the way you'd image the Swiss alps. Great grandeur and absolute simplicity.

We saw practically no cars with American license plates, and that was fun, too. Mother kept saying that it really did remind her of Switzerland, that there were the same spring flowers, the same feel to the way the grass grew and the sun shone while snow still lurked in the shadows, so that sometimes you weren't certain whether a patch of white was left-over snow or spring flowers.

When we got to Kootenay National Park (it's still in British Columbia, but it runs right into Banff at the B.C.-Alberta line) we saw nine bears, three of them darling little cubs. These were our first bears since the one in Tennessee, the night I met Zachary, and we were all very excited to see them. The cubs were so cute and cuddly they looked almost like toys, as though you could get out and play with them. But Daddy reminded us that they're wild animals, no matter how domesticated they look, and their mothers would soon put an end to any fun and games with human beings! We also saw one moose, one grey timber wolf, and five longhorn mountain sheep. Earlier that morning we had seen one mink, two deer, and innumerable chipmunks, so it was a red letter day for Suzy. Her Travel Book was dirty and worn and rapidly filling up with animals, birds, and bugs—though nothing else.

Half the road through Kootenay-Banff National Park was under construction and miserable for Mother, Daddy, and John to drive through, in spite of the fun of seeing bears, and the magnificent scenery. When we got to Banff the town was mobbed, and we discovered that Queen Elizabeth and Prince Philip were arriving the next morning! Ever since we'd reached Canada Mother and Daddy had carefully been planning to avoid them, in spite of our pleas to see a real queen, because of the crowds they'd attract.

We'd expected a lot of Banff, but it was by far the poorest National Park we'd been in. It was huge, and *jammed* with people, though I suppose this was mostly because of the Queen, and if it hadn't been so crowded it wouldn't have been so bad. There weren't any separate campsites, which made things worse. You simply had to find a space big enough for car and tent. There weren't any tables or fireplaces, and there was as much dust as there had been at Palo Duro or Grand Canyon. If you looked up you saw the tops of the pine trees and the mountains rising above, with their grand, snow-topped crests, so we didn't regret being there, but it wasn't going to be the more or less luxurious two days we'd looked forward to. No chance to wash clothes, or even ourselves, for that matter. Cooking wasn't easy, either, because of the mobs of people. There were communal kitchens, with four tables in each, and two wood stoves, and far too many people in camp for the kitchens, so we planned to eat at odd hours. Also it wasn't really convenient for cooking because we were geared to set everything up around the tent. The lavs didn't have any lights, which you don't expect in State Parks, but do you expect in National ones, and there weren't nearly enough lavs to go 'round, so we were always having to stand in line, which was miserable if you happened to be in a hurry. We didn't complain out loud after Mother and Daddy shushed us up, because, they explained, we were visitors in a foreign country and it wasn't courteous to make cracks. But the Canadian campers around us complained loudly, and the louder they groused, the better it made us feel.

After dinner there was a campfire program. We were ready early—the kitchens were so full we'd managed to cook some dinner on Uncle Douglas's stove, unhitching the tent and using the tailgate of the car as a kitchen. While we were waiting for the movies to begin the younger kids played in the playground, and it was the best equipped playground we'd seen in any of the parks, I'll have to say that for it. The trouble was that it was un-supervised, and the bigger boys kept shoving Rob off the swings and seesaws, and if he hadn't had the rest of us around he wouldn't have had a chance at anything.

So, what with one thing and another, none of us was too happy when the movie began. And what happened next was that the very first film they showed made us feel for the first time that we were strangers in a foreign country. I know I said that in Victoria we felt that we were in a foreign land, but we weren't *strangers*. In Victoria we were *visitors*, we were with friends, and we met a lot of interesting, hospitable people, and everybody was wonderful to us, and interested in exchanging ideas and finding out about each other. All through British Columbia we had fun talking with people, and learning from them. There was one girl with a long pigtail, who came from Vancouver, and who was biking *all alone* all the way to Montreal, where she was going to college. She and John had some wonderful talks. Then there were people from Calgary, in Alberta, who were leaving because of the Calgary Stampede. We'd thought something of going there, but they advised us not to, saying that in one day there'd be as many as a hundred thousand people there, and they always got away at that time if they possibly could, because it was like suddenly having all those people descend on Thornhill. They had twin boys just Rob's age and the three of them made a magnificent fort out of twigs and rocks and had to be dragged away from their project when we all left in the morning. Anyhow, what I mean is that everybody was friendly and we loved meeting them and we didn't feel out of place or different.

But that first night in Banff the first movie was called *The Two Kingstons*, and it was about Kingston in Ontario and Kingston in New York, and the man who played the typical (so they said) American looked like Porky Pig and was always telling the Canadian off and trying to boss him around and showing off. All of a sudden, sitting there on the bleachers, surrounded by Canadians, we felt disliked, the way we'd heard Americans are abroad, and we felt very funny about it, funny peculiar, not funny haha.

"What did they *mean* by it?" John said indignantly as we walked back to the tent. "Why would they *show* a picture like that?"

Daddy said calmly, "After all, there's a certain amount of truth to it, even if it isn't very tactful, and even if it's only a half truth."

Rob and Suzy ran and played as usual on the way back to the

tent, but I felt as though someone had scrawled in large letters on a wall, "AMERICANS GO HOME!"

That night it was noisy, and it was the very first campsite we'd been in where there was any noise at night at all. People were in the kitchens talking in loud voices till long after midnight, with the result that we, and everybody around us, were kept awake. I hoped the people making the noise were Canadian and not American. People in other tents kept shouting out, "BE QUIET!" but there wasn't any quiet, and finally at almost one o'clock Daddy got up and went up to the kitchen and then it was a lot better. We were glad it wasn't our introduction to Canada, because we'd have had a very bad impression.

In the morning we slept late because of having been so disturbed during the night and Mother didn't wake us up, because the kitchen was crowded, and so were the lavs. When we finally were dressed and went up to the kitchen to cook our breakfast there were only two other families there. One family left as we got started, and the other family didn't seem to want to talk or make friends; they seemed to be deliberately ignoring us, but I realized later that that was because we were sensitive from the movie the night before. They had three kids, the youngest a boy about Rob's age, and two girls, the oldest about Suzy's age. The five of them got together (the *kids* weren't worried because Rob and Suzy were American) and asked if they could go down to the playground while breakfast was cooking. Mother and Daddy said okay as long as I went along to keep an eye on them. The Canadian parents (their name was York) didn't seem too keen on the idea, but finally they said the kids could go if they were back in fifteen minutes sharp.

We ran down to the playgrounds, so they'd have as much time as possible, and I sat on one of the bleachers and watched while they see-sawed and swang and ran around and had a marvelous time and didn't seem to be thinking about being Canadians and Americans at all. I really don't think kids think about things like that. It's all dumb grown-ups. Why is it that some grown-ups just seem to go on getting dumber and dumber year by year instead of *learning* anything?

All of a sudden the middle little York kid tripped and fell and, instead of getting up laughing, she started to scream. I ran across the playground to her. Suzy was already there and I could see that the little kid's wrist was spurting blood. Not just bleeding, but spurting.

Sixteen

"Shut up," Suzy said to her roughly, "and be quiet so I can stop you bleeding."

The kid shut up. Suzy grabbed her wrist and began pressing. Somebody's mother came running up. "She needs a tourniquet. Here, I'll make a tourniquet for you."

Suzy glared at her. She was holding the York kid's wrist and the spurting had stopped, though Suzy's hand was all red from blood, and there seemed to be blood all over the place. "Sorry," she said sharply, and she sounded almost like Daddy, "but a tourniquet's the worst thing you could possibly do. Vicky, go get Daddy quickly and tell him to bring the first aid kit. I'll go on applying pressure till he comes."

"You ought to get a doctor," the mother said nervously. "Let the poor kiddie's wrist alone. You're hurting her. You don't know what you're doing. I'll report you to the authorities."

"My *father* is a doctor," Suzy said between clenched teeth. "Go ahead and report me."

It wasn't very polite of her, but I didn't blame her. I ran as fast as I could up the hill to the kitchen, panted out to Daddy to get the first aid kit and come *fast*, which he did, without asking any questions. Mother and John and the Yorks came running along, too, because of course nobody knew who was hurt. I tried to explain to them as we ran, but nobody seemed to understand just who was hurt, or how.

We all got there at about the same time, and there was a crowd around Suzy, all of them telling her what to do, and a couple of women yelling at her, and the York kids all crying, especially the one who'd fallen, and Suzy, looking all bloody, was still holding on to the cut wrist with grim determination and crying, too.

"Everybody's *yell*ing at me," she sobbed as Daddy came up, "and wanting to put on tourniquets, and I *know* it's the wrong thing. I'm applying pressure and please make them all go away and leave me alone, Daddy!"

Daddy squatted down beside Suzy, and John and Mr. York shooed the mob away, but I heard Mrs. York mutter, "If she's hurt my child—"

I'd had about enough. I turned on her. "She *has*n't hurt her! Your child fell on a piece of broken glass which shouldn't have been *on* the playground, anyhow, and my sister's keeping her from bleeding to death, and you just leave her *alone*!"

"Vicky!" Mother said in a surprised voice.

But I don't think Mrs. York even heard.

"Everybody thinks Americans can't do anything *right*!" I shouted.

"Vicky," Mother said again, but quietly this time, and took my hand.

I just stood there by mother, my mouth shut tight so I

197

wouldn't say anything more, while Daddy fixed up the York kid. In a couple of minutes he said, "I'm going to take her into one of the lavs. Will you come along please, Mr. York, and keep people out while I clean her up? She's going to be all right. Don't worry. You did exactly the right thing, Suzy. Good for you for sticking to your guns. You come along and wash up, too. The rest of you go back before breakfast burns up. We'll be along in a few minutes."

"How do you *know* she's all right? What do you know about it?" Mrs. York demanded.

"I'm a doctor," Daddy said quietly, as if it oughtn't to have been *ob*vious. "She'll be better off if you'll go along and get some breakfast ready."

Mrs. York turned without saying a word, as though she thought an American doctor couldn't know what he was talking about, and we walked back to the communal kitchen, Rob and the other two York kids running half-heartedly on ahead. When we got back to the kitchen Mrs. York's batch of sausage was completely shriveled up and blackened, and so was our bacon. I watched, without saying anything, while Mother and Mrs. York took paper towels and wiped out their frying pans and put in more sausage and bacon.

Then I said, "If I was rude I'm very sorry. I don't want you to get the idea that Americans are rude. But I knew my sister was doing the right thing."

Mrs. York seemed occupied with her sausage. I didn't think she was going to answer at all, but then she said, "Perhaps I jumped to conclusions." It wasn't really very gracious.

Mother briskly whipped some eggs in the smallest pot. "My

daughter was upset by the picture last night. This is the first time she's come up against any feeling against Americans. One of our faults as a nation may be our very friendliness, and our eagerness to have everybody love us."

John was squatting in front of the stove, shoving in little bits of resiny wood. "Is there really feeling here against the Americans?"

Mrs. York still seemed very busy with the sausage. Sausages don't take that much tending. If you run off to playgrounds when your daughter's cut herself, then they burn up, but when you're right by the stove you don't have to watch them that closely every second. She said, "Well, yes, I think there is, a bit."

"We didn't feel it in British Columbia," John said. "We talked with lots and lots of people and everybody was friendly. Is it just Alberta?"

"Oh, I shouldn't think so," Mrs. York said. "You'll probably find more of it, not less, as you go east."

Daddy and Mr. York came back then with Suzy and the middle York kid. She had a nice neat bandage around her wrist, and Mr. York had his arm around Suzy and began praising her all over the place to Mrs. York, and going on about how lucky it was that Suzy knew just what to do, and Daddy's being a doctor and all, and what a great kid Suzy was, beauty *and* brains, and more should be made like her, and on and on. Mrs. York rushed to her little girl, and as soon as she realized that she was really all right, that all that blood hadn't meant she was going to be brought back on a stretcher, she began to relax. Daddy said the little girl hadn't lost nearly as much blood as it seemed from the mess, but they'd better have her checked by their own doctor when they got back to Edmondton the next day, and get a tetanus booster.

The kids all started playing then, but this time right in the kitchen, the little girl the happiest and noisiest of anybody. The rest of us went on talking about the differences between Canadians and Americans. I think the Yorks had thought there were lots of differences, but the more we talked the fewer and smaller the differences seemed to become, and the more everybody relaxed and got all friendly and normal. Mr. and Mrs. York brought their breakfast over to our table, and the younger kids took their tin plates and mugs over to the York's table, and we began to feel comfortable with them and to have an interesting time. The Yorks had thought that the average American was terrifically wealthy, sort of like Zachary's parents, I guess, instead of being people like us, or like them.

"I think the main difference I've noticed between Canada and the United States," Daddy said, "is that so far in Canada there hasn't seemed to be any nervousness about war." He handed his plate to Mother and she gave him the last strip of bacon and a small piece of coffee cake that was left over.

"War?" Mr. York took a mouthful of sausage and mashed potato. His face and body were relaxed—he was a big man, as tall as Daddy, and quite a lot heavier—and he looked very comfortable. "Why? What about it?"

Daddy looked at John, and John said, "Don't your kids have air raid drills at school or anything?"

Mrs. York was frying more sausage. She was shorter and plumper than mother, and she wore rather baggy slacks and a sweater and a big gingham print apron over all. Now that she'd relaxed and decided that Suzy wasn't killing her child and that Americans were just people, not bug-eyed monsters from Mars, she looked a comfortable sort of person, the kind of person you could easily cry on, even after you were big, and she'd just enfold you as though she were a feather bed, and everything would feel better. Now she looked horrified as she looked over at her children playing at the other end of the kitchen with Rob and Suzy. "Those little tykes? Goodness, no! Why would we put them through anything like that?"

Mother said rather bitterly, "Our children have drills and they're taught to crawl under their desks. In New York, where we'll be living next winter, a warning siren screams fear every day at noon. Each time there's a newscast on the radio there seems to be a new and terrifying crisis."

"We don't listen to the news much," Mrs. York said. "Would you kiddies like a little of this sausage?" John and I both had some, and Mrs. York called out to Suzy and Rob. Rob brought his plate over, but Suzy didn't have any, of course, because of Wilbur the pig.

"We never even think about things like that," Mr. York said, "up where we live. You people going to see the Queen?"

So we got to talking about the Queen and Prince Philip, and on the way back to the tent we saw a big brown bear strolling right through the campgrounds and we stopped thinking about wars and differences between Canadians and Americans.

While we were eating our sandwiches for lunch, which we did sitting around the car, because the kitchens were crowded again, we talked about the Queen and the Prince who were coming by the campgrounds right after lunch, which was why we hadn't gone off on a trip to Lake Louise that day. After all, if the Queen of England was going to be driving right by, we might as well stick around and see her.

"Have you ever met the Queen, Mother?" Rob asked.

"*Hon*estly, Rob," Suzy said.

But Mother laughed. "Well, as a matter of fact, I have."

"*Mother!*" Suzy and I shrieked. "When?"

"It was in England, when I was a little girl, and the Queen was only a little princess. I was visiting some friends of Grandfather's—you know how grandfather has friends everywhere, from dukes to dog-catchers—and these people were minor royalty, and they belonged to the Bath Club. They took us children swimming there, and it so happened that day that the only other people in the pool were the little princesses."

We were properly impressed.

"What are you going to say when you see her again?" Suzy asked.

Mother laughed, "Suzy, darling, the queen wouldn't know me from Adam."

"But you know her!"

"It was a long time ago, and you can hardly call being in the same pool with somebody knowing her."

"But did you *talk* to her?" Suzy persisted.

"I don't remember, Suzy. Sorry to be such a disappointment to you."

"But suppose she speaks to *you*," Rob said.

"She won't, Rob. Don't worry."

"But I wish she would. I'd like to speak to her. If she should speak to me what should I do?"

"She's not going to speak to you, silly," Suzy said.

Rob's face fell. "But I thought they were coming right through camp. Aren't they going to speak to anybody?"

"Honestly, Rob! They just drive *through*, dopey."

I always get mad at Suzy when she talks to Rob that way, and I guess John does, too, because he said, "If you meet the Queen, Rob, what you do is give a deep bow."

"Oh," Rob said. "Okay. Did you ever meet a queen, Daddy?"

"If you count meeting Princess Grace when she was plain Grace Kelly," Daddy said.

Now John was impressed. "You've met Grace Kelly?"

"Just about the way your mother's met the Queen of England. She happened to be visiting in the hospital where I was interning. But it did give me enough personal interest so that I'm apt to watch her and Prince Rainier when they're on TV."

Rob looked up at Mother. "Is Grace Kelly beautiful like you, Mother?"

By the time we'd finished tidying up after our sandwiches people were beginning to wander past us on the way to the road that edged the camp and along which the Queen and Prince were supposed to drive. The Yorks stopped by and we all walked over together. The grassy bank at the side of the road was already filled with people from all parts of the camp, and Mounties in their gorgeous red uniforms were wandering up and down. Every once in a while one would come by on a motor cycle instead of a horse, and everybody would begin to buzz because it might be announcing the Queen's car. Daddy had Rob up on his shoulders, and Mr. York had his little boy, but after almost an hour of waiting in the blazing sun the boys must have been very heavy, and Daddy and Mr. York put them down, saying they'd pick them up again when the time came. The Queen's car was supposed to go by at one o'clock, but by two-thirty she still hadn't come, and everybody began to get restless, but nobody left. After a while we missed Rob and the little York boy, and John discovered them up a tree.

"They were buzzing around me like gnats," John grinned, "so I told them to go climb a tree, and they did."

The branches hung out over the road, and the little boys had a perfect view, so Daddy and Mr. York didn't have to worry about picking them up again. Suzy and the York girls wanted to get up in the tree, too, but Daddy and Mr. York said it wasn't strong enough and they were all big enough to see, anyhow. There didn't happen to be many trees right there by the roadside that were close enough to give a good view, and the few others were already filled with other children. Rob and the York boy had managed to pick the best tree of all and were having a fine time playing Tarzan. John and I played Botticelli, and then some easier word games with the younger ones, and all of a sudden a lot of motor cycles came by, slowly, and in formation, so we knew that the Queen's car was coming.

I saw Suzy and the York girls climbing up in the tree with the little boys in spite of what Daddy and Mr. York had said, but just then people down the road began to cheer loudly. I knew that the Queen was coming, so I forgot about the little kids and craned my neck with everybody else. A couple of closed cars drove by, very slowly. I suppose they must have been the mayor and stuff of Banff. And then, behind them, came an open car with the Queen and Prince Philip, smiling and waving at everybody.

Just before the car reached our part of the road there was a tremendous CRACK and suddenly in the middle of the road right in front of the car was a branch of a tree and a lot of green leaves.

And Rob.

Everybody shrieked, and the car with the Queen and Prince Philip stopped suddenly. Rob picked himself up out of the leaves, stood up in front of the car, and bowed, deeply, and solemnly.

At that the tension broke and everybody laughed, and the Queen and Prince gave Rob a special wave and smile. A mountie scooted up and brushed Rob off and got him up on the bank, the car started up again, and in a moment the Queen and Prince Philip had gone around a bend in the road and were out of sight.

Behind us we heard Suzy and the York kids being excited, and in front of us the mountie was scolding the kids all around, though not as though he really meant it, because, after all, nothing awful had happened, it hadn't been an international incident or anything. Suzy and the York girls had tried to climb up in the tree with the little boys to see better, and of course they were too heavy, and one of the branches broke, the one with Rob on it. He was the only one to go tumbling down, and the branch broke slowly enough so that it softened his fall, and he wasn't hurt a bit, just breathless, and excited because he'd bowed to the Queen. Daddy and Mr. York apologized to the trooper; Mr. York did most of the talking, and made a big joke out of the whole thing, and then he went on about how Suzy had saved his little girl's life that morning, and Suzy got pink with embarrassment.

But he didn't say anything about our being American, and I think I'm just as glad.

Seventeen

What with all the excitement of the day we gave up all idea of going to Lake Louise. Daddy suggested that we go instead to a pool where the water came from natural hot springs. The Yorks said they'd gone the day before, and swimming in the hot water was wonderfully relaxing. That it was. The water in the pool was tested while we were there, and it was 100°. There were signs advising people not to stay in the water more than twenty minutes at a time, but we couldn't even take it that long, but would inch in and stay for a few minutes, and then climb out and lie stretched supine in the sun. It was absolutely gorgeous, as close to being ancient Romans as we'll ever get. At the shallow end of the pool were lots of elderly people, just standing there in the water. It was kind of sad, and I was glad to see Mother and Daddy swimming in the deep end.

What with a whole afternoon of being ancient Romans (John said he missed a gorgeous slave girl to rub him down with oil afterwards) we were all so relaxed that after the movies (which were plain, uncontroversial science films that night) we all went right to sleep in spite of the noise.

We got off quite early in the morning and had an exciting drive over the Kananaskis Mountain Road and Pass. It's an unpaved road, a hundred and fifty miles long, and so sparsely traveled that you have to sign in with a ranger when you enter, and sign out again at the other end. I suppose if you don't come out they send search parties for you. It's completely uninhabited, no stores or filling stations or any sign of civilization. We passed a few fishermen's tents down by the river, but that was all. At one of the points on the pass we got out and threw snow balls, although it was so warm that Rob started to have prickly heat again and was stripped to the waist.

I'd really been in a very good mood ever since we reached Victoria. Once a day I'd read Zachary's love song in the lav, and I thought about only the nice part of him, his gentleness, and his liking me the way he used to. And because he wasn't with me, saying things to frighten me, I didn't think about his heart condition, or Anne Frank, or any of the things that had upset me in Laguna.

But then that afternoon we drove through the town of Frank in Alberta. First of all there was the name. Frank. Like Anne Frank. And it was as though Zachary were there standing by me and grinning because I was so dumb and so ignorant and I'd never even heard before of what had happened to the town called Frank and everybody in it.

What happened was that about fifty years ago half of the mountain crashed down in the middle of the night, burying most of the town and the seventy people in the section it covered. There wasn't any warning for those people in the town of Frank; they didn't have to sleep all night with their ears half open, listening for the sound of storm troopers' boots. They went to bed without worrying about anything at all, just the way we do in Thornhill. The mountain was there, strong and secure, when they went to bed, and in the middle of the night it fell on them.

I thought of the psalm again. *I will lift up mine eyes unto the hills*. The people of Frank must have thought of their mountain as being strong and permanent and reliable. They probably knew that over millions of years mountains rise and fall, but it takes millions of years, and this mountain fell all of a sudden in the middle of the night.

The mountain was so huge that they never tried to clear up the rubble; they just rebuilt over and around it, the people who were left to rebuild. The remains of the huge slide are still there for everybody to see, with the railroad tracks and the road simply going over it.

I wasn't the only one to be silent after we'd driven through the town of Frank. For several miles nobody said anything at all, and then nobody really noticed that I wasn't doing much talking. Just Vicky and her moods.

By the middle of the afternoon we were back in the United States again, in Montana, at Glacier National Park. I suppose because it was well into July and right in the middle of the camping season all the parks were at their most crowded, but we did manage to find a fairly good campsite by some nice people, two rather elderly Greek professors and their wives. Their tents

209

were old and battered and their equipment was as elderly as they were, but they seemed to be having as good a time as though they were kids. Both the professors taught at Harvard, but they seemed really pleased about John's going to M.I.T., and when they discovered he'd studied a little Greek and loved it, you'd have thought he'd given them an enormous present. They were really fun to camp next to, and when we discovered we were both going to have stew for dinner, we put all the stew into their big old iron pot and ate together.

The next day we went up beyond Logan Pass, across the Continental Divide once again. We were even higher and closer to snow than we had been the day before on the Kananaskis road. We went through banks of snow more than twenty feet high, on a road that was opened from the winter only a week or so before. And here it was the middle of July!

At one point when we'd left the station wagon and were walking along the road, Rob shouted out, "A bear! A bear!" A shaggy looking bear was sitting on the snow bank right by the car, peering at us in a much more friendly manner than the bears in Kootenay. Daddy told us to get back in the car, and we had just shut the door when the bear got up, lumbered over, and stuck his head in the window by Mother. I don't think she was happy about this at all. He was an awfully *big* bear. She very gently rolled the car window up almost to the top, so the bear was left on the outside, his paws up against the car, his wet nose smearing the window.

We drove on, and came on the Greek professors looking through binoculars up at something high on the mountain. They managed to point out three white moving dots to us, which they said were mountain goats, and quite unusual to see. So Suzy had some *more* animals for her book. After that we stuck with the Greek professors and they let us look at everything through their binoculars.

Montana was a state we really loved. We spent one night near a marvelous cave filled with stalactites and stalagmites. Rob really got a bang out of this. Then there were great, fertile, gently rolling plateaus, bounded in the distance by the snowy peaks of the Rockies. Everything was green and lush, with beautiful strip planting, and the farms all absolutely enormous in comparison to the little ones we were used to at home. There weren't very many trees, which was surprising, but there were loads of cattle. Every once in a while we would see wild horses running along beside the road, their manes flying behind them, swift and beautiful. These were very exciting to all of us, and of course Suzy could hardly contain herself. The one thing in the world she wanted was to have a chance to tame one of them. I didn't see this at all. The whole reason I loved them, the whole reason they made me shiver with their beauty, was that they were *wild* and *free*. Maybe feeling this way is what makes me more of a beachcomber type than somebody who's planning to be a doctor, like Suzy.

From Montana we went into Wyoming, to Yellowstone National Park. We knew Yellowstone would be crowded, and Daddy almost decided to skip it. If he had it would have changed the whole course of my life. Well. Maybe it's a little early to say that. But Yellowstone made a lot of *difference* to me.

I wasn't feeling particularly glad about it, though, when Daddy said it would be too bad to miss Old Faithful, when we

211

were so close. We drove in, a little before lunch, and wandered around and around looking for a campsite. At the big parks you had to get there before lunch at the latest if you wanted to get a campsite, and we began to think even that was too late at Yellowstone, when we finally saw some people driving away, down at the far end of the camping section, and slid into their place, with a couple of cars behind us still looking for sites. We were in a new section of campground that had just been opened that spring, and that, as recently as a couple of months before, had been bears' territory. As far as the bears were concerned, it was still their territory. While we were setting up camp two large brown bears lumbered along the road right by us, looked inquisitively in the car windows, then methodically went through the supposedly bear proof garbage containers across the road. I was glad we weren't camped right *by* one of the garbage containers. I'm not Suzy.

We were very close to whoever was on our right; the campsites at Yellowstone weren't made for privacy. We saw three pair of bathing trunks out on a line, and there was a very weatherworn tent and a beat-up old grey car with a New York license plate. We were just getting settled when three kids, boys, came sauntering up and took their trunks from the line. They looked over at us, saw that John was about their age, and came over to say hello.

They were brothers, two straw-colored blonds, and one with red hair, not dark red like John and Uncle Douglas, but bright orange red. I figured he was probably the youngest, but you couldn't really tell, except that from something they said I thought the other two, Don and Steve, were in college, and

Andy still had another year to go. Their last name was Ford, and they were camping by themselves. No parents or anything with them. Just on their own. I was very impressed. But *they* seemed kind of impressed that John was going to M.I.T.

Suddenly Steve said, "*Cave*, kids, watch it, here comes the suicide blonde."

"Hunh?" Suzy asked.

"Dyed by her own hand," Andy said, and the three of them dived into their tent and vanished into the shadows.

I looked around and an enormous woman was bearing down on us. She must have weighed two hundred pounds, and she had on bright red slacks that were too tight, an orange shirt, and the brightest yellow hair I've ever seen. But she was as friendly as could be. As a matter of fact, she didn't give anyone a chance to get a word in edgewise.

"Hi, you nice big family," she started out. "My, but campers are so friendly, don't you think so? Those are the nicest boys right by you. You'll just love them. My girls all have crushes on them." She kind of batted her eyelashes and leered at me. "You will, too, so watch yourself, cutie-pie, watch yourself." I thought of the boys right inside their tent hearing every word, and writhed, but she went right on. "Joe's gone off fishing, my husband, Joe, that's his boss Joe's gone with, they were gone all day yesterday, Joe went with his boss, and today the girls wanted to go fishing, too, so they went with Joe and his boss, and I thought I'd write some letters, my mother-in-law gets so worried, and I didn't have any writing paper, so I wondered if I could give you a quarter for a couple of pieces of paper. . . . Oh, thank you, but can't I give you something for it? . . . I know what, I'll bring the kiddies some ice cream. . . . Well . . . you'd better watch out for bears here. The rangers say they're nastier this year than they've ever been before. This is our fourth year here and we always used to try to get close enough to a bear to take a picture. Well, like I said, Joe and his boss went fishing, Joe took the car, and I didn't want to leave the food on the table, so I put it in the tent. The girls had picked up a lot of children and they were playing charades, and I was playing right along with them, like a dumbbell, except for my oldest girl, she was lying in the tent reading, Jo-Bette's thirteen, all five of my girls are named after their Daddy, Jo-Bette, Jo-an, Jo-Belle, Jo-Blanche, Jo-Lee. And a bear went after the food right into the tent with Jo-Bette, and I was so scared I picked her right up and said, 'Run, Jo-Bette, run!' and all the time I was holding her tight and almost throwing her at the bear. Well, we couldn't get that bear out of the tent. One man hit at it with a hatchet, but it wouldn't budge. Another man threw a couple of big firecrackers at it, but it didn't even act like it heard them. All the men came running because I was screaming so. 'Mother,' Jo-Bette said, real mad at me, 'you kept telling me to run and how could I run with you throwing me right at the bear?' "

We took everything she said with a whole keg of salt. I can't imagine Daddy hitting at a bear with a hatchet, or throwing a firecracker at it. As soon as she'd gone the boys came out of their tent, wearing trunks.

"There are more darned fools around here," Don, the oldest, said. "One of her kids is going to get hurt by a bear, and she's not even going to understand why."

"They have to drive *in*," Steve said impatiently. "You'd think

214

they could read the warnings. After all, if she can write a letter she ought to be able to *read*."

Don laughed. "Doesn't always follow. About a hundred and fifty people have to be treated for bear wounds every summer, and it's all their own fault. They think bears are just too cute for words and will eat right out of their hands like pets. You can't tell 'em a million times that bears are wild animals, *not* domesticated, and they won't believe you."

Steve started to lean against the hood of their car, then jerked away because the sun had made it so hot. "Last night this girl across the road went to bed with a chocolate bar and only ate half of it. So a bear smelled it and went right into the tent after the chocolate."

"Not that we want to scare you, or anything," Don said. "Just a friendly warning. A man where you're camped now had an unopened carton of milk in his tent. One of the bears ripped a neat little hole in the tent with his claws, reached in, got the carton of milk, very carefully sliced off the top, and drank it. They're the biggest gluttons you'll ever find. The main thing is *never* to leave a crumb in the tent, and to shut your car up tight at night. We're off for a swim. See you later."

We shut the car up tight and went sightseeing.

I seem to have felt about lots of the places we visited that they belonged on another planet, but Yellowstone really did. If you could take away the trees and the few green patches, the surface of the earth would look like a Bonestell painting of Mercury, rust and yellow crust, boiling waters, some blue, some an emerald green from the yellow algae. The weirdest was a pool of bubbling clay, pink and ivory and grey, oozily gurgling.

When we got back to the tent the boys were cooking their dinner, hamburgers, which was exactly what we were having that night. A large bear was hovering over the boys, and Andy, who was the one who seemed to talk the least, kept banging two tin plates in the bear's face, and then it would retreat a few inches.

The minute our hamburgers began to send up their delightful aroma the bear moved away from the boys and came over to us, so Mother grabbed two tin plates and whacked them together, and Andy came over with *his* tin plates and managed to drive the bear across the road. But at Yellowstone you never just sat down and relaxed. You were always looking around for bears.

The boys walked over to the campfire program with us. Steve and Don walked with John and talked college. Don went to Oberlin and Steve to Swarthmore, and one of the things they'd been doing on their trip was give Andy a chance to look over some colleges.

Andy fell into step by me, but he wasn't very talkative. He did point out a mule deer for Suzy. But mostly he didn't say anything. John said afterwards to me, "Why didn't you *say* something to Andy? I mean the whole time we were waiting for the program to begin you just *sat* there, like a bump on a log."

"He didn't seem to want to talk."

"You yakked enough with that dumb *Zach*ary. Couldn't you have asked him a few questions or something?"

"It didn't seem necessary." I tried to sound lofty. But it was true. I had this funny feeling with Andy that you didn't have to talk all the time. It was perfectly all right just to sit and look around and appreciate things. Anyhow, the others talked enough for Andy and me, and I listened to them, and I think he did, too. It was all right when they talked about college and New York and jazz like that, but I didn't like it when Don told about how some people just won't heed the warnings to stay on the wooden paths. The crust of the earth at Yellowstone is so thin that if you step on it you'll go right through into boiling water, but every once in a while somebody'll forget to watch a child, and the child will step off the path, and get scalded. To death. I think they were warning us about Rob. But they needn't have. Mother never let go his hand while we were wandering around. What with people being hurt by bears and scalded by boiling water I didn't feel too happy about Yellowstone.

The next morning we all took showers—pay ones again—and then went to look for geysers. We didn't see the Ford boys, though their tent was still there, and their bathing trunks hanging out on the line. In the afternoon we saw Andy at Clepsydia Geyser, and just as we said "hello" the geyser began bursting forth, shooting up out of four holes simultaneously. Andy and the ranger who was standing with him there got very excited. The ranger told us that we were seeing the geyser in its wild stage; this was only the fifth time this year it had come shooting up that way, and very few tourists ever see it.

When Clepsydia had stopped spurting Andy turned to me and said, "How about ditching your family and coming to Great Fountain with me? It'll mean just sitting and waiting because it doesn't spout on time like Old Faithful. Most people don't have the patience to wait for it, but Don and Steve saw it last year, and it's supposed to be the most spectacular of all the geysers, so I'm determined to see it."

"I'd love to," I said.

Andy turned to Daddy. "Okay if I kidnap Vicky for the afternoon? I don't think Suzy and Rob'd be interested in sitting around waiting for Great Fountain."

He didn't mention John, and Daddy said it was okay, he thought they'd all go for a swim.

Andy and I set off. Again we didn't say anything, and again it didn't seem necessary. I had the funniest feeling of being comfortable with Andy. There wasn't anything comfortable about Zachary. He was exciting and scary and I was always a little afraid he'd stop liking me. But Andy didn't say anything about liking me or not liking me. I couldn't even tell whether he did or not. It didn't seem to matter. I just felt that while he was around everything was okay.

Suddenly he grabbed my arm and said, "HEY!" in a loud, startled voice. I looked around and there was a little kid with a frizzy permanent holding out half a sandwich to a bear.

Eighteen

"It's that dratted Jo-Lee," Andy said, and started to run towards her. The bear reached for the sandwich and grabbed Jo-Lee at the same time, and the kid began to shriek. A fat man standing near with a cigar in his mouth began to shout and jump up and down. He looked like the American in the movie about the Two Kingstons, and he swotted ineffectually at the bear. People came running, and Jo-Lee shrieked louder and louder, and I could see that the bear had her by the arm.

Andy sprinted to the fat man, grabbed the lighted cigar from his mouth, and held the glowing end to the bear's nose. The bear dropped Jo-Lee and rubbed his nose in a surprised way. Then he turned and waddled off.

Jo-Lee kept on howling and Andy looked at her arm. A ranger came hurrying over, and Andy said, "It's just a scratch. Not too bad a one. She was feeding the bear, the dumb kid, after all we've told her."

"She your sister?" the ranger asked.

Andy looked horrified at the thought, and explained that Jo-Lee belonged to a family camping nearby. The ranger wanted us to come along with him to the first aid station, and then wanted Andy to look up Jo-Lee's mother.

"What're you doing wandering about *alone*, anyhow?" Andy asker her crossly.

Jo-Lee just howled. She made an ugly face when she cried and even though she was a *little* kid, about Rob's age, you didn't want to pick her up and comfort her. You wanted to smack her bottom. At least I did.

"This is their fourth year here, for crying out loud," Andy said indignantly to the ranger. "Some people just never learn. Stop crying, Jo-Lee. You're okay. And if you *dare* ever go off by yourself this way again I'm going to wallop you. Somebody has to."

"That was quick thinking about the cigar, son," the ranger said, taking Jo-Lee by the hand and dragging her down the path.

"It wasn't my idea," Andy explained. "I read about somebody doing it once in Central Park Zoo when a bear reached through the bars and grabbed a kid who was teasing it. I can tell you I was glad it really worked."

Jo-Lee made Andy go in with her to the first aid station, so the ranger and I went off to find the rest of the family. The kids were all scattered somewhere, and Joe was probably off fishing with his boss again, but the mother was sound asleep in her tent, with a carton of orange juice beside her. The ranger took the orange juice and chucked it into one of the garbage cans in a kind of fury. Then we wakened the mother and took her back to the first aid station. She gabbled so all the way we never had a chance really to explain what had happened. We left her with Jo-Lee, who started to howl again the minute she saw her mother, and Andy said, "Come on, Vicky," and grabbed my hand and we set off for Great Fountain.

"If that darned kid's made us miss it I *will* wallop her. See if I don't." Then he didn't say anything and we half ran, half walked down the path leading to Great Fountain. After a while he growled, "I didn't mean to seem brutal with that kid, but I just don't have any patience with deliberate stupidity. *Any*body with the intelligence of a three year old ought to be able to understand that the warnings they give you when you come into the park mean just what they say." Then he snapped his jaws closed again.

When we got to Great Fountain there wasn't any sign of activity. "She spouts once a day, about," Andy said, "but there isn't *any* regularity at all." He asked around, and there were a couple of people who'd been waiting there since morning, so at least we hadn't missed anything. Andy led me over to a patch of grass away from the others and we sat down.

"We can see from here if anything starts," Andy said. "I don't feel like getting into conversations with anybody."

I just nodded and we sat there. The sun was warm, but not too hot, just vital and comforting. Andy started to whistle. The melody was familiar and at first it seemed to me that it was Zachary's awful song. I thought, —Oh, no, not *you*, Andy! Then I realized that it wasn't Zachary's song at all, but Daddy's "Tumbling along with the tumbling tumbleweed," and for some reason the fact that *this* was what Andy was whistling made me intensely happy. He lay back on his elbows, his lips pursed out in his whistle, and I tried to look at him out of the corner of my eye

221

so he wouldn't realize I was doing it. His face was all freckled with the freckles mixing in with his tan. His eyes were a *very* bright blue. He had on chino shorts and a blue cotton shirt and he looked and acted about as different from Zachary as could possibly be. I certainly couldn't imagine Andy in a black leather jacket.

Zachary's poem was back in the tent. I'd worn it out too much to keep it in the pocket of my Bermudas. I didn't need to look at it.

> *They're rioting in Africa,*
> *They're starving in Spain.*
> *When will I see*
> *My Vicky bird again?*

You couldn't possibly, not possibly, imagine Andy writing anybody anything like that.

"What I like about you, Vicky," Andy said so suddenly that I jumped, "is that you don't talk all the time the way most girls do. It's not that I have anything against talking. In fact I propose to do a good deal of talking while we're waiting for Great Fountain. We may have a long wait. Do you mind?"

"No," I said. I thought I probably should have said something more, but I was kind of waiting around to see what Andy was going to talk about.

"I just don't like to talk," he said, "unless I have a *reason*. I mean there's no point yakking just to see if your jaw's still hinged. When I talk I want to find out about things. Or impart useful information." He grinned. "Did you know Yellowstone's the only other place besides Iceland and New Zealand that has geysers?"

"Nope. Live and learn," I said.

"I have a summer project in science for my school, and I'm doing it on geysers. They load us down with all this summer homework. It's a good school, though."

"Where is it?"

"In New York, where we live. St. Andrew's. So of course it was the only logical place for me to go. Add to that, it's only a few blocks from our apartment. My father teaches Chaucer and all that gluck at Columbia. He and my mother are in England this summer. They'll probably come back *speaking* Chaucerian. *A nyghtengale, upon a cedir grene, Under the chambre wal there as she lay, Ful loude ayein the moone shene* . . . kookie stuff, but my father makes it sound as though it had *some* sense. Your father's a doctor?"

"Yes."

"John says you're going to be living in New York next year. How d'you think you're going to like it?"

"It's going to be different from Thornhill, that's for sure," I said.

"Know where you're going to be living?"

I shook my head. "When we get back Mother and Daddy are going to look for a place, and see about schools and stuff."

"You sound kind of nervous about it," Andy said.

"I think maybe I am."

"I'll give you my phone number. You give me a ring or drop me a line or something when you know where you're going to be, and maybe I can show you around. I know New York inside out, and believe me, there isn't any place in the world like it."

"Is this good or bad?"

"Both. Some people hate it and some people love it. As for me I wouldn't want to live any place else. If my father didn't *work* at Columbia, and if I didn't want to go away from home for college, I'd stay right there. But after I get out of school I'm coming right back. And if I have to do graduate work or something I'll do it right there."

"Graduate work in what?"

Andy flung out his arms in a wide, kind of despairing gesture. "You got me there. I haven't the faintest idea. Don's all set to teach English and write and stuff on the side. He's really good. He's already sold a couple of stories. Steve wants to do something overseas in the diplomatic service or the U.S.I.A. or something. Maybe the Peace Corps for a while. As for me, I'm no dope, I've got a perfectly good mind, and I haven't the faintest idea what to do with it."

I rolled over on the grass and felt so grateful to Andy I could have hugged him. "Oh, Andy!" I cried. "Me, too! John's always known he was going into physics or chemical engineering or something. And Suzy thinks she's practically *through* medical school. Zachary's going to be a lawyer. And I just don't know where I'm going."

"Who's this Zachary?"

"Oh, he's this boy in California."

"Old friend?"

"No, we just met him this summer. The thing is, *he* knows what he's going to do, *John* knows what he's going to do, *Suzy* knows, everybody knows except me.

"I bet you're no slouch in school, though," Andy said.

224

"I get good enough *grades* and stuff. I just don't have any *talent*."

Andy extended his hand. "Shake. You're in good company. I don't let it worry me. After all, we've got till the end of sophomore year in college before we have to make up our minds what we're going to major in. The main thing is to find a good general college, with high scholastic standing, take as wide a range of subjects as possible during the first two years. And then, by golly, inspiration had better descend. Listen, if your parents haven't done anything about schools they could do worse than look up St. Andrew's."

"Isn't it a boy's school?"

"Co-ed. Nursery school right on through. It's run by these Episcopal nuns but they're really swell. Most of them have Ph.D.s and stuff. Then there're a lot of lay teachers, too. Some really good men. Take our Latin guy. He's this Mohammedan from Indonesia and he's teriff. Another thing, it's not too expensive as schools go. I don't know if you're rolling, or not."

"We're not."

"And if John's going to college and there're three of you going to school that's going to take quite a hunk. If you want to get into a good college you've *got* to have a good education. Steve took *four* languages before he ever went to college. French, German, Latin, and Russian. Not many schools give you that. He wanted to take Spanish, too, but they wouldn't let him carry that heavy a load, because he had to do all the regular stuff, math and history and all, along with the languages. And you don't have to be an Episcopalian or anything. I mean, the kids are *every*thing. All races and colors and all that, too. Last year Head of School was from Sao Paolo, Brazil, though he's lived here for six years. His father's in the embassy. This year it's just a plain old New Yorker."

I looked at Andy and he looked kind of self-conscious. "Such as you?"

"Well. Yah."

"Congratulations. I think that's swell."

He grinned and began pulling up little pieces of grass. "I have to admit I'm pleased. Don was Head of School his year, and Steve was valedictorian, so the competition was pretty stiff all around. You see, I happen to think it's a great school. It's not just like being the head of any old school. Listen, where are you going next? I don't mean after school, I mean after Yellowstone."

"I don't know," I said. "Daddy wants to go to some place that isn't crowded."

"He *does?* We know *the* place. Honest. It's a little campsite hardly anybody knows about in the Black Ram mountains. It isn't in any of the camping books or anything. It's this beautiful sort of plateau way up high in the hills and there're never more than a couple of tents there. Want me to tell your father about it?"

"Sure. It sounds like fun."

Some people came strolling up, then, to ask about Great Fountain, so we sent them off to ask the people who'd been there ever since morning and seemed to know all about it.

Mother and Daddy and the others came by after swimming, and Daddy said I ought to go back and help Mother get dinner.

Andy said, "Sir, she's waited all this time, wouldn't you consider letting her off just this once? She's bound to start spouting soon. Not Vicky. Great Fountain. And I'll treat her to a hot dog or something afterwards. Not Great Fountain. Vicky. And we could meet you at the evening program."

Mother said, "We're not going to have anything exciting for dinner and I can get along without you perfectly well, Vic. This kind of patience ought to be rewarded. Anybody else want to stay and watch?"

I sat very still in concentration. No. No. I want to talk to Andy alone. I love you all but I don't want you here now. No.

I was concentrating so hard I didn't realize they'd all decided not to stay until they'd gone. Old Faithful was due again in a few minutes and they were going to watch that.

Then Don and Steve came wandering by and announced that they were going to get dinner, and Andy said to go ahead without him, we'd just pick up a hot dog and a coke.

After they'd gone he said, "Bored or anything, Vicky?"

"Nope." I felt happy and peaceful. Andy was so relaxed about everything you couldn't help being relaxed, too, when you were with him. And I was excited, too. But it was a very different kind of excitement from being with Zachary. There wasn't any fear in it.

After a while I realized that it was growing dark, and Andy said, "Oh, come *on*, isn't she *ever* going to spout?" And then there was a sort of bubble and gasp from the geyser and great lacy curtains of spray began to rise, to fall, to rise, until finally there was a tremendous high fountain of silver, shivering and pulsing and flinging itself up into the sky and then falling down in a delicate shower and then shooting up again.

We sat and watched it in silence, and it seemed to go on and on, and finally it just drifted down and disappeared.

"Now *that's* what I call worth waiting for," Andy said in a satisfied way. "Come on, Vicky, I'm starved. We'll miss most of the evening program, but I don't think anybody'll mind."

After we'd eaten we went back to the tent to get sweaters and the others had all skipped the program, too, and were sitting around the fire, gabbing. Just as we came up we heard a commotion down the road. Suzy ran off to see what it was, and came back, full of excitement, to report that there was a cub up a tree and the rangers were trying to get it down.

"Grab a sweater, Vicky," Andy said. "Let's go."

We didn't even wait for the others but ran down the road and joined the group watching. Luckily almost everybody in the tents around was at the evening program, so we had a really good view, because what had happened was that during the day a mother bear had ripped up several tents. If a bear goes into a tent with food in it, that's just rough luck. They give you enough warnings so you *deserve* what you get, like that brat Jo-Lee feeding the bear her sandwich. But this bear had gone after a couple of tents with no food, and when that happens the rangers go after the bear. They had managed to get the mother bear into an enormous trap, but they hadn't been able to get the cub, who had run up a tree.

There were four rangers out after the cub. One was up a tree with a lasso. Two others, also with lassoes, were standing on the ground just below. The fourth ranger was back with the campers, probably to keep some dumb jerk from trying to get in the hunt and getting hurt. Everybody watching had flashlights trained on the bear. The ranger with the campers was the one who'd come along that afternoon when Andy stuck the lighted cigar against the bear's nose. He yelled "Hi!" at us as though we were old friends, so Andy and I stood by him, and soon Suzy had slipped through the crowd to stand close to the ranger so she could ask questions.

The cub hunt was like something out of Disney. Half way up a tall, slender pine, looking cute and adorable like something in a cartoon, was a fat little cub. At first you couldn't imagine why the ranger had to climb gingerly up a nearby tree, why he couldn't just climb after the cub, pick it up, and bring it down to its mother. But in a minute you saw why. As soon as the ranger in the tree got his lasso anywhere near the cub, the little thing stopped looking like a stuffed toy and turned into a wild animal, and a fat little bear cub is plenty big enough to rip a grown man to shreds. I realized for the first time how lucky that darned Jo-Lee was to have somebody with presence of mind like Andy around when the bear grabbed her.

Suzy wanted to know why they were trying to catch the poor little cub anyhow, and our ranger explained that in the first place they wanted to give the cub back to its mother, and in the second place if a mother is captured and the cub isn't then the other bears kill the cub.

Maybe, I thought, man isn't the only species who isn't good to his own kind. I still had Zachary and his darned song lurking in the corners of my mind ready to spring at me. *What nature doesn't do to us will be done by our fellow man.*

Andy obviously wasn't thinking scary thoughts the way I was, but he must have been thinking along the same lines, at least about *life* and all, because he turned to me with a big, happy grin, and said, "This guy Santayana, I was reading him in school this year, he says, 'There is no cure for birth and death save to enjoy the interval.' I'm sure enjoying it. I hope it's going to be a good long one."

Suzy turned pleadingly to the ranger. "Then when you catch the cub what are you going to *do* with it?"

I could just imagine Suzy begging Daddy to let us take a bear cub home with us.

The ranger explained, "We band both the mother and the cub, and then we take them a hundred miles out into the wilderness. Most of them stay there and everything is fine. But if a banded bear—and these are the bears that are apt to be vicious around human beings—is seen in a campgrounds, then we have to destroy it."

"You mean you *shoot* it!" Suzy wailed.

"We have to, honey," the ranger said. "We've given it its chance, and we can't risk people being hurt. Look! They've got a couple of lassoes around the cub."

That diverted Suzy and we turned back to the cub hunt. It was really thrilling: the small group of us standing around in the moonlight with flashlights aimed at the cub as it ran up and down the tree; the rangers with their lassoes; the cub switching trees in desperation, and the ranger very quickly switching, too! And Andy holding my hand in a calm, protecting sort of way.

The cub would slide slowly almost all the way down the tree, nearly within reach of the lassoes, and then give a jerk of his head and shinny back up the tree, while everybody let out a sort of groany sigh. Poor little thing, you couldn't help feeling sorry for him because how could he know that the rangers were trying to put him back with his mother so the other bears wouldn't kill him?

People were beginning to drift back from the campfire program when the rangers finally got three lassoes around the cub. He fought, he snarled, he thrashed about ferociously, and I realized that I was clutching Andy's hand hard. The rangers held the cub off from them with poles, and finally managed to get a barrel over him, so they could then get him into their truck. There was a lot of wild growling, scuffling, shouting and then it was over.

Everybody relaxed, and I thought I ought to let go Andy's hand, now that the excitement was over. But he took my hand again very firmly and walked me back to the tent.

Nineteen

The next day we went to Andy's campsite in the Black Ram mountains. Don got out their map, and Steve took a red pencil and marked in the rather wind-ey, back-tracking course for us. Just as we were leaving Andy gave me a slip of paper with their address and telephone number on it.

"Now promise you'll call when you get to New York," he said. He turned to John, "Make your dumb-cluck of a sister call me, hunh?"

Suzy stuck her head out the car window, "*I'll* call you if she doesn't, Andy. I like you lots better than Zachary."

I almost belted her one.

We drove off, and, except for feeling mad at Suzy, I was all warm and sort of glowy over Yellowstone, in spite of the fact that nothing really had *hap*pened. But I had Andy's address and phone number in my pocket. And there was Zachary's poem. I had *two* unforgettable souvenirs of the trip if nothing else.

It was real western country all day, quite different, *again*, from anything we'd seen. There were great stretches of range, with barren, lava-like mountains rearing up on the horizon. Up, up, up, along the most curvy roads yet, if that's possible. More of the beautiful wild horses, and enormous herds of sheep, and well-fed cows and bulls. Up on the plateaus were lush, green fields, clear streams, evergreen trees, early *spring* wildflowers, and quite a lot of snow in the shady, protected corners. There were quite a few ranchers' chuck wagons, and the only people we passed were cowboys, real ones, and some of them Indians. I felt that Thornhill was a very small world to have spent so much of a life in. I wonder if we'll feel that way about our earth when we get into interplanetary travel?

We stopped about four thirty at Andy's campgrounds, and it was just as nice as he'd said it was. It was just a little green shelf below the mountain's crest, bordered on one side by the peak of the mountain, on the other by a stream that ran icy cold from melting snow. There was a riot of wild roses all in bloom and the grass was speckled with buttercups and daisies. When you were right out in the sun it was wonderful and hot, but the stream, swollen with melted snow, was much too cold for swimming. There was only one other tent there, and who did it turn out to be but the nice Greek professors and their wives from Glacier!

Then.

We hadn't even finished setting up camp when there came the familiar sound of a station wagon being driven too fast for the roads. And there was Zachary, this time with his parents. We hadn't actually *seen* his parents since that first night in Tennessee.

He parked the station wagon in the campsite next to ours,

got out, and demanded, "Who is this Andy?" I must have looked very startled, because he went on with elaborate patience, "This guy at *Yell*owstone. Andrew *Ford*."

Suzy bustled up to him and said, "Andy's *nice*. How'd you find out about him anyhow?"

I usually wished Suzy'd keep her nose out of my affairs, but she'd just asked a question I wanted to know the answer to and pride would have kept me from asking.

"How do you suppose I *found* you?" Zachary asked impatiently. "I was at Yellowstone last night and I didn't even *see* you. Why weren't you at the campfire program?"

"But how did you know we were *here*?" Suzy asked.

"I cooked up a very convincing story about having to get hold of my cousins because of family illness and this morning they let me look at the register so I knew you were there. So I went around *ask*ing people, for crying out loud, and these three boys said you'd been camped right by them, and they told me you were coming here, and that red-headed one seemed kind of annoyed that the others had told me."

"*Relax*, Zach," I said, much more calmly than I'd have been able to before I met Andy. "Suzy and I have to get the air-mattresses in the sleeping bags. Either help us or get out of the way."

"I'm going to help Pop." Zachary looked stormy. "I'll see you later, Vicky."

"He talks as though he *owned* you or something," Suzy said indignantly. "I like Andy much better."

"As Christopher Marlowe said, comparisons are odious. Hold the sleeping bag *straighter* so I can shove the air mattress *in*."

"Don't spray it, say it," Suzy said.

My heart was kind of thumping. I was glad to see Zachary

234

and I wished he hadn't come. I wanted to go on enjoying the relaxed feeling Andy had given me, but I was excited that Zachary
was still following me, that he'd gone to all that trouble, inventing
cousins, and all, and that he and Andy didn't seem too happy
about each other. I *mean*! Nobody in Thornhill had ever gone on
that way about me!

I pretended to be very calm, and as though nothing important had been happening, and helped Mother get dinner while
Zachary and his father went through the long rigamarole of lay-
ing the linoleum carpet and tying the plastic cover over their
tent. The Greek professors were bug-eyed.

We ate early, because we were all hungry, and when we
were through one of the Greek professors came over, eager as a
kid, to suggest we all play Hide-and-Seek. They even got
Zachary's mother and father to play and it was really a blast.

Once Rob was it and he'd found everybody except one of
the Greek professors and Zachary, and the rest of us were loung-
ing around, eating cookies and drinking ginger ale as a sort of
extra dessert. It was still sunny, though the sky was beginning to
get that golden look it does when it's just about to be evening.
Rob finally found the Greek professor way up a tree. As a matter
of fact he was stuck up there. We had to help him down and he
could hardly get down at all, he was laughing so hard.

After we got the professor down Rob kept on looking for
Zachary but he couldn't find him, and after a while he began to
get unhappy about it, so we all called, "Okay, Zach, you win, you
can come home free," but he didn't come, so we all started looking for him. I could see that John was annoyed, and I wished
Zachary would turn up.

After we'd all been looking for about half an hour I noticed that Mrs. Grey was getting a strained, anxious look, and I was beginning to feel worried, too. One trouble was that you didn't know just where to look. This was not a campgrounds with definite boundaries like the regular campgrounds, and nobody'd thought to set any limits to where you could hide. The logical places were all in the little plateau where we were camped. Up above there were pines, and the shadows were already deep in there. After the trees the mountain ended up with coarse, sharp grass, and finally just rocks on the very top. Below the camping plateau was the stream, and below that a big, green field, and then a long, thorny barbed wire fence.

Mrs. Grey came up to Mother. She was clasping her pudgy hands (how could Zachary be so *thin* with his parents so well fed?) and her eyes looked as though they were about to fill with tears.

"Mrs. Austin, I'm frightened," she said. "Zachary's so wild, you never know what he'll do next, and he hasn't been well lately, and he wouldn't go to a doctor. He has a heart condition, you know."

"I know," Mother said. She looked at me. "I wouldn't worry about him yet, Mrs. Grey. The whole point of hide-and-seek is to stay hidden as long as you possibly can."

"But the game's over," Mrs. Grey said. "He ought to realize it's over by now."

Mother sounded very calm. "Sometimes young people don't know when too much is enough." She put a hand on my shoulder. "Vicky's a prime example of that."

When Zachary hadn't turned up after another few minutes of looking and shouting for him, the Greek professors organized where everybody should look. John and I were to stay in camp

236

while Suzy and Rob got ready for bed and in case Zachary should come sauntering in. Everybody except the Greys was very annoyed; the Greys were worried; I was annoyed *and* worried.

After Suzy and Rob had washed up, were in their night clothes, and in the tent, reading (we knew it was no good telling them to go to sleep) John and I sat by the remains of the camp fire.

"It's just a kid's trick," John said disgustedly, "pulling a disappearing act like this."

I didn't answer. I sat there, looking from the embers to the rambler roses that would have been over long ago at home but here were just bursting into fullness and drifting their fragrance all around us. "The Greys are very worried," I said after a while.

"He worries them on purpose. He *likes* worrying them." John poked at the fire. "I hope this shows you, Vicky."

"Shows me what?"

"He isn't worth your getting all stewed up about."

I thought of Zachary. Then I thought of Andy. Then I thought of Zachary again. "Take his parents," I started.

"You take them."

"That's just the point. You wouldn't want them for parents."

"As far as I'm concerned he's a chip off the old block."

"He's a lot more than that. I mean, there's something there, John, something terrific, there really is."

"You're the only one who's seen any sign of it."

"You haven't given him any *chance* to show it. I've *talked* to him. You know how we feel about Mother and Daddy. How would it be if we *couldn't*? It would have an ef*fect* on us, wouldn't it?" I didn't tell John that Zachary knew his father made all that money in kind of shady ways. I didn't tell John Zachary's reasons for wanting to be a lawyer. I didn't believe Zachary's reasons. Because Zachary himself had told me not to. But John would believe them. "Suppose he's hurt himself?" I asked.

"He's not Rob's age. What could he do?"

"He could have fallen and broken his leg or something. Or he could have had a heart attack. I think that's what his mother's afraid of."

"Serve him right if he has."

"John, *please!*"

"I'm sorry, Vicky. I just don't like him. I don't like what he's done to you."

"It isn't Zachary. It's everything. It's *life*."

"Most people manage to face life without getting into a swivet."

"I'm *not* in a swivet." Then I said, "John, do you mind if I kind of go around and look for Zach?"

"What for? That's just what he wants."

"I don't think Zach gets what he wants very often."

"He gets it *all* the time. That's what's wrong with him."

"I don't mean that kind of thing," I said. "I mean the—the *real* things. I mean the kind of things we take for granted. And Andy and Don and Steve, too."

"All right," John said. "If you want to. Just don't *you* get lost. Stay within shouting distance, will you?"

"Okay."

I got up, but he stopped me. "Listen, Vicky."

"What?"

"One thing I hope you realize, speaking of Andy—"

"What?"

"I hope you realize that all during this trip you've had the male population at your feet. Everybody was too *used* to you in Thornhill."

"Yah. The whole male population. Big deal. Zachary. And I watched a geyser with Andy."

John gave me his very nicest grin, so that I forgave him for everything he'd said before. "I mean what I say. The whole male population. That's what I allege," he said, going into a family joke.

"So? That's what you allege?"

"Yeah, that's what I allege."

"You make these allegations?"

"I'm the alligator."

"See you later, alligator."

"In a while, crocodile."

"Olive oil."

"Abysinnia. Get lost!"

I waved at John and set off.

Suzy loves the dark and it doesn't bother me. I don't have a dark phobia like my acrophobia or anything. But by now it was awfully dark in the pines, and I had to go through the pines to get to the mountain top. For some reason I had a feeling that Zachary would have climbed up to the top of the mountain to hide, if only because it was the worst possible thing for him to do. I knew that Daddy had gone up and yelled from the mountain top, but I also knew that Zachary mightn't have answered if the yeller was Daddy.

I didn't much care for it in the woods. It wasn't the trees or the deepening shadows I was afraid of, but bears, after all the bears in Yellowstone. I remembered that Don had told us that this wasn't supposed to be bear territory, and I tried to stop my heart from thumping each time I saw a shadow and thought it was a bear. Luckily I was so worried about bears that I didn't even think about snakes. I'm not sure I wouldn't rather see a bear than a snake, even though Suzy has told me over and over again that snakes won't bother you unless you bother them first.

I got out of the trees without being attacked by bears and started up to the crest of the mountain. It was so high that the sun was still golden on the coarse grass, and the rocks were warm to touch, though it would be completely night by now down in the valleys. Whenever I saw a big rock I looked behind it, but I didn't see Zachary.

As I neared the top of the mountain I began to yell, "Zachary! Zach! Come on, the game's over, everybody's worried, it isn't funny any more. Come on, Zach, don't be a dope!"

By now I was panting and tired and my stomach was churning with worry. I was sure Zachary'd capsized somewhere. If he'd climbed up here it would be enough to give him a heart attack.

Suddenly I thought I heard something, as though a voice far away were calling, "Vicky!"

I scrambled up to the crest of the mountain and stood there, calling and looking. My stomach gave an awful jerk as I looked down, because it was much steeper on the far side, and I felt acrophobia-ey. I closed my eyes for a minute, and then opened them carefully. The sun was sinking, way below me. I turned around so I wouldn't have to look down the steep side of the mountain, and the tents were still bathed in light. I seemed to be standing on a mountain peak way above the sun, and yet with the sun's light still streaking across the rocks and grass, at the same time that shadows were deepening and stretching out everywhere. I suppose light must be something like this in Alaska, or Norway, at the times when the sun doesn't set at all. Only this sun was setting swiftly, and I wanted to hurry back down to camp, with or without Zachary. Our tent roof was golden with sun, and then suddenly it was in shadow. I knew that John would be furious with me if I didn't get back before dark.

But just as I was ready to start down for the camp I heard it again, behind me, down the other side of the mountain. "Vicky!"

I shouted. "Zachary! Where are you?"

Silence.

I was sure that I hadn't been mistaken, that I'd heard him calling me, and that it wasn't John or anybody from camp calling me to say that Zach had been found, because their voices would have come from the opposite direction.

I turned around. The shadows were deepening again, and as I looked down the rocky mountain I felt a surge of acrophobia.

"Vicky!" The voice sounded lost, and far away, and hurt, and I knew that I would have to control my acrophobia and climb down. Of course what I should have done was to go back to camp and get Daddy. What earthly use would *I* be if Zachary'd had a heart attack or broken a leg? But I was so busy trying not to feel sick at my stomach, and so terrified of climbing down the mountain side, that I never thought of the logical thing. I gritted my teeth and started down, mostly backwards. Actually, backwards it wasn't too bad, because I didn't have to look down, even though I seemed to slip and slide a lot. It was getting darker every minute, but it wasn't that quick darkness that seems to come with a bang, and I was grateful; now, instead of being golden, everything was a soft grey.

"Vicky!"

"Hold on, Zach!" I shouted. "I'm coming!"

Not too far below me was a field, much bigger than the one where the camp was, and across the field a huge mound of rocks, and it was from these rocks that the voice seemed to be coming. I reached the field and started to run across it to the rocks. "I'm coming, Zach!" I called.

And then he came strolling out from behind the rocks, cool as a cucumber. "About time," he said.

I was *furious*. I didn't know I *could* be so furious at Zachary. "What do you *mean*!" I shouted. "Everybody's been *look*ing for you! Your poor mother is *fran*tic! What do you mean, just *sit*ting down here!"

"Well, hey, hold it!" Zachary said. "How'd I know everybody was looking for me?"

"Didn't you hear us *yell*ing? Daddy went up to the top of the mountain and yelled. You *must* have heard him."

"Sure I heard him," Zachary said, "but you were the one I was waiting for."

"You were so sure I'd come?"

"I figured if I waited long enough you'd appear."

"So you just *sat* and let your mother get scared out of her wits?"

"What's all this worry about my *mother*? She ought to know by now not to have fits. She never knows when I'm coming back at home and it never seems to bother her. Why all this parental agony all of a sudden?"

"Because she *loves* you," I said. "Because she thought you had a *heart* attack or something. Well, I'm going back to camp. You can come along if you feel like it."

"No, you don't," Zachary said. "Why do you think I waited down here all this time? I want to talk to you about this Andy."

He made a grab for me, but I jumped out of his way. "Good-bye," I said, and started across the field to the mountain. Out of the corner of my eye I saw Zachary shrug and go back to the rock pile.

Then the ground wiggled under my feet.

It was a most peculiar feeling. The solid ground under my feet gave a shudder. I stood still. It kept on feeling as though the ground were shivering. Then suddenly there was a jerk under me. It was something like when you go water skiing and some-one cuts the motor and then suddenly speeds up again, trying to throw you.

The next jerk did throw me. It was a much bigger jerk, and I fell flat on my face in the soft grass of the field. Underneath me the ground seemed to heave the way your stomach does when you're terribly, terribly sick. I clung to the grass because there wasn't anything else to cling to. It was as though the whole earth, the whole planet, were jerking out in space, veering wildly out of course, and I was on its back, clinging to its mane.

Behind me there was a terrible noise. It was louder than thunder and it seemed to keep on and on until I thought my head would burst. Then the noise began to break into separate parts, a sound like thunder, a roar like the ocean in a storm, great crack-ings, crunchings, and finally all the noises got smaller and with spaces of quiet in between, and then they stopped. The silence was so complete that it was as frightening as the noise had been.

I managed to turn my head, and the top of the mountain wasn't there any more. It didn't seem to be anywhere.

Then I remembered the town of Frank in Alberta, the mountain that had fallen on the town. I pressed my face into the grass of the field, and, as the earth heaved beneath me, I thought I was going to throw up, too, from terror. But I didn't.

I looked around again. The top of the mountain was still gone. Everything looked different. I realized that most of the mountain had fallen into the field, because the mountain was much closer to me, the field was much narrower, than it had been before.

I lay there, clutching the grass, not daring or even able to move, even if the rest of the mountain should fall on me. But after a while I realized that the tremors were less violent, that the earth was becoming quiet again. I staggered to my feet. The ground seemed quite solid beneath them. I looked for Zachary. The pile of rock was still there, but it was a different shaped pile. I didn't see Zachary.

I simply accepted the fact that he was dead, that he was buried under the rocks. I didn't want to scream or anything. All I felt was a terrible, resigned calm, as though something in me were dead, too.

"Vicky!"

It was Zachary's voice. It was quite strong, and it was coming from the rocks. I ran across the rest of the field. Now the dark was on top of me. I couldn't see anything except rocks and shadows of rocks. "Zach, where are you?" I wasn't sure whether the heaving came from me, my chest racked with gasps, my heart pounding, or whether the earth was still shaking. I thought it was mostly me.

Zachary's voice came from inside the pile of rocks. "Vicky! Here!"

I couldn't see him, but I could hear his voice, coming from somewhere inside the rocks. "Are you hurt?" I called.

"I don't think so. How about you?"

"I'm okay." I kept looking for the voice, and finally, in the darkness, I saw two great rocks leaning together, with a space about a foot wide at the bottom. I got down on my hands and knees and tried to peer in.

Zachary's voice came from the darkness. "Here, Vic."

"Are you all right? Are you sure you aren't hurt?"

"I'm all right. But I don't think I can get out."

I tried to keep my voice from shaking. "What happened?"

"Must have been an earthquake. I got whammed down to my knees, and then two rocks shifted and fell against each other, and I'm in a sort of small cave, trapped, but good."

I pushed and shoved at the rocks, but they were huge ones and they wouldn't budge.

"It's no use, Vicky," Zachary said. "Don't exhaust yourself. You might as well try to move the mountain."

I shivered. The mountain. "Are you sure this is the only hole?"

"No, there's some sky above me. I can see a star. But it's too high. There isn't any place I can get a toe hold to try to climb up. I tried until I got a pain."

I stood very still there by the pile of rocks with Zachary nothing but a voice in the darkness. He sounded a great deal braver than I felt.

"I never thought I'd die this way," Zachary said. "I always planned to have a certain amount of control over it. Are you *sure* you're okay?"

"Yes. Zach, what'll we do?"

"You'd better go back and get the others. Maybe they can get me out."

"Zach," I said. "The mountain. It fell."

Zach's voice sounded too reasonable for comfort. "Yeah, I figured something like that must have happened from the noise. How about the campgrounds?"

"I don't know."

"Vicky," Zachary said quietly. "Did the mountain fall on this side?"

"A lot of it did."

"Then they're probably okay."

I didn't answer.

"Listen, Vicky," he said after a while. "I'm stuck in here. There's not a thing I can do to get out. I tried. I've still got a pain. I don't dare try anymore and I don't think it would do any good anyhow. You've got to go back. I'm sorry, darling, but you've got to try." His voice was gentle.

"I don't want to leave you."

"I'm all right. There's nothing you can do by staying here, and your parents must be having fits about you."

My voice almost went out of control. "If they're okay."

"If the mountain fell on this side they're okay."

My voice galloped towards hysteria. "When I climbed the mountain to look for you only John and the little kids were in camp. The grown-ups were all out looking for *you*. I don't know where anybody *is*."

"All you can do is go look for them. Vicky, you have to try."

I knew he was right. "All right."

"Have you got your flashlight?"

246

"No. It was still light enough when I left." I looked up at the sky. "There's going to be starlight, anyhow." My voice was back in control.

"It's full moon time," Zachary said. "That'll be up later. Can you see your watch?"

I tried to squinch my eyes so I could read my watch, but it hasn't an illuminated dial, and I couldn't see it. Zachary has a very elaborate watch, so I asked, "Can't you see yours?"

"It seems to have been broken in the sturm und drang," Zachary said. "It's probably about nine. Not that it really makes much difference at this point."

I looked up at the sky. It wasn't completely dark around the edges. There were green bands of light stretching across the horizon. Up above it was night, with more and more stars coming out every minute.

"Vicky. Go on," Zachary said.

"All right." I stood there by the rock pile without moving. Then, "I'm off."

I started to walk across the field. Every step I took I expected it to start jerking under my feet again, but it didn't. It was solid and very slightly springy, the way a field ought to be. I tried not to think about the top of the mountain that wasn't there. Most of it did seem to have fallen on Zachary's and my side, because the field was less than half the size it had been, and if I'd been further away from Zachary's rock pile when the earthquake started I might have been under the mountain just like the people in Frank. Zachary would have blamed himself, and if Andy ever heard about it I thought he'd be sorry. I kept thinking about things I knew *hadn't* happened, so I wouldn't have

247

to think about the possibility that all the mountain hadn't fallen on our side, that some of it might have fallen on the campgrounds, that the tents might be hidden under rocks like the town of Frank. I couldn't think about this and keep on going.

Soon I came to little bits of gravelly stuff, and then little bits of rock, and then bigger pieces of rock, and then I was climbing over boulders, and it was all still in the field. I hadn't even reached the mountain or started to climb upwards. Every once in a while I would look back over my shoulder to Zachary's pile of rocks looming up black against the night sky, to keep my bearings.

I'd been at least half an hour and had gone what seemed a long way before I realized that I wasn't going to be able to get up the mountain. In the starlight I could dimly make out a sheer wall of stone in front of me. Uprooted trees seemed to stick out of it here and there, but there weren't enough of them, and they weren't low enough, to be of any help in climbing up. I stood and called and called and called.

"Mother! Daddy! John! Suzy! Rob! Oh, everybody, help, please help! Mother! Daddy!"

I called and called and no one answered. I realized that one of us would have to be up on top of the mountain for the other to hear, that what was left of the mountain was between us and would cut off the sounds of voices, but I kept on calling till I was hoarse.

At last there wasn't anything to do but turn around and head slowly back across the rocks to the field. The field had become drenched in dew in the time I'd spent climbing over rocks. A couple of times I fell in the darkness, but all I did was scratch and bump myself a little. I wanted very much to cry, and at the same time I was too frightened and unhappy to cry. This was beyond tears. It was something that couldn't possibly happen to the Vicky Austin who'd grown up in Thornhill, Connecticut, and who was now on a nice, leisurely camping trip with her family.

But it had happened.

I wondered if it would be on the newscasts, and if Uncle Douglas would hear about it in Laguna, and if he'd wonder if we were anywhere near where the earthquake was. I wanted Uncle Douglas.

I got back within communicating distance of Zachary and called, "I'm back."

"Did you find them?"

I leaned against one of the rocks. "No, Zach. The earthquake kind of messed up the mountainside. I couldn't climb back up."

"I wish I could have a shot at it," Zachary said.

"For heaven's sake," I cried irritably. "A whole hunk of mountain fell off into the field. There's a wall of stone I couldn't climb up even in daylight unless I were a fly."

"Vicky, I'm sorry," Zachary said. "I keep getting you into messes."

I still leaned against the rock as though I couldn't possibly stand up by myself. I'm not sure I could. "Stop blaming yourself. What good does it do?"

"None. I just thought you might like to know that I'm sorry. I don't apologize easily."

"So what're we going to do?" I asked.

"Wait until morning. Then maybe someone will come to look for us. Or maybe when you can see better you'll see a way up."

Night had completely fallen now, and the sky was crusted with stars. There were as many stars as there are at home on a cold, frosty winter night. Looking at the stars I realized that I was cold. I didn't have anything on but Bermudas and a shirt, and the night air cut against me like ice.

Zachary said, "Hey, Vicky, have you got on a sweater?"

"Nope."

There was a sound of movement from inside the rocks, and a kind of sharp grunt, as though he'd hurt himself, and then I could see something being shoved out the small hole at the bottom of the rocks. "Here."

"What's that?"

"My jacket. Put it on. I'm protected in here. I don't need it."

"I don't either."

"Put it *on*, I said."

After a minute I reached for the jacket and slid into it. The leather felt cool, but the lining was comfortable with Zachary's body warmth. I buttoned it up tight. Then I sat down and leaned against one of the rocks. It was still faintly warm from the sun, but I knew it wouldn't stay warm all night, and I didn't trust rock any more. I leaned against it, but I couldn't relax. My back was tense, waiting to feel the rock shake underneath me. I thought I'd probably be safer lying out on the dew in what was left of the field in case another earthquake came. But I stayed where I was.

"Hey, Vicky," Zachary called.

"What?"

"Ever read much science fiction?"

"Sure. Why?"

"Suppose it wasn't just an earthquake? Suppose we're the only people left on earth?"

"At this point your sense of humor doesn't amuse me."

"I wasn't trying to be amusing. It's barely possible, you know."

"We're in enough trouble with an earthquake without making up extra trouble. But——"

"But what?"

I clamped my jaw shut. "Nothing."

"But that's a habit of mine. Making up trouble. That's what you mean, isn't it?"

I didn't answer and there was silence from the dark hole out of which Zachary's voice had come. I kept on leaning against the rock. Above me more and more stars came out, filling the sky. Inside the rocks Zachary shifted position.

"Hey, Vicky."

"*What?*"

"This Andy——"

"What about him?"

"Do you like him better than you do me?"

"I only *met* him day before yesterday." Day before yesterday? It must have been longer ago than that. It was longer than years ago. It was outside time ago. The earthquake had split time in two as well as the mountain.

"Do you like him?"

"Yes. I like him."

"Much?"

"I told you I only met him."

"I don't want you to see him again."

"What's it to you? We're not going steady or anything."

"I just don't want you to see him again."

"Doesn't seem likely at the moment, does it? I'm tired, Zach. I don't want to talk any more. I want to sleep."

When Zachary didn't say anything else the hole in the rock seemed to get darker and smaller. I didn't like it. But I didn't want Zachary talking Andy at me. Or science fiction.

"Sleepy?" he asked after a while.

"Nope."

He began whistling. That stinking song. But this wasn't anything our fellow man had done to us. This was plain old nature. Unless he was right with that science fiction stuff about our being the only people left alive. No. That was nuts. There hadn't been a violent light or a mushroom cloud. *That* idea was Zachary making up trouble, like thinking he was dying of the Black Plague before he ever *got* it. He kept on whistling.

"Shut up," I said.

"What d'you want me to do? Sing a hymn? Recite a prayer?"

I didn't answer.

Silence.

Every once in a while Zachary would stir, as though he couldn't get into a comfortable position. I couldn't tell just how much room he had in his cave.

Then, over the mutilated remains of the mountain I saw a glimmer of light, and my heart leaped within me. It was a search party! It was Mother and Daddy and John, or even the Greek professors, it didn't matter, we were found!

But it was the moon.

It came up, a great, almost round golden ball, suddenly seeming to shoot up over the broken crest of the mountain into the sky. All the shadows became stronger and darker, and yet I could see everything more clearly. I looked at my watch, and the moon's light was so bright I could read it. Not eleven o'clock.

A terribly, terribly long time till morning. I sat there with my back against the cooling rock, listening, listening.

Inside the cave small, uncomfortable shiftings from Zachary. Outside all the usual sounds, the insects chirping happily as though nothing had happened, as though the earth hadn't had a terrifying convulsion, as though the mountain hadn't fallen.

Zachary's voice came softly, "Vicky?"

"What?"

"Are you asleep?"

"Yes."

For a while he took the hint. Then he said, "What're you doing? Saying prayers or something?"

"*No.*"

"Why don't you, then?"

I didn't say anything.

"Why don't you ask your God to get us out of this? The way he got Anne Frank out of all *her* troubles?"

"Anne Frank doesn't have anything to do with it."

"Why not?"

"That was *people*. This was an *earth*quake."

"So what's the difference in the long run? I told you life wasn't going to go on being all easy and cozy for you."

"I never said it was."

"But you thought God would get you out of any hole you got in, just like your mother and father, didn't you? So why doesn't he get you out of this?"

"I haven't asked Him."

"Go ahead and *ask* Him, then. And see what happens. Go

253

ahead like that family in Anne Frank, always saying psalms. I *will lift up mine eyes unto the hills,* or whatever it is."

"Shut up," I said.

There was no longer any help from the hills. There hadn't been ever since I met Zachary. Now the hill had fallen. And even if our help came from the Lord, not from the hills, what about the town of Frank? What about all those people sleeping there innocently and unaware and suddenly the mountain fell on them? What *about* the town of Frank? What *about* Anne Frank?

"Whyn't you go ahead and say a psalm or something?" Zachary sounded very nasty. "It'll make you feel better."

I stood up. I sounded just as nasty as Zachary. "So you want me to say a psalm, I'll say one." I turned my back on the pile of rocks and cried at what was left of the mountain.

> *"I will lift up mine eyes unto the hills*
> *From whence cometh my help.*
> *My help cometh from the Lord*
> *Which made heaven and earth.*

I stopped. "Very pretty," Zachary growled. "Go on."

> *"He will not suffer thy foot to be moved,*

I went on,

> *"He that keepeth thee will not slumber.*
> *Behold, he that keepeth Israel*
> *Shall neither slumber nor sleep.*

I stopped again. Why didn't He wake up, if He was? Why did Anne Frank die in a concentration camp after her mother had said those words, after her mother had cried out those words? Why did the people of Frank die when the mountain without any warning, fell? Why were Zachary and I here? Where was God? Didn't God have any warning? Couldn't He have stopped it?

"Go on," Zachary said.

"The Lord is thy keeper,"

I cried,

> *"The Lord is thy shade upon thy right hand.*
> *The sun shall not smite thee by day,*
> *Nor the moon by night."*

But the moon was smiting us. Its light, cold and impersonal, was splashing me, so that I shivered, and the Lord was doing nothing about it.

Uncle Douglas! You believe in God! Where is He?

I raised my head to the sky and the icy moon and the distant impersonal stars, and I called out,

> *"The Lord shall preserve thee from all evil;*
> *He shall preserve thy soul.*
> *The Lord shall preserve thy going out and thy coming in*
> *From this time forth, and even forevermore."*

Then I began to cry. I cried loudly, because I hated Zachary, and I hated God. I cried and I cried and Zachary didn't say a word.

Finally I stopped crying. Zachary was still silent. The moonlight was still smiting us. The insects were still singing merrily. I reached in the pocket of Zachary's leather jacket but there wasn't anything to blow my nose on.

My anger was all gone. I got down on my hands and knees in front of the dark hole that was the entrance to Zachary's cave, but I couldn't see anything inside except further darkness.

"Vicky?" Zachary's voice came very soft, very gentle.

I made a small sort of noise in response so he'd know I'd heard. After all my shouting it was all I could get out.

"Vicky. I want to live."

When the earthquake came the ground beneath me had seemed to tremble and heave. Now everything was very still.

"So help me," Zachary said, "if I ever get out of here I'll go to the doctors and I'll do what they say. Maybe it takes an earthquake and you yelling your fool head off to make me know. . . . Hey, Vicky. . . . You still right there?"

"I'm still right here."

"Reach in if you feel like holding my hand, hunh?"

In a moment I felt his fingers around mine. Strong. I didn't understand anything. I didn't understand why Zachary wanted to live. I knew I was glad. But I didn't understand.

I remembered Uncle Douglas saying that we're always yelling, *Do it MY way, God, not YOUR way, MY way.*

Sometimes He picks most peculiar ways.

I looked up at the sky and at the stars and at the moon, and the moon was no longer smiting me. I didn't know why. I didn't know what the difference was. I didn't understand the psalm any better now, and I still didn't understand about Anne Frank and the town of Frank, and I'd probably go right on yelling at God to do it my way when I got upset about things.

The point was that now I knew it didn't matter whether or not I understood. It didn't matter because even if I didn't understand, there was something there to *be understood*.

That's all. That's all I can say. It didn't really have anything to do with Zachary. It didn't really have anything to do with the earthquake.

Still holding Zachary's hand I got off my knees in front of his hole and lay down. I closed my eyes and I went right to sleep.

I couldn't have been asleep more than a few minutes when I heard a noise. I opened my eyes quickly and looked at the mountain. I looked at the mountain and I saw a light, and I thought, —it's just the moon, rising.

Then I remembered that the moon had risen, that it was shining high and bright in the sky.

In one quick movement I was on my feet, shouting.

"What is it?" Zachary asked.

"Vicky! Vicky! Vicky!"

It wasn't one voice, it was several voices. I recognized Daddy's voice, I recognized John's voice.

"Here!" I shouted back. "HERE!" I stood up and leaped up and down and waved my arms.

"*Go*," Zachary urged from his dark hole. "Go *to* them."

Now there were more lights hovering at the edge of what was now the top of the mountain. I ran stumbling across the field. "HERE!" I shouted again. "Zachary and I are here!"

"Can you hear me?" a voice cried. "We'll lower someone down in a minute. Wait!"

"I can hear!" I called back. "I can hear! I'll wait!"

I ran back and told Zachary. Then I ran across the field again and started climbing over the rocks. I could see the shadows of two people slithering down the mountain side. I think they were on ropes. Then one of them dropped to the ground and I could see that it was Daddy and we scrabbled across rocks to get to each other and then I was in his arms, hugging him and clinging to him and crying like a baby.

"Is everybody all right?" I asked, pressing my face against the roughness of his sweater. "Did the mountain fall on you?"

"Everybody's fine," Daddy said. "It all fell on your side. Oh, Vicky. Vicky." The other shadow came over the rocks to us. It was a ranger. "Where's Zachary?" Daddy asked.

I pointed to the mound of rocks. "In there. He's trapped in a sort of cave."

We went hurrying across the field, calling out to Zachary. He called back once, to tell Daddy and the ranger he was okay. Then he was silent.

When we got to the rock pile I got down on my hands and knees in front of the hole again. "Zach. Daddy and a ranger are here. They'll get you out."

It took about half an hour, but they did it with ropes, through the hole in the top. What Zachary hadn't told me was that when his watch was broken his wrist was broken, too. He never said anything about it, all that time there in darkness and in pain.

When they got him out his face was very tight and strained, and Daddy had him lie down on the grass. I could see that Daddy was taking his pulse as Zachary asked, "Everybody really okay?"

"Everybody's fine," Daddy answered. "The tent pegs weren't

even uprooted. There's a good fire going and enough hot choco-late and coffee as though we expected a returning army. We'll get you to the hospital and get that wrist fixed up. And we'll check on a few other things at the same time."

"Yes," Zachary said. "Anything you say, sir. I'm sorry to have caused so much trouble."

The men managed to get Zachary up the mountain with ropes and blankets. Then they came back for me, and I did pretty well by myself with the rope, and Daddy and the ranger telling me just what to do.

At the camp the fire was blazing so brightly that it lit up the whole area, but it wasn't half as bright or as warm as my wel-come. I was surrounded by everybody all talking and laughing at the same moment, Suzy and Rob tumbling over each other to hug me, John thumping me on the back, the professors pumping my hand, and Mother waiting a little on the outskirts until things had calmed down and then holding me in her arms, tight, tight, and just murmuring "Vicky. Vicky." We were both crying and we didn't even know it. At least I didn't.

Zachary was lying on a cot in his tent, drinking coffee, while Mrs. Grey fluttered about, crying, and Mr. Grey tried to calm her down, and Zachary kept telling them both to get out, he didn't want anybody near him but Daddy. Mother and the pro-fessors' wives must have used up every piece of bread everybody had, because there was a whole enormous pile of sandwiches on our picnic table, and Rob insisted on leading me over there as though I were an infant and poking bites of sandwich into my mouth. Then he went into the tent and got Elephant's Child and wound him up and put him in my lap. I sat there, leaning against

Mother, still too excited to be tired, and so happy that it took me a while to realize that I was drinking out of two cups, one hot chocolate and the other coffee. Mother's arm was firmly around me and everybody else was hovering and I relaxed into comfort and love.

Then Daddy called, "Come here, Vicky. We're going to take Zach down to the hospital now."

I went back to the Greys' elegant tent and stood looking down at Zachary.

He was very white, almost grey, and he spoke as though he were so tired he could hardly shape the words. "Just want to tell you I meant what I said, Vicky. Be seeing you."

Then they lifted him into the ranger's truck, Daddy got in beside him, and they drove off, the Greys following in their station wagon.

The rest of us sat around the fire and ate, and, just the way it did on the beach the evening Uncle Douglas and Aunt Elena got married, food seemed to put everything back into perspective again. One of the professors recited "Jabberwocky" in Greek and got us all laughing, and then Mother insisted that we all get some sleep for what was left of the night.

Even though it was so late Mother read to us, I think mostly to get us calmed down enough to go to sleep. It worked with the little ones, but after we'd said prayers and Mother had turned out the lantern I felt very wide awake, happy, but not a bit sleepy. When I did start to get sleepy I'd drift into a dream of being down on the other side of the fallen mountain again and that would jerk me into being awake. I whispered, "Mother?"

"Yes, darling?"

I crawled out of my sleeping bag and climbed down off the tailgate of the car and sat on the double sleeping bag by her.

"Lie down," she said. "Daddy won't be back for a while."

So I lay down and held Mother's hand, the way I used to do after a nightmare when I was Rob's age, and then I was able to fall into a quiet, lovely sleep.

Twenty

When I opened my eyes I could tell that the sun was quite high, and I'd waked up only because I heard the sound of a car coming up the hill to the campgrounds. I thought it was Daddy coming back from the hospital, and I went sleepily to the door of the tent, my hair a mess, my face all twisted up in a yawn.

But it wasn't the ranger's truck with Daddy, it was a beat up old car with Don at the wheel, and Steve and Andy leaning anxiously out the windows.

Then there was excited hellos all around with everybody hugging as though we'd known each other forever, and Andy had his arm about my waist and we were waltzing around the picnic table and the fireplace.

Well. You probably read about the earthquake in the newspapers. It hit mostly Wyoming and Montana, and because the worst of it was in the wilderness not many people were hurt. Yellowstone had quite a bit of it, and from what Andy, Don, and

Steve told us I was just as glad we were where we were instead of Yellowstone. Quite a few geysers stopped spouting, and new ones sprang up where there hadn't been geysers before, but it wasn't so much the geysers that worried me as the idea of the bears. I'm sure those bears who lived right by our campsite must have been very much upset by the earthquake, and I wouldn't have wanted a bear trying to get into the sleeping bag with me for comfort.

Andy hadn't been worrying about bears or geysers, though. They'd heard that the Black Ram section of Wyoming had been hard hit by the earthquake, and Andy felt he was responsible for our being there, so, the first minute they could, they set off to see if we were all right.

I've never felt so protected. Or so happy. It was a peak of happiness I don't suppose I'll ever reach again.

We all got dressed and made a communal breakfast. The bread had been used up the night before, but we had pancakes, dozens and dozens of pancakes. You should see Andy eat pancakes!

"What about this weird-o who came looking for you yesterday?" Andy asked, his mouth full.

So then we told him about how Zachary and I were on the other side of the mountain when it fell, and Zachary getting trapped in the cave and all, and Andy said, just about the way Zachary had said it, "I don't want you to see him again."

We were finishing up when Daddy and the ranger came back, so we made some more pancakes for them. Zachary's wrist had been operated on and was in a cast. His heart had stood the operation and he was getting along all right. They were going to keep him in the hospital and give him a lot more tests he should have had long ago and had refused to have, and Daddy thought that if he really took care of himself the way he'd promised he'd be okay. He'd never be able to climb the Himalayas, but he could live a perfectly normal life.

We all, the Fords, the Greek professors and their wives, and us Austins, decided to spend at least another night right where we were. Everybody was exhausted and felt the need to recover from the events of the night before, and Daddy seemed to think that I particularly needed to recover, but, except for feeling a bit achey, and discovering scratches all over my arms and legs, I'd never felt so wonderful in my life. I took a long, deep nap in the afternoon, and in the evening Andy drove me to the hospital to see Zachary.

I sat beside Andy in the car and we didn't talk. It was the kind of silence I had with Andy, warm and complete in itself. As we got to the hospital Andy said, "I'll go in with you for just a minute, and then I'll leave you alone with that clunk. But don't stay long. Your father said only five minutes, anyhow."

"He isn't a clunk, Andy," I said.

We walked down a long, quiet corridor to Zachary's room. He was lying flat in the bed, his eyes closed, his face as white as the bedclothes. I knocked gently on the door and his eyes flew open and he smiled.

"Vicky!" And then, to Andy, "Oh. Hi."

"Hi," Andy said. "How you doing?"

"Fine," Zachary said. "Wind that crank at the bottom of the bed, will you, please, so I can sit up?"

Andy cranked him up, and then the two of them sort of looked at each other, Zachary all white and black like a moonlight night, with his pale skin and dark hair and fringed eyes, and Andy like a summer morning, with his brilliant red hair and blue eyes. Zachary and Andy looked at each other, and I looked at them, and I could just hear Mother saying, "As John Donne says, Comparisons are odious," and suddenly my heart lifted because it was absolutely true. There wasn't any need of comparisons.

Zachary picked up the newspaper that was lying on the bed as though he'd been reading it before he got tired. "What's black and white and red all over?"

"A newspaper," Andy answered disgustedly.

"Nah," Zachary said. "An embarrassed zebra." He closed his eyes, then opened them again. "That's me, Vicky-O. I'm very embarrassed about all this."

"There's nothing to be embarrassed about," I said uncomfortably.

Andy tapped me on the arm. "I'll wait downstairs, Vicky. Take it easy, Zach."

Zachary waited until the sound of Andy's footsteps had diminished down the corridor. Then he said, "What, for cripes sakes, is *he* doing here?"

I'd forgotten that Zachary wouldn't know that the Ford boys had come to look for us, so I explained. "After all," I ended up, "Andy blamed himself because we'd *gone* to the Black Ram campsite."

"It was just an excuse," Zachary said, "to go chasing after you all over the countryside, and that's *my* business. Where's he live in the winter?"

"New York."

Zachary let out a yowl, a loud one, and I heard footsteps

hurrying down the corridor, and a nurse stuck her head in the door. "What's going on in here?"

"Somebody's trying to steal my girl," Zachary said.

"Is waking up the entire place going to keep her?" Then she smiled at Zachary. "I admit she's probably worth howling about, but no more tonight, huh? You're supposed to be keeping quiet." She cranked him down briskly. "I'll give you two kids three more minutes, then I've got to put baby to bed. Be good now."

"Vicky," Zachary said. "I'm going to do exactly that. Be good. I promised. And I'm going to keep my promise. . . . Vicky. About last night. I'm sorry." He reached out gropingly with his good hand and I took it in mine.

"It wasn't your fault. You didn't start the earthquake or anything."

"Yes, but if I hadn't lured you over the mountain top you'd have been safely in the campgrounds with your family. And so would I."

I looked at him carefully. His words had come out with an effort. As he'd said, apologies didn't come easy to Zachary. "The whole thing," I said, "is if you really mean it about taking care of yourself and not trying to dig yourself an early grave any more. If you really mean it, then none of the rest of it mattered. I'm glad it happened."

"For some reason I really mean it," Zachary said. "So help me I can't tell you why, but I mean it. I think it's something of you rubbed off on me. Hey, you're all scratched up. Was that last night, climbing over rocks and stuff?"

I nodded. Then I said, "Zach, there's something I have to tell you."

266

"What now?"

"I'm—I'm not quite sixteen."

"You mean you're only fifteen?"

"Well—not quite."

"Only *four*teen, for crying out loud?"

I nodded.

He reached out with his good hand and for a moment I thought he was going to hit me, but he only took my hand in his and pressed it. "You're quite a kid," he said softly. Then, "Vicky, in this bed table thing here. There's a piece of paper and a pencil. Now write me down where you're going to get mail next. Okay. Now we're going to keep in touch, see? Promise?"

"I promise." I leaned over and kissed him on the forehead. *I* did it. I kissed a boy myself and I didn't even feel funny about it. It wasn't like Zachary kissing *me*, or anything. It wasn't exciting or disturbing. It just meant we were going to go on being friends.

That's really all.

That's really all that happened that summer.

Andy took me back to camp and the next day we headed for home. Andy was full of plans for seeing me in New York, and before we left he must have handed me at least ten slips of paper with his address and phone number. It looked as though it was going to be a busy winter.

As we drove away from Black Ram Suzy said, "I like Andy *lots* better than I like Zachary. I'm glad it's Andy who lives in New York."

All I said was, "As John Fortescue said, compari—"

"Oh, shut up, Vicky," Suzy said.

I'm not going to tell about the trip home. It was beautifully uneventful. We loved going to a real, working cowboy's rodeo in Sheridan, Wyoming; we loved the ships going through the locks at Sault San' Marie; and the Retreat at the big fort in Quebec. But nothing exciting happened. We'd had more than enough excitement for one trip.

After Quebec we went right to the Island where we kids were to stay with Grandfather while Mother and Daddy found a place for us in New York.

It was wonderful to see Grandfather again, with his white hair blowing in the ocean breeze, and his face all lit up from inside with pleasure at seeing us all. We hadn't been in the stable for five minutes before Mother had the *Fifth Brandenburg Concerto* going on the phonograph; Daddy was going over the mail, which Grandfather had been holding for us; yes, I had letters from both Zachary and Andy, and I put them in my pocket to take down to the beach where I could sit on my rock and read them in peace ("I suppose you realize, Vicky," Daddy'd said as he handed me the letters, "that you now know boys from A to Z?" No, I hadn't realized it. It was quite a thought!). Suzy danced up and down and asked if she could make a milkshake, and if Mother would bake an apple pie for dinner (it was almost six o'clock); Rob and John went up to the loft and got into their trunks so they could have a dip before dinner; the phone rang, long distance for Daddy from New York; Mother was collecting all our dirty laundry to take to the laundromat in the morning, and then she got a steak out of Grandfather's freezer to celebrate; and we all went around turning on lights and trying all the electrical equipment just the way we used to do in Thornhill after an ice storm had broken lines and caused a power failure.

This was even more fun because we'd been so long in the wilderness. Suzy said, "Mother, why do you keep looking in the refrigerator and at the stove?"

Mother said, "Want to build a fire on the beach for dinner tonight, Suzy?"

"Sure," Suzy said enthusiastically, and couldn't understand why everybody jumped on her.

Daddy called in for everybody to be quiet, he couldn't hear on the telephone.

We tried our best to calm down, and Mother said *all* of us go down to the beach for an hour so she could talk to Grandfather and get dinner in a real kitchen in peace and quiet.

I sat on my rock in Grandfather's cove and read Zachary's letter and Andy's letter. Z to A. John and Suzy and Rob waded into the ocean where the breakers were coming in with slow majesty, long, lacy, deliberate rows of them, delicately crested and proud, and very different from the wild surf at Laguna Beach. After a while John took the little ones and went around into the bigger cove next to Grandfather's cove, so that I seemed to be entirely alone, a small speck in the vastness of beach and ocean.

The last time I'd sat on the rock in Grandfather's cove was before Uncle Douglas and Aunt Elena were married and I'd been full of fear and confusion. I had thought that life was over, and now I knew that it was only beginning. It was amazing that covering the distance between the Atlantic and the Pacific and back again could make so much difference. Somehow all those miles had stretched me, too. Not just the distance, but the things that had happened. It was the big things like Zachary and Andy and the earthquake. And the little things like filling a pot of water to boil from a rushing stream in the mountains of British Columbia. Or lying in my sleeping bag at night and listening to a coyote crying across the canyon.

The last time I'd sat on the rock all the pieces of the puzzle that made up my picture had been scattered, and now they had come together and I knew who I was. I was myself.

I was Vicky Austin.

The L'Engle Cast

THE AUSTIN FAMILY

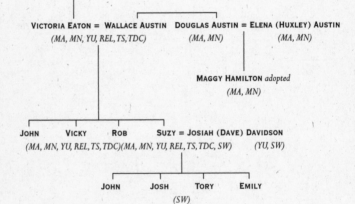

GRANDFATHER EATON = CARO EATON
(MA, MN, REL)

VICTORIA EATON = WALLACE AUSTIN   **DOUGLAS AUSTIN = ELENA (HUXLEY) AUSTIN**
(MA, MN, YU, REL, TS, TDC)   *(MA, MN)*   *(MA, MN)*

MAGGY HAMILTON *adopted*
(MA, MN)

JOHN   VICKY   ROB   SUZY = JOSIAH (DAVE) DAVIDSON
(MA, MN, YU, REL, TS, TDC)(MA, MN, YU, REL, TS, TDC, SW)   *(YU, SW)*

JOHN   JOSH   TORY   EMILY
(SW)

BOOKS FEATURING THE AUSTINS:

Meet the Austins (MA)   *Troubling a Star (TS)*
The Moon by Night (MN)   *The Twenty-four Days*
The Young Unicorns (YU)   *Before Christmas (TDC)*
A Ring of Endless Light (REL)   *A Severed Wasp (SW)*

# of Characters

THE MURRY-O'KEEFE FAMILY

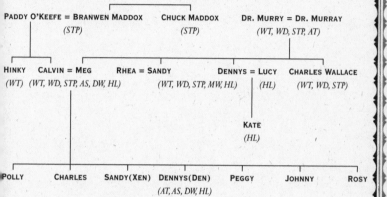

PADDY O'KEEFE = BRANWEN MADDOX   CHUCK MADDOX   DR. MURRY = DR. MURRAY
       (STP)   *(STP)*   *(WT, WD, STP, AT)*

HINKY   CALVIN = MEG   RHEA = SANDY   DENNYS = LUCY   CHARLES WALLACE
(WT) *(WT, WD, STP, AS, DW, HL)* *(WT, WD, STP, MW, HL)* *(HL)*   *(WT, WD, STP)*

KATE
(HL)

POLLY   CHARLES   SANDY(XEN)   DENNYS(DEN)   PEGGY   JOHNNY   ROSY
                               (AT, AS, DW, HL)

BOOKS FEATURING THE MURRY-O'KEEFES:

A Wrinkle in Time (WT)	An Acceptable Time (AT)
A Wind in the Door (WD)	The Arm of the Starfish (AS)
A Swiftly Tilting Planet (STP)	Dragons in the Waters (DW)
Many Waters (MW)	A House Like Lotus (HL)

CHARACTERS WHO APPEAR IN BOTH SERIES:

CANON TALLIS *(AS, YU, DW)*   MR. THEOTOCOPOULOUS *(YU, DW)*
ADAM EDDINGTON *(AS, REL, TS)*   EMILY GREGORY *(YU, DW, SW)*
ZACHARY GREY *(MN, REL, AT, HL)*

GOFISH

MADELEINE L'ENGLE

What did you want to be when you grew up?
A writer.

When did you realize you wanted to be a writer?
Right away. As soon as I was able to articulate, I knew I wanted to be a writer. And I read. I adored *Emily of New Moon* and some of the other L. M. Montgomery books and they impelled me because I loved them.

When did you start to write?
When I was five, I wrote a story about a little "gurl."

What was the first writing you had published?
When I was a child, a poem in *CHILD LIFE*. It was all about a lonely house and was very sentimental.

Where do you write your books?
Anywhere. I write in longhand first, and then type it. My first typewriter was my father's pre–World War I machine. It was the one he took with him to the war. It had certainly been around the world.

What is the best advice you have ever received about writing?
To just write.

What's your first childhood memory?
One early memory I have is going down to Florida for a couple of weeks in the summertime to visit my grandmother. The house was in the middle of a swamp, surrounded by alligators. I don't like alligators, but there they were, and I was afraid of them.

What is your favorite childhood memory?
Being in my room.

As a young person, whom did you look up to most?
My mother. She was a storyteller and I loved her stories. And she loved music and records. We played duets together on the piano.

What was your worst subject in school?
Math and Latin. I didn't like the Latin teacher.

What was your best subject in school?
English.

What activities did you participate in at school?
I was president of the student government in boarding school and editor of a literary magazine, and also belonged to the drama club.

Are you a morning person or a night owl?
Night owl.

What was your first job?
Working for the actress Eva Le Gallienne, right after college.

What is your idea of the best meal ever?
Cream of Wheat. I eat it with a spoon. I love it with butter and brown sugar.

Which do you like better: cats or dogs?
I like them both. I once had a wonderful dog named Touche. She was a silver medium-sized poodle, and quite beautiful. I wasn't allowed to take her on the subway, and I couldn't afford to get a taxi, so I put her around my neck, like a stole. And she pretended she was a stole. She was an actor.

What do you value most in your friends?
Love.

What is your favorite song?
"Drink to Me Only with Thine Eyes."

What time of the year do you like best?
I suppose autumn. I love the changing of the leaves.
I love the autumn goldenrod, the Queen Anne's lace.

Which of your characters is most like you?
None of them. They're all wiser than I am.

READ THE ENTIRE
Austin Family Chronicles

MEET THE AUSTINS

For a family with four kids, two dogs, assorted cats, and a constant stream of family and friends dropping by, life in the Austin family home has always been remarkably steady and contented. When a family friend suddenly dies, the Austins open their home to an orphaned girl, Maggy Hamilton. The Austin children—Vicky, John, Suzy, and Rob—do their best to be generous and welcoming to Maggy. Vicky knows she should feel sorry for Maggy, but having sympathy for Maggy is no easy thing. Maggy is moody and spoiled; she breaks toys, wakes people in the middle of the night screaming, discourages homework, and generally causes chaos in the Austin household. How can one small child disrupt a family of six? Will life ever return to normal?

978-0-312-37931-5, $6.99 US/$7.99 Can.

THE MOON BY NIGHT

As if simply being fourteen-years-old weren't bad enough—what with the usual teenage angst and uncertainty—Vicky Austin's always comforting and reliable home life is changing completely. Her brother John is going off to college in the fall. Maggy has gone to live with her legal guardian. And the rest of Vicky's family is moving from their quiet house in the country to the heart of New York City. But before the big move, the entire Austin family is taking a meandering trip across the country in their station wagon, stopping to camp along the way, with no set schedule and not a single night of camping experience among them. Wild animal attacks. Life-threatening natural disasters. Cute boys on the prowl. Anything can happen in the great outdoors.

978-0-312-37932-2, $6.99 US/$7.99 Can.

THE YOUNG UNICORNS

The Austins are trying to settle into their new life in New York City, but their once close-knit family is pulling away from each other. Their father spends long hours working alone in his study. John is away at college. Rob is making friends with people in the neighborhood: newspaper vendors, dog walkers, even the local rabbi. Suzy is blossoming into a vivacious young woman. And Vicky has become closer to Emily Gregory, a blind and brilliant young musician, than to her sister Suzy. With the Austins going in different directions, they don't notice that something sinister is going on in their neighborhood—and it's centered around them. A mysterious genie appears before Rob and Emily. A stranger approaches Vicky in the park and calls her by name. Members of a local gang are following their father. The entire Austin family is in danger. If they don't start telling each other what's going on, someone just might get killed.

978-0-312-37933-9, $6.99 US/$7.99 Can.

A RING OF ENDLESS LIGHT

After a tumultuous year in New York City, the Austins are spending the summer on the small island where their grandfather lives. He's very sick, and watching his condition deteriorate as the summer passes is almost more than Vicky can bear. To complicate matters, she finds herself as the center of attention for three very different boys. Zachary Grey, the troubled and reckless boy Vicky met last summer, wants her all to himself as he grieves the loss of his mother. Leo Rodney has been just a friend for years, but the tragic loss of his father causes him to turn to Vicky for comfort—and romance. And then there's Adam Eddington. Adam is only asking Vicky to help with his research on dolphins. But Adam—and the dolphins—may just be what Vicky needs to get through this heartbreaking summer.

978-0-312-37935-3, $6.99 US/$7.99 Can.

TROUBLING A STAR

The Austins have settled back into their beloved home in the country after more than a year away. Though they had all missed the predictability and security of life in Thornhill, Vicky Austin is discovering that slipping back into her old life isn't easy. She's been changed by life in New York City and her travels around the country while her old friends seem to have stayed the same. So Vicky finds herself spending time with a new friend, Serena Eddington—the great-aunt of a boy Vicky met over the summer. Aunt Serena gives Vicky an incredible birthday gift—a month-long trip to Antarctica. It's the opportunity of a lifetime. But Vicky is nervous. She's never been away from her family before. Once she sets off though, she finds that's the least of her worries. She receives threatening letters. She's surrounded by suspicious characters. Vicky no longer knows who to trust. And she may not make it home alive.

978-0-312-37934-6, $6.99 US/$7.99 Can.

ALSO AVAILABLE:

A Wrinkle in Time, 978-0-312-36754-1
A Wind in the Door, 978-0-312-36854-8
A Swiftly Tilting Planet, 978-0-312-36856-2
Many Waters, 978-0-312-36857-9
An Acceptable Time, 978-0-312-36858-6

SQUARE
FISH

Available at your local bookstore, or visit
www.squarefishbooks.com.